Also by Patricia Powell

Me Dying Trial

A Small Gathering of Bones

THE
PAGODA

THE PAGODA

A novel by

Patricia Powell

Alfred A. Knopf   New York   1998

THIS IS A BORZOI BOOK
PUBLISHED BY ALFRED A. KNOPF, INC.

Copyright © 1998 by Patricia Powell
All rights reserved under International and Pan-American
Copyright Conventions. Published in the United States by
Alfred A. Knopf, Inc., New York, and simultaneously in
Canada by Random House of Canada Limited, Toronto.
Distributed by Random House, Inc., New York.

www.randomhouse.com

Library of Congress Cataloging-in-Publication Data
Powell, Patricia, [date]
The pagoda / by Patricia Powell. — 1st ed.
p.   cm.
ISBN 0-679-45489-6
1. Chinese—Jamaica—History—19th century—Fiction. I. Title.
PR9265.9.P68P34 1998
823—dc21   98-14568   CIP

Manufactured in the United States of America
First Edition

For Winnifred, my mother
And for Teresa

Acknowledgments

A million thank yous to the Corporation of Yaddo, the MacDowell Colony, Cottages at Hedgebrook, and the U Mass grant that brought me to Jamaica again, for research.

A million more thank yous to Teresa Langle de Paz, Jonathan Strong, Carmen Sanguinetti, Victoria Wilson, Charlotte Sheedy, Neeti Madan, Geeta Patel, Robin Lewis, Shay Youngblood, Carlesa Coates, Kate Rushin, Becky Johnson, Kiana Davenport, Elizabeth Hadley, Faith Smith, Makeda Silvera, Stephanie Martin, Nevin Powell, Barbara Schulman, Reyes Coll, Jennifer Stone, Suze Prudent, and the books that were essential to this project: *China Men; The Yellow Emperor; Anthology of Chinese Literature; A House for Mr Biswas.*

THE
PAGODA

1

That morning, after the clock's iron music buckled out its final tone and the house had again tumbled into dead quiet, Lowe rose. He was still weary from the torrid dreams, the visions of hurricane and wreckage, though neither deluge nor drought had struck the island in some time. The lamp was out and a blackness had invaded the room, deepening the corners and empty spaces so it seemed suddenly enormous. Balancing himself on one elbow, he leaned into the fuzzy outlines of Miss Sylvie's shoulders and chest, as he had done every morning for the thirty years of their marriage, listening for the steady rise and fall of her breath. It wasn't that she was ill, or that she was prone to maladies, but there was always the fear steep in him that she'd die sudden and abandon him. At first there was nothing, no gentle wind slipping from her lips, slightly ajar, no muffled murmuring, just his own roaring head and the infernal heat that steamed off her skin. He burrowed even closer, till he could pick out the raspy rhythms of her shallow breathing, then he eased back with a relieved sigh into the cushioned lap of his bed, allowing the darkness to assail him, fill up his nostrils and the void before his eyes.

Last night the heat had turned liquid. No breeze stirred through the arms of trees, and the insects, driven mad by the molten fire, shrieked and thrashed themselves against windows and doors that had been shut, their crevices sealed with cloth, as Lowe couldn't bear to sleep underneath the mosquito netting or with the house doors flung wide open. A swarm of carnivorous mosquitoes still managed to slip in, and they clung to the walls, leaned up against the ceiling, sometimes circling round and whining, but mostly they clung to the walls, too anguished even to move. The razor heat, egged on by hot winds, had broken in, sucking air from the rooms, swelling locks on the doors, blistering the cream-colored paint on the walls. But now, in that hour right before dawn, temperatures had eased, the house had cooled down, and a light breeze had stolen in, gently billowing up corners of the bedspread and turning over loose pieces of paper.

Lowe slipped out of bed, quietly hauling on his slippers, parked at the foot, and groped along the mantel top until his fingers stumbled on the box of matches. He struck a match and the room was immediately bursting with the smell of sulfur, and blocks of shadows scattered across the floorboards. He lifted the lampshade and moved the flag of flame onto the wick. Soon it gave off a moonglow, lighting up the metal posts of the bed and the embroidery of the carved headboard, and making the bones of his face more prominent with shadows. Clutching the drawstrings of his voluminous pajamas with one hand, the slender waist of the lamp with the other, he wended his way through the maze of solemn English furniture left over from Miss Sylvie's first marriage, plunging the light ahead into the swirling darkness.

In the narrow passageway of the drawing room, he stopped

to wind the pendulum clock pressed up against the wall, which read a little after four, and to turn over the page on the almanac hung there beside Miss Sylvie's old organ. It was the start of a new month. April first, eighteen hundred ninety-three. He lingered there as well to fasten on, from the pile he kept in a cigar box, a fuzzy tuft of bristle-black hair that trembled over his slightly protruding top lip. Then, with a face ravaged by life and the false and hairy handlebars, he made his way clumsily over to the desk, pulled out the chair, and sat heavily, resting the lamp near his hand. The unfinished letter to the daughter was there, several sheets of paper that stared up at him from among the yellowing piles of old newspapers and magazines, ledger accounts, invoices, and IOUs from customers down at his shop, dried-up inkwells and pens that no longer wrote, squat bottles of pills and cough medicine without labels but which he knew by heart and swallowed regularly.

Lowe coughed quietly into his hands and cleared his throat several times, balking at the sweet sickening smell of Miss Sylvie's incense and lilies that pervaded the room and reminded him of funerals. He reread, lips moving slightly, the lines of his gnarled handwriting. Not much, though he'd started it close to a month ago now and had been coming here, in fits of urgency, night after night, like the frenzy of dreams chopping up his sleep, leaving him fidgety and impulsive. He had never written a letter before and had had to rifle through Miss Sylvie's moldy and decaying correspondence in order to find the correct form. He noted that his address—Actingbeddy District, Rose Hall Postal Agency, Manchester, Jamaica, West Indies—had to be placed in the right-hand corner, and underneath that the date, skipping one line, and underneath that, to the far left-hand corner, half inch or so from the margin, "Dear So-and-so." After much deliberation over the term of salutation, ranging from Mrs. J. Audley Drinkwater to Amoy, the nickname he'd given her, he finally settled on "My dear Elizabeth," a title that was neither far nor near.

He had asked after her health, and that of his grandson and the husband he disliked so much he'd refused to meet him in person all these years. Then he told her Miss Sylvie was hearty and that the old organ was there catching dust, as there weren't many students these days. Himself, well, he couldn't complain. The shop was doing well. The people hadn't cut his throat yet. At this he chuckled, his face folding into a hundred vertical pleats, narrowing his eyes, though it was no laughing matter. His people, the few Chinese living on the island, had been meeting hell, at the hands of the Negro people and the few Europeans that controlled the country, ever since they arrived. Some forty to fifty years now. But often one had to turn bad things into laughter.

He'd gone on to tell her why he was writing her after all these years. Twenty years exactly since he'd last seen her. After so much silence and bad feeling and malice between them, time had come to put things behind and start again, he had written. He was growing old, and arthritis was snaking up his spine and down through his fingers, his asthmatic chest rattled more than ever, his bones ached when it got cloudy or made as if to rain, and his heart wasn't as steady and dependable. All these years he had kept his life private, hidden, but there were things now he wanted her to know, secrets he could no longer hide inside; besides, his memory too was quickly eroding. He hadn't gotten farther. He hadn't mentioned the confused and tormented nightly cogitation, the dreams.

Lowe paused to drink a glass of water standing there by his elbow; it was old and tasted of the mustiness of the room. A voice, raspy and mannish, reeled off a string of invectives, then stopped. It was Miss Sylvie, still deep in the clutches of sleep. He heard the groaning bed as she turned, the loud frightful sigh, then the house plunged back into marble stillness. He cleared his throat; he scratched his scalp and thigh; he picked up the pen. It quivered in his hand, jumped out, and clattered on the desk. Against the wall, shadows from the wick wavered back and forth, filling the room with diffused and swaying colors, as the wick steadily sucked what was left of the kerosene oil.

The light hovered over the faded portraits on the wall: pouring down the shoulders of Victoria, the old Queen; snagging on the governor-general's rough-cut silver medals; illuminating the glinting enamel eyes of the last Manchu emperor, whose face had been clipped from the newspaper and was rapidly fading; spilling into the handsome gilt frame that housed the wedding picture of Lowe and Miss Sylvie, his mustache then a black and shiny contraption, with the waxed edges curling together like tails. A row of Miss Sylvie's family covered one corner of the wall. The side made up of dead politicians, plantation owners, ministers. Then there was the daughter, the husband, and several pictures of the grandson, a few still lifes Miss Sylvie had commissioned from a retired Englishman who had had some claim to artistic fame, none of which Lowe could recall at that moment, and a watercolor of Cecil standing on the deck of his ship, *Augustina*, the very same ship that had brought Lowe to the island.

They gleamed at him from the pale-yellow wall, at the top of his head, which was neatly trimmed and steadily turning metallic, and at the tattered collar of his flimsy white pajamas. He picked up the pen again and without a pause began to write, wildly, feverishly, the nib clawing across the white sheet, head tottering with the movements of his hand.

It does not make sense to put this aside and hope it will go away. It makes sense simply to say it now. To tell you myself, before someone else does. I know you will probably find all of this hard to believe, but at some time or other we all do things to save our lives. Some more drastic than usual.

Suddenly it occurred to him that maybe the husband would receive it first and read it. Worse still, maybe the postmistress would steam it open. Then what? A load of silence settled on his head, until he decided that what had to be done simply had to be done.

I am not your father like you think. It is a long story, full up of a lot of deception, a lot of disguises, but try to understand this was all so I could live. All so I could be free. Have a life. Maybe a letter is not the right thing. Maybe I should meet up with you in person and explain face-to-face, so you can see for yourself. I am not what you think. It wasn't so easy to just leave Kwangtung, though foreign vessels clogged the waterways of South China, ready to take people. To North America, Australia, Singapore. Anywhere people wanted. The villages had grown so poor and overcrowded. So destitute. People left China in droves. For me, though, it had to be different. I know it must be hard, fixing your head now to think this way, when for so long you called me Dada. But you are older now, the hope is you will understand. There isn't a record of any of this. Of what I am in truth. No certificates. No registration. Everything had to be quick and hush-hush. Nothing was written down. We delivered you at home. Miss Sylvie . . . Well, she is not your rightful mother either. I . . .

A cry escaped his lips. He crumpled the sheet and it sat tortured in his hand. He looked out into the lamplit silence, willing his racing heart to quieten, willing his shaking and wet hands to be still, the roar in his head to cease. A trembling hand reached up to tug at the puffy brush of mustache, to push away hair that had fallen on his forehead, now damp and warm. He fondled his throat in alarm, wondering if a fever had started. And his throat too and chest were damp.

Beside him, the lamp started to smoke, shooting monstrous shadows against the walls. Frustrated moths charmed by the light heaved themselves at the window. Lowe looked up with crowded eyes. It was as if voices, growing taller, more passionate in his head, daily, were choking him, threatening him to speak. Sometimes the voices lulled, but this week they had rioted his dreams, commanded that he signify, give testimony, and so now here he was. Here he was. With his roiled-up memories. With his labyrinth of feelings. He flung the chair away from the desk and staggered to the glass doors, pushing aside curtains that smelled of camphor balls. He pressed his nose against the glass and stared out into an inky night, his lithe, thin frame a dead weight braced against the door. He remained there till he was calm, then turned back to face the desk, his face white with exhaustion. There was so much to tell her, so much to write, and it seemed almost impossible to set everything down all at once. Almost impossible to reveal all of who he was. There was so much.

As the years flew by, Lowe had grown increasingly hard of hearing in both ears, according to Miss Sylvie and some of his customers down in the shop, and so the thin thread of a wail that sounded out his name didn't strike him as strange at first. From time to time he heard circling echoes of sounds he couldn't always distinguish. Other times everything throbbed a flat, monotonous hum. Furthermore, if someone was out there calling, the dogs would've been barking, unless he couldn't hear even that. Or perhaps it was Cecil, who had arrived stinking drunk late last night just when he was about to lock up shop and had immediately fallen asleep on the rice in the storeroom at the back. It was still too soon for Dulcie, the housekeeper, to begin her early morning duties, and earlier still for the cries of villagers down the road, whose flattened shouts often drifted up to the house and through the open windows.

So without even turning to pull back blue muslin curtains and glance out the window into the impenetrable night, Lowe remained in the drawing room, hunched over the desk, chopping and mincing with a ratchet knife the fleshy meat of a rope of tobacco Miss Sylvie had hung to dry on a nail. The letter he'd been writing, by this time, had rolled and settled underneath his chair. And so the only sounds that could be heard were the tap-tap of metal knocking against the wooden skin of the desk, the wailing chorale of bats and crickets and frogs that pervaded the night, the rattling of his own asthmatic chest.

There was that sound again, that whispering wail strung along by the breeze, and what was that smell? Roast yam, smoke, roast corn? Lowe chuckled softly to himself at his neighbors, who could start fire and put on pot to boil at any hour of the day or night, and anxiously yearned for daybreak to arrive so he could tidy himself and walk the ten minutes down through the rough, winding snake path to his shop, which he had tended ever since he arrived on the island, thirty-two years now. The shop—and Cecil had paid for it in cash—had been half in ruins, with patches of grass sprouting up through the cracked concrete that covered the floor and rain pouring down the holes in the corrugated zinc, which he first had to patch with tar that dripped on customers during the middle of the day when the heat boiled. Over the years he'd raised the ceiling, replaced the cement floors, added on three rooms and a large outside piazza with Doric columns, where people could sit and carry on a conversation while they finished up their drinks.

Mister Lowe.

Lowe lurched, unsettling the lamp by his elbow, the knife spilling from his hand and clattering to the floor underneath the desk, where his feet were frantic, searching for the letter, the letter that would reveal him, point him out, disgrace him in front of everybody.

Mister Lowe.

He tried to answer, hand reaching out to steady the lamp that had swerved onto its side, cracking open the glass shade, plunging the house into complete darkness.

Mister Lowe.

He tried to answer. Voice barely a squeak. And rotten. Almost breaking. He fumbled for matches in the pocket of his gown, lit the lamp again, pointing the light toward the darkened corners of the room, to where he heard sound, spinning with the circles of sound, the letter pinned under his slipper.

Mister Lowe.

Then finally it dawned on him that the voice was calling from outside, a fevered cry he didn't recognize, moving from window to window, circling the house, and for a fraction he just sighed, relieved. But it was short-lived, for then he began to wonder about the two watchdogs. And why they weren't barking. Here it was, a stranger outside in the yard, calling. He heard the footsteps too, stealthy but sure, moving about the yard, coming up the steps of the veranda and moving away again, and still the dogs weren't barking. Then it all came to him. Then he knew. His skin grew damp, then cold, and dots of sweat walked great gaunt steps along the thin shaft of his neck. He'd heard of setups, where they distracted you to one direction and took everything in the other. He'd always known he was there on sufferance. They told him to his face. When he wouldn't give credit to somebody who didn't even have pot to piss in. Plus they didn't like him living up there with Miss Sylvie. After all these thirty years. But where were the damn dogs—why they weren't barking, that was the thing, why they weren't barking. And Dulcie, the housekeeper, up there in the buttery, sleeping on her coconut-brush mattress, she didn't hear. And her big rusty-skinned son, Omar. Always caustic. Always walking round sullen with that sharpened cutlass as if itching to chop someone. He didn't hear.

Mister Lowe.

Lowe didn't answer. He stared out ahead of him into the rapacious blackness. He hauled back the curtain, and his distorted reflection peered at him several times from rectangular panes of glass in the door. It was still dark. Darker than ever. Even for five. Not even a glimmer of copper light peering through the canopy of branches, creeping over the top of great hills. He'd feared death before, but tonight was different. He plunged his tongue rapidly over his lips, trying with all his might to calm the raging in his chest.

The shop burning, Mister Lowe.

The shop?

Yes, sir.

The shop, Lowe! Dear God!

That was Miss Sylvie behind him, round and strapping and white-skinned, in a pink nightgown that trembled over her blue fuzzy slippers.

Lord have mercy, poor Cecil!

And with a strength he didn't know he possessed, he was swinging into yesterday's breeches and the black rubber galoshes. Snatching doors and windows open, he bellowed out for help and fire, help and fire. Rounding the corner by the side of the house, next to the troughs where the animals fed, he stumbled into the dogs stretched out stiff and twisted and dead at the foot of the wooden washstand. Last night's dinner rushed up into his mouth, and he convulsed. There wasn't time now to stop and weep over the dogs; he had to save Cecil. Save the shop for the grandson.

And so he ran, bounding through the dark, fear traveling in his feet, the whispering wind beating his cheeks. His rubber boots leapt over tufts of grass, piles of stones, sloshed through mud, and his arms flayed against trembling leaves that grew in profusion and flogged his face. Morning sky was still cloaked in darkness. No moon. No stars. Behind him, Miss Sylvie's opera of shrieks, the distant croaking of frogs, and the call of an owl with the voice of a woman. Birds and bats shot past him, the frenzied conversation of insects deafened him momentarily. His nostrils grew clogged with the sweet-smelling sap that dripped from trees, with the humid rotting decay of the forest floor, with the odor of nutmeg and cashew that drifted through breeze. Insects clung to his skin and burrowed holes in his flesh. And still he ran, zigzagging through the winding forest, his chest pounding, his head pulsating with an infernal heat, his mind only on Cecil in the back room on the rice, Cecil who had brought him here to the island, Cecil who had given him the keys to the shop and the bag of money he was to use as capital, Cecil who had dictated his life up till that very moment.

He could hear people down the road bawling, could see plumes of gray smoke pillowing toward a black sky, hear the cackle and spit of unresisting timbers and concrete. He could smell it, although only faintly. He knew it couldn't be saved, Cecil or anything, that the villagers had done it finally. As if he hadn't been good enough to them, hadn't lived there side by side with them. When drought struck and the land couldn't bear, hadn't he fed them? There wasn't one funeral he had missed. He locked shop early and attended every wedding with a box of hard-dough bread and a carton of white rum underneath his arm. He knew every child by name. He knew who was carrying belly for who. He knew who had money in bank and who was working obeah for who. They left it all there in the shop under the spell of liquor. And those years before Miss Sylvie came, he'd slept there underneath the counter on a bed of flour bags and old carton boxes.

Yes, he'd come to catch his hand, to make something of his life. But he was no poor-show-great. He didn't see himself better than them. Above them. But now they had burned it down. Flat. Flat. He was there only on sufferance. Himself and the other five thousand Chinese on the island. He realized now how the Negro people must have secretly despised him for being there, how secretly they must have envied him and his shop and his relationship to Cecil and Miss Sylvie, for here now was the proof. And the whites didn't give one blast if the others burned it down. So long as their houses were untouched. Their daughters. Their wives and the plantation equipment. How he knew! Whoever hath eyes, let him see. Whoever hath ears!

He watched the crowd of people, his neighbors, men and women alike, gangs of children, still in nightclothes, sleep etched in their faces, dousing the dying cinders with buckets of water from corrugated-steel drums attached to gutters at the sides of the shop. They gave orders, shouted, cried out for more

buckets of water. They doused. Sliding and spilling and collid-
ing in the dark, their clothes shifting like wings, their copper
skins the color of zinc in the approaching dawn. In the noise and
confusion he heard a woman wailing, a low deep moaning, and
although the woman had never liked him, would always fire a
spit when she walked past his shop, he started to cry at the way
of the world, for these very same people had burned it down.
These very same ones dousing. The women especially, for they
were most notorious, when prices rocketed and their children's
plates shone empty.

Rooted in the orange orchard next door the shop, his face a
network of wrinkles, his eyes muddy and dull from exhaustion,
his hands bunched in the pockets of his torn and ragged
trousers, he heard their voices rising and falling in sharp parox-
ysms of sound, saw the small bundles of their animated gestures.
Patches of them, with eyes feverish from the sparkling cinders.
These—the bottom of the bottom. The ones who didn't have
land: who eked out a living picking peanuts today on Mr.
McClean's property; cutting cane tomorrow on the estates; carrying belly for Mass Charles, whose house they cleaned, with
the hope that the brown baby would bring them prosperity; the
ones who chopped grass for a living or trimmed hedges. Mass
Hanif. Missa Alphonso. Miss Irene. Mass Dermot. Missa Cole-
ridge. The ones who set the fire and those who sat by and
watched with folded arms and crumpled faces. Those who didn't
know anything at all. But everybody was dousing nonetheless.
For it was theirs too. He watched them with their arms folded
across chests, listening to the tick and crack of the last pieces of
wood, their eyes glued to the dying embers, as if the destruction
had somehow eaten away parts of themselves. He watched their
loose empty gentle faces, withdrawn and tucked under.

Idlers set it, man. Damn thieves and idlers.

Our people are wicked. Look how Mr. Chin good to us.

Payback time. Him thief enough from us.

Elders' shop so far. How we going feed the children them? At least the Chinaman will trust till payday. Not Elders. Not Miss Cora.

A moan swept through the crowd and wove in and out of the leaves of trees.

You hear that blasted idiot moaning like is her shop burn down? She don't see how the Chinaman take advantage of we. How the backra put them between we. All the hell we set at they tail, now they bringing in Coolie and Chinee.

Who you think set it?

You know how much weevil me find in the cornmeal. And that bad rum him sell. Mix with water. Hot oil.

Them say Cecil burn up inside.

You mean Cecil the white man, Lowe's sweetheart?

Eh, the nasty life they lead up there. The ungodliness. I see that Lowe. I see them. Devil workers!

Lowe fled beyond their talk and thought of his daughter. His grandson. The shop had been for her, if she wanted it, for him, if he wanted it, and the Chinese who had escaped the sugar estates with broken backs from working twenty hours a day for close to nothing. They came with hands twisted and chewed from water pumps, scarred by deep grooves left over from cane leaves that cut like knives. They came with spit bubbling with blood, asthmatic and tubercular chests from the dust. They came without flesh, with holes in the skin, half starved from inferior food, lashed and mutilated by overseers under the muscle of plantation owners. The shop was there so if they wanted they could come and apprentice with him, till they'd pay off their contracts and with a small loan open up a little shop, selling half flask of rum, a stick of cigarette, big gill of coconut oil, two inches of tobacco, quarter pound of rice, repaying monthly and with interest.

Just two nights ago the shop had been full of people. Music flowed from the gasping bellows of Blind Belinda's accordion as the drunken men in the corner ordered more rum, danced and dropped coppers in the kerosene tin at her feet. The women in harsh sweet voices haggled and teased him. They abused him about the high prices. They laughed at his slanted eyes and told him to read the scale properly and stop from tipping it. Stop watering the rum and the kerosene oil. Outside in the road their waiting children played hopscotch from the yellow glare of the tilley lamps that swung from the rafters. Just two nights ago, and now this.

He watched as they laid out Cecil on his back in the grass at the foot of an orange tree. He watched them back away from the white glare of Cecil's luminous eyes, which were still wide and surprised and staring at the sky. A snarling clot of flies immediately sprung on his dead face, which was riddled with furrows, and a white handkerchief briskly waved them away. Someone pressed his eyes shut. Someone else covered his stiff and twisted body, which had suffered no visible burns, with a thin white sheet. He watched them hover round the body but at a respectful distance. He watched the women fuss about, wailing and muttering funereal songs in cracked voices. He watched their quivering lips and gray cobweb faces.

Then he looked at Cecil, and at the big pink toe that peered out the hole of his left sock. And he thought only of the ship Cecil had mastered and on which Lowe had been a stowaway, living for weeks crouched inside a fish barrel that vibrated with the shudders of the ship, sneaking out only to empty his bowels and bladder alongside rats bloated and dizzy from fermented grain. And each time he snuck out, the onslaught of air, sour with the smells of rotting timbers and mildewed beams, dizzied him, his unused legs wobbled, and his ears rang with the melodies of strange instruments.

Yet he had learned how to stifle sneezes and hold back coughs, how to lock the muscles in his rectum and tighten his kidneys, how to squat for long hours behind crates of shimmering silk and handcrafted fans, dodge between cargoes of fine tea and silver dishes wrapped with ropes, dart between towering columns that divided the ship into small, neat boroughs. And always there was the fear clanging in his chest, thudding in the veins by his head.

Sometimes sailors were so close he could taste the salt on their legs, smell the musk inside their shoes, his eyes dazzled by their shimmering oilskins. How their strange language with its harsh and discordant tones came to sound like music. He didn't know, then, that the ship was full up of stolen Chinese. That thin men spare as bones were piled in like prisoners and stowed tight with the chests of tea and silk, for sale to the highest bidder in the West Indies. He didn't know then that that was common accord, that not long before, the Negro people had met a similar fate and that now it was big business again, for the sugar estates were there devastated, broken down in financial ruin. Emancipation had come. Nobody was working for nothing anymore. And so the planters, to save face, had now turned their gaze east, looking for the cheapest labor they could find.

He didn't know then that people like Cecil, who had a little ship and some capital, could disregard the contract system, where they'd have to dole out money per head at immigration for each Chinese, and could instead pay little or nothing to men desperate for food and work, to kidnap anyone they could find. It was only later that he found out. Long after Cecil found him hiding in the bowels of the ship, flattened alongside planks, roasting from fever. Long after Cecil kept him locked up in his small hot dark cabin. During his entire life on that island Lowe had been indebted to Cecil. The shop was Cecil's, except that Lowe had been running it all these years. He provided the costumes for the drama Lowe lived out in that house all these years with Miss Sylvie. And now Cecil was lying there at the foot of the tree, dead. And Lowe wasn't sure what to make of it all, wasn't sure what the next step was. There was his life spinning and spinning and spinning away with no bottom at all under his feet and no rails against which to clutch or lean up, no compass to steer, no supervision, no bolts or bars.

He turned to observe the scattering crowd, the diminishing

shuffle of feet and muted babble broken up by faint bells of laughter and lamentation. He turned to observe the rubbish heap of destruction that was his shop, at the blackened Doric columns, the wooden rafters holding up the zinc roof that had melted down to nothing, the rusty yellowing zinc tumbling after that. Wooden shelves leaning against the wall, holding cakes of soap and boxes of detergent and oats and bottles of beer and stout, aerated water, white rum, boxes of clothes peg, hairpin, button, phensic, tins of condensed milk and mackerel in tomato sauce, corned beef, sardines in vegetable oil, two- and three-pound bags of rice and flour and sugar and cornmeal, the closet filled with spiced buns and bread and water crackers, two unopened tins of New Zealand cheddar, the glass case leading out to the doorway, with home-sweet-home glass lamps and shades and tilley lanterns and bolts of calico and silk, spools of thread, brand-new Wellingtons, unused machetes, the oil drum, exploded. Nothing.

He turned again. To Miss Sylvie's hands drawing his head roughly against her shoulders, his cheek and ear rubbing up against the sharp cloth of her floral dress, against the heaving ribs. At first he stiffened, worried, even after so many years, about what the villagers might say, how they'd see him, but he was so weary, so weary and broken, that he wanted to sob into her loose and tangled hair, into the square shelf of jaw, wanted to weep all over the column of neck and into her ample back. But he checked himself. He looked past her clear and grave eyes, he looked past the deep lines around her mouth. He looked past the fragrances of oils and herb, the harsh wet smell of tobacco and the barks of great trees that perfumed her skin, and thought it strange that it'd been so long since he noticed any of this. He looked past Miss Sylvie and at the upside-down world turning topsy-turvy at his feet.

Overhead the splendor of dawn had broken over the sorrowful grayness of the village. Light the color of smoke crept from behind low, horizontal hills, seeped languorously across the long, spacious sky, unfolding into patches of burnished Indian red and then into mauve. The sun had already begun sucking back moisture, preparing the earth for a slow scorch. Then he heard the conch, and the shrill screech of it drowned the early morning dialogue of birds and made him shiver. He thought quickly of the letter balled up there underneath the desk in the drawing room and of his daughter. Sadness overwhelmed him.

The conch sounded again. And he wondered nervously at the power of that shell, how years ago it used to ignite the Negro people to rise up and fight, how at the sound of it they would tumble out of bushes in the blackness with only torches in hand, but by morning entire plantations would be flat, flat. He heard the funereal toll of the church bell. By midday the whole district would know. And the police inspectors would come, not because of his insurmountable losses, but because Cecil, one of their own, had died. They would come with their reddened and drenched faces, with their black notebooks and bristling mustaches, with their tired mules. They would talk in solemn and subdued tones to Miss Sylvie, nodding and jotting down notes, all the while glaring suspiciously at Lowe, at the bristle-black brush of hair pasted there above his thin lips, and at the villagers, especially the women, who would have crowded round to listen and to watch.

2

Those days following the funeral, after the last grain of dirt had been sprinkled on top of the coffin, after the hole had been packed up again with fresh earth and made to look neat and untroubled, after the diggers had parked their shovels and pick-axes, washed their hands, and drained the bottles of the final taste of rum, after the mourners had wiped dry their last streaks of tears and the village had plunged back into its dull and indifferent routine, Lowe kept to his bed, leaving only to drown himself in the roiling steamy water Dulcie prepared for his baths and to take his meals in the smoky kitchen, squatting by the door of the woodstove and staring blindly into the crackling firewood. Sometimes he went outside for a walk, and either Miss Sylvie or Dulcie would find him standing up by the washstand for hours, stiff and straight, his eyes wide open, unmoving and unblinking.

Sometimes he went outside for a walk, moving slowly and

unwieldily, for all of a sudden his joints had become swollen and arthritic. And each time he went outside he saw devastation wreaked everywhere. He saw the heads of black cats teeming with maggots dangling from guava trees. He saw crushed poinsettias sprinkled all over the yard, torn up feverbush, shrubs of croton and clumps of moist earth streaked with blood. He saw swelling gutters of bilge water running through the yard, and the mangled and bloated bodies of dogs and goats floating quietly on the brim, and, swimming not too far behind, the small neat bundles of their rotting entrails, green with flies. He saw all this each time he walked outside, and so he stayed indoors, trembling underneath a mountain of sheets packed onto his stomach and legs even though it was the middle of the dry season and the heat outside boiled and raged, relentless in its oppressiveness.

He took to seeing spectacles of Cecil all hours of the day and night. He looked out the window and saw him walking past the rosebush down below and whistling. He looked out the window and saw him squatting in the yard, a square of light boxing his jaws, which worked up and down. One afternoon he saw Cecil sitting in the doorway of the room, his face hidden behind a mist of smoke from his cigar, his hat cocked low over the brim of his eyes, his skin a very leathered brown, pitted from sea cuts and boils and sunburns and wind smites. He remembered the letter he had been writing to his daughter and turned to the image across the room.

"You know, Cecil." His voice was serious and his face was placid. "I getting old." He coughed, and the asthmatic chest rattled and then stopped. "One day I might drop down sick and then she going have to take care of me. Then she'll see. Then she'll know the whole story. And then what! She not going to forgive me. Instead she going to call me all kinds of nastiness and perversions. She not going to forgive me at all."

Cecil tipped off his hat to scratch his head, which was bald and freckled and leathery. The hat dropped on the unpainted floorboards, and waves of dust billowed up and swam through shafts of light seeping in the window and sloping sideways across his plaid trousers. He was slow to respond, and when he spoke his lips hardly moved and the cigar shook slightly, the tip glowing like a petal. He swallowed. "I don't envy you."

Lowe was quiet. He cleared his throat nervously and stared in front of him. "Look, man, is not just me. Is the two of us. You forget?"

"I don't envy you."

"That's all you can say." Lowe grew dizzy, his voice a thin whisper. Bile rose up into his throat, and he remembered again Cecil's ship and the ropes wrenching his wrists and Cecil's short quick breaths in his neck and Cecil's hands on his waist, the buckling and unbuckling of fingers. "That's all you can blasted say!" His chest hammered. He flung off the blankets that were all of a sudden hot and unbearable. He rolled up the sleeves of his shirt that constricted his muscles, and he bolted upright in the four-poster iron bed. He pushed back toward his elbow the copper bangles that drew arthritis, and lathered his hands vigorously with soap and a nearby bowl of water that waited there on the bed. "You forget me and you down in the belly of that ship. How you loved me as you like. Treated me as you want. Lock up inside that cabin for days!"

He was shouting now at the thin frail back leaning toward him, at the long shaft of neck, at the thin blue line of smoke coiling into sunlight. Spots of sweat bubbled on Lowe's forehead, and he heaved himself out of the mountain of sheets and out of the swaying bed. He shot toward the doorway with the basin. "You should envy me. You never had to take responsibility for nothing in all you life! You spent all you blasted days on the boat. On the sea. That's where you hid. Fuck! Shit! You never had to . . ." He pitched the basin of dirty water violently through the open window, and the scrawny and diseased chickens dawdling below scattered noisily.

Then he caught the man staring at him, the housekeeper's son, Omar, with the eyes not quite as hard, only curious. The basin shook unsteadily in Lowe's hands. He heard a ringing in his ears and wondered if he'd been shouting. He lashed out at Omar: "What is you damn problem! What the hell you looking at! What the hell!" He flung the empty basin to his feet, and it bounced against the floor, chipping off pieces of wood. Omar coughed and slipped out of sight.

The scene was to repeat itself every Tuesday for a month, until Dulcie, the housekeeper, steeped him quarter pound of an herb she found growing in the forest at the back of the house, which made him sleep. Sometimes he slept for twenty hours without dreaming, sometimes he spent all night searching for people appearing then disappearing, his dreams dripping with the voices of the villagers, the electric flashes of their eyes, their amber skin, the dying embers in the metallic morning. And when he woke up again his eyes were red and delirious from exhaustion and full of big green and blue veins.

Six weeks passed, him confined to his bed, until one morning he woke up bright and early, and with no signs at all of his symptoms, though huge tufts of his hair, which had turned completely white, had fallen out and his face was crinkled with brand-new pleats. He had no recollection of the nightmares, recalled only the burning shop and Cecil's passing, the profound absence of the two black dogs. He wandered over to his desk, which had been locked up since that night, and found lying there among the squat silver bottles of pills and old receipts the crumpled-up pieces of paper that were the letter he had begun. He sat down on the hard-back chair and with swollen, clumsy fingers began to straighten out the sheets, poring over his crabbed handwriting.

It all seemed so far away and indifferent now, nothing at all compared to the throb of tragedy that had so ravaged his life, the ungrateful and malicious people who had so turned on him all of a sudden. People who for over thirty years he thought were his friends. Soon it would be the house set ablaze, with him and

Miss Sylvie burned up inside. Soon the same fury that had been unleashed on Cecil would be directed at him and Sylvie. And then what would it matter whether or not his daughter knew how he'd arrived there on the island exactly and why? What would it matter how he and Cecil had lived down in the gut of that ship? How he and Miss Sylvie lived up there in that house all these years? How the daughter was born and who were the rightful parents?

Lowe sighed, so weary, so aged and frightened and sickly all of a sudden. He peeled off the ridiculous mustache and put it in his shirt pocket and vowed never to wear it again. He coughed in his hands, and his chest rattled. Inside his stomach he felt a deep tunneling begin to flare up, and he wrapped his belly with both hands and remembered again his village back in South China and his father, whom he'd not thought of in years. Twenty to be exact. They had been bench and bottom, eye and socket, but that was when Lowe was still wide-eyed and before his limbs suddenly shot up and his body started turning against him.

His father had been a thin wicker figure of a man, who had no hair at all on his shiny head dotted with liver spots, barely any vision at all behind his milky eyes, only a flowing white beard that settled against his rounded bird chest. In his day, he had been a shipbuilder, a shoemaker, a sign painter, a professional boxer, a snake charmer, and by the time he was sixty and Lowe was conceived, in the heat of an unusual passion that flared up between him and his wife, he had opened a four-by-four lean-to crouched on the hillside, where he made coffins and walking sticks with elaborate designs carved into the handles.

And Lowe remembered again the parchment maps that lined the walls of his father's coffin shop; the wiggly blue lines winding through a dry and hilly terrain and emptying into rivers through which his father used to navigate a sampan. And he was skillful, his father, though weak and shaky from old age, but he would guide the boat with tremendous grace, passing between muddy sandbanks and deceptive rapids, the water swelling and churning around them, while off to the sides, wheat and bean and rice fields raced by, endless against a backdrop of heaving blue-black mountains.

From his chair in the drawing room, the curtains drawn to shut out the glaring light and heat, Lowe felt his cheeks reddened by the breeze of the delta on whose banks he used to sit while his father recited by heart and with his eyes closed soliloquies from plays and entire books of love poetry. For though the station allotted him in life was low, he was an avid reader and through literature must've received a greater vision. He explained to Lowe in a breathless and compelling voice his ideas for a book he'd been making for twenty-three years. It was to be a collection of nine short stories, all of which had already been titled, all the pages numbered, some with illustrations; only the stories were left to be written.

Lowe remembered too that, unlike his brothers, he had not been sent to school and had had to learn the brush strokes of his calligraphy under his father's tutelage, sitting in the unfinished coffins under the yellow glare of oil lamps before the first streaks of dawn appeared, when mist still covered half the world, and in the dead of night, when the shop was bolted. And after the lessons ended his father brought out the decaying sheets that were the maps, and Lowe, lost in the smells of fish glue and wood shavings and mildewed fabric that inhabited his father's shop, trundled along the stubby route of his father's forefinger, listening to the faltering voice outline expeditions by sea.

Always they were the same. They would haul out of the docks at Canton early morning and with a tranquil sea. They would slip silently out of the harbor and across the straits and down the treacherous South China Sea, the ship sublime and gallant, with every sail careening over the coiling waves. The route too was always the same; the goal was America, not to work but to explore, by way of the Malay Archipelago, then down the Indian Ocean and up and around the lip of the Atlantic. Always they would pass a succession of clippers heading into China for workers to the American West, schools of porpoises frolicking in the blue-green waters. And they would travel like this until right off the coast of Mauritius, when the wind suddenly whipped up the cold green sea and icy sprays sprang up and lashed the boat, which lurched and pitched as it climbed crest after crest of foaming rollers, groaning and straining against swords of lightning scarring the sky. They would continue like this, with waves as tall as eleven houses rolling up, crashing against the ship, all day, all night, and it was never clear to Lowe, on those days when the edges of his mind wavered, if it was only he and his father commandeering the ship or if there was a crew his father mastered.

It was never clear to Lowe if the brig they sailed, with the bronze woman vaulting off the bowsprit, was on loan or if his father had made it by hand, plank by plank, the way he made the coffins, with elaborate carvings and adorned with the shiniest brass handles and red silk lining that clung to the dead as if it were a second skin. But it always felt criminal to interrupt his father's feverish imaginings with such frivolous yearnings for details, for his father was never more animated. His eyes momentarily lost their milky glare, his crooked arthritic fingers straightened, the low gravelly hum of his voice cleared, and so Lowe plugged in clues as they suited him, peering with salt-stung eyes into the furious seas ahead, the endless fog, swaying to the staggering of the ship, listening all night as they lay awake to the wailing winds, great thuds of waves hammering the deck and the chaotic sea leaping around them.

On none of their expeditions had they reached America, as the ship was too battered by storms, planks splintered, rails and wheelhouse smashed in, beams and davits flattened, and for hours they had to repair the wreckage, beat back creeping water, whistling and singing so as not to show their snarling nerves.

For years and years and years the stories continued, always underneath the shadow of night or the smoky mist of morning, always in animated but subdued tones and especially hidden away from the reproachful eyes of the mother, until one morning Lowe awoke to the riveting stench of puberty. One day

Lowe turned thirteen and saw that the aromatic petals of his childhood had been replaced with thin wisps of hair that lodged themselves underneath his arms and between his legs. His voice, which had once murmured and trickled like a stream, had erupted into a noise so sharp and brutal he couldn't recognize it. Was that his nose, round and smashed like a lump on his face, and were those unshapely logs shooting out from underneath him his legs? And why had people taken to staring at him so, the young girls hiding their ugly smiles behind their hands? And there was his skin rising and rising each time the men's eyes moved on him.

He saw that his father had grown more gaunt, more silent and sullen and hostile, more abstract. He felt for the first time the mother's glare searching the arches of his limbs and the cut of his clothes, which mimicked his father's, her glare on his disheveled hair. One day Lowe turned thirteen and realized that over the years he had acquired no playmates at all, his only companion had been his father, and now all of a sudden his body had changed and his father had disappeared neatly into himself and there was no one now, nothing at all but his head full of stories, his head full of dreams.

Lowe stirred uneasily from his daydreams. The smell of lime was stagnant in the humid house and weighty on the bark of his hands, which he brought slowly to his face. It was wet. He glanced at the letter again and rose unsteadily from his chair, the pair of suspenders that had belonged to Miss Sylvie's late husband despondent at his sides. A hand passed through his hair, which was jumbly, and he made a mental note to remind himself to tell Dulcie to ask Mass Clement for a trim next Sunday. He gathered the mutilated sheets together and straightened out their creased lines and curling ears. He tapped the shabby edges on the desk and then fumbled for matches in the drawers. Now wasn't the time for letter writing, that was clear to him. Furthermore, he had mistaken the significance of the dreams. He had misinterpreted the rising slate water sweeping through the village, the repetition of images night after night, he had mis-read the scene with his daughter turning away each time he tried to save her from the deluge, preferring instead to meet her own death in the deep and headlong storm of current. He had misunderstood the talking voices in his head, commanding him to bear witness.

He looked out at the room and saw with unseeing eyes Miss Sylvie's Oriental rugs that lined the floors, her columns of texts fitted into ceiling-high shelves, and her hand-woven tapestries and gilded oval mirrors scarred by mildew that covered the walls. From the deep recesses of his mind, he thought he heard the ticking of the pendulum clock in Miss Sylvie's hot and silent house. He waited until it sounded its iron music, then he gathered the letter, lit a match to one end of the sheets, and watched them burn down to curlicues of ashes. He carried his cupped hands to the doorway of the drawing room and looked out toward the clump of trees, toward the hilltop, toward the mountains and sky, as an incredible sadness rocked him. He scattered the dust on the heads of the sprouting rosebushes below and walked swiftly toward the forest, pillared with palms and coconut trees on which clusters of brown and green nuts clung.

The ground was soft and padded with dead leaves and dried guinea grass. Prickly blades raked his arms and legs, and a warm wind blew hard around him. Cattle walked in the distance, but he heard neither their plodding hooves nor their soft lowing. He didn't hear the crowing roosters or the miserable cackling hens. But he glanced behind him often, searching for movements in the tall and dark and crowded branches of trees, among the shrubs and plants that thrust themselves out of the earth and hovered around his ankles. He listened for footsteps other than his own and heard voices ringing in his head. He remembered the night of the burning shop and the savage murder of the dogs. The voice of the caller came to mind again. He turned it over and over, listening to its range of tones, its timbre, the fevered impatience. Sometimes he thought he recognized it, other times he wasn't sure.

When he reached the clearing at the edge of the forest and saw Cecil's grave, now fenced round with barbed wire and a ring of wild pink roses, his profuse melancholy so overwhelmed him that he threw himself on the concrete covering, buried his head in his hands, and wept, his voice a piercing lament. He wept for his life, which was cornered with disappointments at every step; for his daughter, whom he had deceived in the most sordid way; for his father, who carried the frustrations of his magnificent dreams on his face; and for Miss Sylvie and her undying affection, which he could never wholly return. He wept until the wells of his tears had emptied, and then he blew his nostrils into the sleeve of his shirt, straightened the mustache, which he'd tacked on again, brushed off his trousers, spotted with cement dust and sprinklings of marl, and wobbled slowly back to the house, his head alarmingly clear all of a sudden.

He had to get away from Miss Sylvie's sighs, which trundled after him all day, all night, throughout the house, her hands, which now were especially restless and waiting to stroke his shoulders and soothe his forehead and pull him to her chest so she could weep into his shirt. He had to get away from the prying stares of the villagers who came every Sunday to offer condolences, with bundles of flowers that littered the room and left horrible smells, and huge bowls of peppered stews, a portion of which he doled out first to Dulcie's Siamese cat, Hazel, just in case. He had to get away from the rambling house, empty without the dogs and suffocating him at every turn. There was no Cecil now and no shop, just the burned-out remains that suffused his nostrils and pierced every detail of his clothes, just the wide empty stretched-out days and the thirty years of silence between him and Miss Sylvie. He had to go and see his people, see Kywing and the community of Chinese that convened once a month at his house in Westmoreland. He had to rekindle his spirit, command his life, think up new dreams, fill up the deep bottomless gaps in his stomach. He had to start again.

3

Before daybreak, and with just a tip of his wide-brimmed hat to Miss Sylvie, who watched from the back door with eyes that seemed to be begging him not to go, not to leave her there alone and so soon, he climbed onto the saddled mule and was rumbling over winding, endless muddy dirt roads with the night at his shoulders and the cool morning air in his nostrils. He could not help her now; his own cauldron of grief was too deep; he had to look for help, look outside himself. Lowe rode quickly, keeping to the shadow of huts and lean-tos lining the hillside, slowing at bridges, mindful of rotting planks as he crossed beds of rivers and creeks, now dry and empty but notorious for rising up, overflowing nearby roads and washing away huts strewn along low-lying areas. He passed district after district, the markets like skeletons without the shouting, quarreling people, only rats and stray dogs and cats prowling through the garbage. He passed churches standing solemn and solitary without the singing, roaring congregation that would descend in less than three hours. It was Sunday, and the short steady clips of the mule's shoes were the only sounds that woke the quiet.

He rode past the bolted doors of unpainted, box-shaped concrete houses with corrugated zinc roofs, his trousers wet with the beast's sweat, until the sky started turning a shimmering rosy hue, and then the world took on life. He passed people, their donkeys laden with buckets of water, who nodded hello or called out "Mr. Chin." He began to smell coffee, pick out fingers of smoke from the pointed roofs of kitchen, smell frying, hear muttering voices. He passed naked children playing in the fine red dirt; thin white lines of smoke that rose from burning rubbish dumps; fat black carrion crows circling overhead; mule-drawn carts; listless donkeys; people drinking coffee from enamel mugs in the blackened doorways of houses and dunking in hardened pieces of bread.

He rode past yellowing pieces of white clothes hooked up on wire lines, and others spread out on jutting rocks to bleach. Now he rode past herds of cows; vegetable plots knee-deep with weeds; hills browned by drought; grass blackened by bush fires; endless fields with tall wire fences, empty now on a Sunday but on any other day flooded with workers. Amid all this, For Sale signs littered the countryside as deserted estate houses and factory buildings lay broken down in financial disaster, turning back to bush, in the wake of Emancipation. A pack of crotchety and emaciated dogs with powerful drooling jaws rushed at the mule, followed it for a while, grew bored, then disappeared.

Up and down, up and down, the road ribboning through wild and untamed hillside, he replayed again and again in his head how they must've done it, the gang of them, stumbling round the foundation under the cover of night, sprinkling the ground with kerosene. He saw the sea of brown faces he'd seen every night since he'd had the shop huddled in a corner, talking softly and plotting. He knew that like the church hall, protest groups were founded right there on the piazza of his rum bar in the dead of night and in hushed tones. That the labor unrest sweeping through the countryside and the workers' rebellion strikes against landholders paying them little to nothing and overwhelming them with work had started up right there with the glassful of rum cocked in their hands and the heads close together.

But he never thought they'd turn on him, though it was common accord for them to burn down the Chinese people's shops. Common accord for them to loot. The more militant types intending to clear his people out of the country. Still, he never thought they'd turn on him. But they must not have known Cecil was inside. Poor Cecil. Or maybe they knew! Poor Cecil. With his eyes wide open like that. He must've leapt awake to the oil drums exploding, his heart giving out immediately. He must've jerked awake to columns of smoke, blazing bars of fire, his heart giving out at once. For there were no bruises, according to the coroner, who inspected him carefully before filling out the certificate. Still, it was strange, his gray eyes wide open like that, wide open and surprised and staring out as if bemused by the turn of events.

Indeed it was a strange turn. Cecil had brought him there, had given him the shop, and now both Cecil and the shop were gone. But strangely enough he was relieved. Though he was flooded with conflicted feelings and earnestly wished that all could've been settled with the daughter before his passing. But he didn't miss Cecil. He felt clean and unburdened from the shop and from Cecil's plans. Yes, he missed the rust of routine that had protected him all these years, for now he just felt naked and empty and listless. But somewhere deep in him he knew that for the first time he could sort out what it was he wanted to do with his life. That fate now, in the middle of all this tragedy, was handing him the reins to his own life. He could rethink again those reasons that had brought him to the island and try to live out some of his dreams. He longed to unburden himself. He longed to walk free, without hampers saddling his shoulders, thwarting his pace. But he wasn't sure how. There was still the daughter to contend with, his marriage to Miss Sylvie, and the fabulous masquerade that was his life.

The mule slowed as they entered a stretch of idle lands, and he thought briefly of investments, then shoved it aside. The savings, and there wasn't much now, was for the daughter. Plus the idea of employing farmhands frightened him. It was hard enough asking a woman as old as Dulcie to boil him a pot of tea, hard enough waking and asking Omar, his age-mate, to feed and saddle the mule. He was always envious of how commands steamed effortlessly from Miss Sylvie's velvet lips, but he knew they came with the authority of near-alabaster porcelain skin. The coppery mass of hair that fell to her waist. With him it was a different story. He was the outsider. The foreigner. The newcomer. He had the burned-down shop there to show, to remind him of his place there on the island.

At this his eyes filled up, and he dug his boots deeper into the animal's gut. He had to see Kywing and the others. He yearned for the music of their frenzied dialects, the euphony of clicking tiles as they played games, and his mouth watered in anticipation of stews Kywing would prepare, embryonic chickens with tender bones in peppered soup, pressed duck and tiny bottomless cups of tea. He longed for vestiges of his family mirrored in the men who came, in their gesticulations and corroded faces, in the Morse code of their languages, which he didn't even understand anymore, but anything to remind him that he wasn't alone there on that wretched island. And then he longed just to see Kywing and his family, with whom he had grown close over the years.

Lowe rode on through the light of haze and heat, stopping now and again to water the mule, keeping away from the centers of towns, eating the lunch Dulcie had prepared, as he traveled endless winding roads that led to new districts, his face darkening under the onslaught of sun strokes.

All over the countryside church bells tolled, summoning sinners to worship. He heard feverish preaching and incredible pandemonium as hymns broke out and the possessed shrieked into the tin roofs. He passed the cluster of buildings sprawling along the hillside that made up Good Hope Estate, with its mills and its boiling and curing houses, and not too far off the thatched-roof barracks where the Negro people had once lived, and still farther off, the hundreds of acres of caneland, deserted now on a Sunday, just dry cane stalks and husks stretching to fill the horizon. Had it been yesterday, the yellowing stalks would've been peppered with glistening bodies: free Negroes; indentured Indian and Chinese laborers pouring in daily by the boatloads; Irishmen fleeing famine—hoeing, plowing, weeding, shielding themselves underneath wide-brimmed hats.

But though it was Sunday and no one was there, Lowe could still hear voices rise and fall to a tune that tiny trembling streams of wind had carried from afar, a song sung in an attempt to ignore assault from the never-ending backbreaking labor; singing to relieve pain in their twisted limbs, stomachs tormented from hunger, skins baking under a fiery sun; anger seething like trapped steam from lips. Sometimes breezes brought the whistling whip on its way to bite and cut and to dig away at the burned and desecrated flesh. But those sounds were no longer common, as there would be fights, murders, torchings carried out at night, households charred, heads wiped off by machetes and lined up by the gate for shiny, metallic flies to attack in the morning.

Lowe rode on, not a hut in sight, just a long, hopeless stretch of thorny acacia trees, an endless range of green hills then gray hills fading into the spacious white of the sky. Drowsy from the heat and from fatigue, he dozed to the steady lackadaisical clips of the mule's shoes, until braids of smell—musty charcoal from wood fires, pungent coconut oil, pickled pigs' feet—shimmered by his nostrils, lulled him to life, and he knew it would be only a matter of minutes and Kywing would be at the iron gate of the stucco house he had built behind the bakery.

He dismounted and let the mule loose in the pen across the road, where one of Kywing's boys would attend to it. He approached the house slowly, his head bowed, his heart broken, his shirt soaked with sweat, his hat in his hand. Sharmilla, Kywing's wife, was waiting. Her majestic arms, swaddled with silver bangles and some gold ones, jangled as she hugged him, the great cascades of her flesh and her sweet-smelling essences hemming him. "Man, we not safe here at all. Not safe at all." Her eyes, rimmed with black, glistened with tears, and Lowe grunted, his face a network of grimaces that meant nothing and everything.

He nodded and shook his head at intervals, not quite ready yet to stir up his grief. Though he wanted nothing more than to have lain there basking in her embrace, nothing more than to have her stroke his head and behind his ears and smother him with sweet tenderlings murmured in his chest. His suffering was so deep. His brokenness so complete. His confusion so enormous. Plus her embrace was never like Sylvie's; it wasn't full up with the same kind of yearning, as if some grave thing had been taken away, so that now she had to walk round with her arms outstretched and aching, and anything she touched she had to hold close, almost to the point of strangulation, just to make sure it didn't disappear.

But still he extracted himself neatly from Sharmilla's embrace and stepped back to admire the florid embroidery on the collar and pockets of her sleeveless cotton frock, and she broke down in laughter, showing the brown roots of her molars, and he laughed with her, wanting only to forget and to distract her curling eyes from lolling along the arches of his limbs, from reading him, a smooth-spined text.

For it was as if she knew exactly what lay behind the costume, though it was nothing she said, nothing she intimated, it was only in the rhythm of her eyelids, tugging at the brush of false hair that trembled above his lips, bursting the buttons of his striped short-sleeve shirt, stripping down his shorts, and so he could never linger long in the snugness of her embrace, never engage her for any length of time. It was always there between them, the overwhelming self-consciousness, the palpable silence, the charged glances. Once, for a brief and furtive moment, he thought perhaps she desired him, but he found the idea so worrisome, so marked with frustration and distress, that he wiped it completely from the shelves of his mind.

From his bag Lowe brought out the little surprises he had carried for the waiting children, twelve in all, who had turned out to greet him, stiff and shy in their starched and bristling Sunday shirts, the stunning frocks, their hair marbled and glistening from scented pomade. He handed out the colored bottles to match the assorted glass of their eyes, pairs of rubber catapults, and gifts from one of Miss Sylvie's husband's old trunks, wet with mildew and rotting in the buttery: three bloated copies of *Pilgrim's Progress*, with passages underlined in ink; a miniature birdcage, rusty and empty and with the gate missing; a magnifying glass with a jagged crack; an atlas with the pictures faded and the names of countries inked in Latin.

Behind them on the veranda, Kywing watched with a long gloomy face and a wide shaggy nose, and shook his head slowly, khaki trousers shimmering in the afternoon glare. Lowe climbed the short flight of concrete steps up to the shade of the veranda. He rested his wide-brimmed felt hat on the floor by his feet and sat down on the Morris chair with the arms peeling. Around them, the insects hummed, wild with the heat. Sharmilla bellowed, and one of the boys appeared with a piping-hot glass full of jasmine tea on a tin tray enameled with bright-red apples. Then she disappeared into the maze and clutter of the house, her slippers dragging on linoleum floors, and Lowe knew she wasn't far.

"Burn down flat, flat, Lowe! Nothing!" They dipped cheeks, then lapsed into island speech. Lowe's Hakka and his Cantonese had long since atrophied, from both lack of use and mindful forgetting, as his only company had been the villagers those early years and he'd so badly wanted to start over. Kywing's face was stern, and he wore a mustache much like Lowe's, a thick black brush of bristles, but unlike Lowe, who never touched his at all, except now and again to check if it was still there and to readjust it by winding the sharp edges thoughtfully, Kywing fingered his at all times, plucking and twining and smoothing as he paced the length and breadth of the veranda.

Lowe shook his head, eyes bright, remembering his neighbors dousing the building in the dense dark of the morning.

"And Cecil, gone too!" Kywing's hands, pale and bony, sprang off his face and clapped at invisible mosquitoes and flies, then he yelled at one of the girls to bring the bottle. The girl came and she had one of the books underneath her arm and she smiled at Lowe and Kywing slapped a handful of the juice on his neck and throat and the smell made Lowe's eyes slowly leak. "They going to turn us mad in this place with they hate, Lowe, seriously." He stopped his pacing to drink from a glass of white rum and light a cigarette from a half-empty pack that lay on the flaky arms of the other chair. Then his voice grew softer, and his meandering and fondling started up again. "Sorry bout Cecil, man, I know he mean much to you. I know."

Lowe didn't say anything. He wondered what Kywing really knew. He had never told anyone about the hell he lived on that ship after he was caught; how Cecil locked him up inside that cabin that barely had air, barely had light for weeks and months.

Kywing's voice changed and it grew confidential. He wasn't much older than Lowe, but the mustache, which drooped alongside the edges of his face and covered his fine lips and broken teeth, gave him an ancient look. "How much you need to start over, Lowe? We have something wrap up inside. How much?"

Lowe looked up. Suddenly he was alarmed. He hadn't even been thinking of another shop.

"Well, maybe you shouldn't start so big again, Lowe. I mean they might burn it down again. And then you just lose everything again. And with the business so little, they don't want insure us. Look what happen to Woo Lee. Look Wong T'in. They asleep in the back. They set them on fire. And the fellows they catch get off light, light. You think maybe you housekeeper, what her name, Dulcie, have something to do with it? Or her son, the young boy there. You can't trust nobody. Not even people inside you own house."

And at that Lowe started, for just the idea that the fingers of death trembled so close to his throat was unbearable. He shoved away the thought and brought again to mind the voice of the caller, and he wondered why now, why after thirty years, and not before, when he had just arrived there, when he didn't know them yet and was so much more vulnerable to their onslaughts. Why now, after he had turned godfather to so many of their children, had trusted goods to so many of them so they wouldn't starve.

"Well, if you want start big again, maybe you should move. Come down this way. More of us here."

Still Lowe said nothing, and Kywing grew desperate. Then he reached over and grabbed Lowe's knees. "I know, man, it hard as hell. And on top of that with Cecil gone. And still nothing yet from the police." He paused and together they said nothing. Together they coughed timid ahems to clear their lungs. Together they took deep breaths that swelled the caves of their stomachs. Then Kywing started up again. "You must have something save up? I mean all these years you working. What bout the wife, Miss Sylvie? She must have something."

"I need to think a little, Kywing." Lowe's voice erupted sharper than he intended.

"Man, you crazy!" Kywing clapped at more invisible mosquitoes and wiped his face over and over with the soiled white towel at his shoulder. "You have to just open up another shop, quick. You have to pretend things not so bad. You can't show them we weak. You have to just accept it as bad luck. Man, you can't stop to think. They going to murder we in this place."

But Lowe didn't hear him; he was thinking of how the Chinese killed themselves over the shops, all so they could send money home, return rich like the dreams that had brought them. They slept back there underneath the counters on top of long-grain-rice and unbleached-flour bags. They didn't buy shoes, didn't buy new clothes, they had the shop open from daybreak till the last customer emptied the bottle of white rum and stumbled out into the darkness. They had everything stored underneath the counters and could marry goods when things were scarce. A cut of butter with one pound of salt fish. One box of detergent with one ball of blue. And how the ungrateful people heaped abuses on them.

"Mr. Chin, big gill of coconut oil."

It didn't matter, his name.

And when their lives hit rock bottom, they came waving their fists. "Chinee, you shortchange me again! You sell me the rotting meat again!"

"Chinee, you thief me again!"

As if a little manipulation wasn't often the nature of trade.

Sometimes a woman would come hollering with a red rag tying up her head, two half-naked thin-limbed children locked onto her hips, their stomachs bloated out with arrowroot, the arms and legs white and spotted with disease. "Chin, I don't eat since Tuesday gone." By then it was Friday. From underneath the counter he handed over half a pound of dried cod and two pounds of rice, for somehow they had become his people too; these women who cursed and haggled him one day and the next laid out their woes, begging for advice on their wayward husbands and lovers. Yet now the shop was there burned flat to the ground. Everything gone!

Lowe broke out into a hard dry sob, and just as abruptly, he stopped. For during those fleeting seconds he allowed himself to rise up from the dregs of his despair; he could see that it was indeed a blessing, this massive destruction. That indeed he could try out another kind of life altogether. Not one that his father or Cecil had routed out for him, but one he could weed out for himself. And then it came to him. And then he knew. "Look, Kywing," he cried out into the blazing heat, his eyes suddenly bright and bursting, "what about a school?"

Kywing didn't say anything at first. He wasn't an attractive man. He also wasn't a sharp thinker. And his mouth turned disappointed and hostile. "A school, Lowe." He said this quietly, slowing down to look closely at Lowe, whose mind had erupted into a torrent of fantastical ideas and schemes. He would rebuild the shop into a school! A school for the Chinese children born on the island. A school and meetinghouse where they could hold weddings and celebrate festivals. All over the country a multitude of schools had sprung up. Mico Teachers Training, Munro, Mannings. Down by his way alone, five more missionary schools, two trade centers, and a teacher training college. Why not one for the Chinese so they could learn Commerce and Geography, Elements of Astrology?

"But that won't bring in any money, Lowe."

"Well, maybe not right away, Kywing." He tried to keep his voice even. It was his first dream. He saw it withering away. He thought of his father and all his bottled-up fantasies. He thought of Cecil and of the mangled bodies in his dreams. He thought of all those years he had so successfully and piece by piece erased himself. He didn't even have language!

"Well, that is damn nonsense, then, Lowe. I mean we not learners here, man. We didn't come to turn learners." Kywing lowered himself next to Lowe on the bench and began to separate, into small neat bunches, the hair on his face. "We just come here to catch we hands, sell a few things, catch we hands." He softened his voice. "Some of us going back home, as soon as the contract finish. Even my big boy there, talking this nonsense bout law, bout sacred and universal history! And the bakery there!"

"But, Kywing, maybe I could teach." He didn't like the whine of his voice, and so he coughed to clear his throat.

"But, Lowe"—he laughed out loud, and Lowe's face burned—"you not a teacher man, you not a scholar. How you wanting to teach?" He clapped Lowe on the shoulder. "You always ambitious, that's what I like about you. Ambitious."

"Well, maybe Wong Yan-sau." He'd been a schoolteacher in Kwangtung Province and now ran a bakery not far from Kywing.

Kywing hissed. He leapt up from his seat next to Lowe and started pacing again. "Look, Lowe, just take my advice and start again with fifty. All right, Lowe. A Chinese school and meeting-house, man. Then they would really chop we up in this place."

In the background, Kywing's wife scolded one of the children, then they heard a cuff, followed by shouts and a loud wailing, and Lowe knew, as if by intuition, in just that slap she had delivered, that Sharmilla had endorsed his plan. Kywing got up and yelled for one of the children to bring more drinks, signaling an end to the conversation. But Lowe's flurry of designs had just sprung to life. Every day now, boatloads of Chinese came. Maybe interested members could pool together what little money they had saved up and offer out loans, give out scholarships encouraging the next generation to take up law and medicine, public speaking and drama, and liberate themselves from shop-keeping. And just so the children would remember, maybe somebody could teach them Cantonese and Mandarin, so they could read literature. If they were still interested in business, then maybe they could form their own wholesale association, and then members could promote business and protect rights.

Further in the future, he saw this club, this benevolent society writing its own newspaper, reporting on events affecting Chinese both here and abroad. There would even be an obituary section and another announcing weddings and births, and still another reporting on those murdered in cold blood by the warmongering people, on those whose shops they looted and burned down, on those opening up new businesses. He would call it . . . And he thought for some time, until he arrived at the title of one of his father's short stories. The Pagoda. Later he would add on one or two extra buildings, a home for the aged, maybe even a kind of sanitarium for the ones maimed on the estates, those who couldn't work, too poor to pay the passage home. Maybe even a cemetery, where Chinese people could visit their ancestors, instead of those public plots where the government dumped poor people. Kywing handed him a tumbler of carrot juice, and Lowe turned it to his head, drinking with both feet stretched out ahead, as the future loomed bright with promises.

By late afternoon a bundle of overworked mules and donkeys and horses had gathered to graze in the field facing Kywing's house. They had come, the Chinese men, from the neighboring villages and towns and had assembled in his drawing room, some on chairs, others on old crates, upturned boxes full of bottles. And the older men, the ones who'd been living on the island for decades, with line-striped faces and bald patches underneath their wigs; the ones married to the Indian and Negro women, to the low-class creoles and hybrids; the ones teeming with prosperity or those just barely getting by from one day to the next; the ones still basking in the sweet waters of bachelorhood and those who patronized whorehouses and those who took each other in love, gathered round Lowe to heap condolences and encouragement on his head in the same rancid breath. And the younger men, the recent immigrants, who were bitter and burnished from beatings and fights on plantations, from overwork and malnourishment, became boys again, asking newcomers—who had just arrived from Macau or Amoy, seven, eight weeks ago, and had survived the three months' journey, the rotten and weevil-infected food, who had survived scurvy and cholera and seasickness, the mutiny that broke out on board—news about their sons and their women left behind, the Chinese women forbidden by law to emigrate. An open window blew in warm air along with droves of mosquitoes and flies frenzied by the furious heat, and the room shrank in size as the men ate and drank and exchanged anecdotes and sweated intensely. Someone brought a pipeful of the opium planters doled out to laborers, and they passed the pipe around, the room suddenly darkening with smoke, and those who wanted lost themselves momentarily.

Soon the conversation eased round to money, and they let Kywing know how much they'd saved, how much they would've earned at the end of the contracted five years, the worth of the loan they needed to start their grocery store. Back home some of them had owned a tiny shop that sold baskets and metal pots, had run businesses, selling hot noodles from a wood cart, fresh fruit. Others had been farmers or had rented a stall in the market butchering pigs and ducks, gathering up entrails in a bucket to sell later on, or poled ferries across the river transporting goods between neighboring villages. They were eager to start again.

In short sharp bursts of sounds, they spilled touching testimonials, variations of which Lowe had heard before, but he listened nonetheless and remembered again the letter to his daughter and all those nights full up of his anguished dreams, and he wished they could've been closer, he wished he had had the courage to tell her everything and that she could've been here now, listening to the virulent histories of their lives and the woeful conditions that drove them from China. With faces haggard and gray and bathed in the scanty light of the semidarkened room, with fingers still glistening from the India ink that bound them to contracts—two pounds a month for five years at seventeen, twenty hours a day, six days a week—they talked about China and about the debts.

They talked about the severe losses at gambling, the hunger that drove them to sign contracts. They talked about the violent clan fights and about the secret societies, how they were captured and taken prisoner, kidnapped and sold to agents with foreign ships. And then they talked about the hunger. Always the incredible hunger that killed their children and forced them to sell wives. And then their voices would hush and the room would plunge into silence and they would brush their hands over faces and over mouths screwed tight as they fought with the memories. Then another man would start, and even before he finished, another one began. Then they would become speechless again, broken down and ashamed at how they had been sold like dogs by their own, crimps working for the dirty foreigners.

By the end of the evening, Lowe could recite all the stories by heart, not because he understood all of what they had said—for the dialects were lost on him now—but because he'd been hearing the same atrocities over and over, all those years he'd been coming, he saw the desperation on their faces: the ones drugged and taken prisoner, others attacked by soldiers with weapons who threatened to drown them unless they got on boats, others tortured. There were the stories, too, of the contracts that promised one thing when they signed in Whampoa but presented another once they arrived on the estates; of Chinese coming to join a brother or an uncle on another island who had a successful business but were tricked here instead, to work the poverty-struck plantations.

"But didn't you come with you own free will?" Kywing blurted out, wanting to rebel against the depression that had plundered the room. "Didn't you sign contracts to come? Five years. They promise riches and food. And don't some of us have it!" He waved his finger around the room. "Don't some of us own grocery store and bakery, don't some—"

"But what is free will?" Sam Chen wanted to know, in a low voice that hummed round the room. He was an aged Catholic priest, whose mission was to convert as many Chinese as possible. "When you don't have one grain of rice to eat, you not free. When you don't have money, you not free. You turn slave to your stomach. Desperation drives you. Is either immigration or death, no!" Then he was still, and they stared at their broken shoes, at the black patches in the white linoleum, at nothing in particular.

Then suddenly it struck Lowe that for the years he'd been coming, all they talked about was home. The treacherousness of the Chinese there, the horror of the conditions that drove them away. It was as if the bitterness they carried could only be directed at the crimps, those Chinese who had sold them per head like rats to barracoon agents, owners of receiving vessels. It was as if that betrayal was greater than any humiliation they had suffered while chained up in those barracoons and beaten daily until their wills were broken, greater than the punishments doled out by the captains of foreign ships during the crossing, where many of the ships fell apart in the ocean—only one third of them ever survived the passage—their bones scattered, sunken in beds in the middle of the Atlantic. They never talked about the man markets that greeted them on the island once they arrived, how they were made to stand naked so the throng of planters could prod their open jaws and hanging testicles before buying them, how planters chopped off their glossy imperial queues and emblazoned, in bold red letters on their skins, the initials of plantations. It seemed as if nothing could be as bad as that, as bad as being sent to this bondage by your own.

The older immigrants never talked about the condition of the lives they lived here on the island, how planters rarely abided by the contracts they had signed back in Whampoa, in the pigpens. They never talked about Chinese on plantations who walked off cliffs from overwork, who hung themselves with pigtails looped round tree limbs, who tied stones to their feet and jumped in rivers or sat on banks waiting for the water to take them, how those that escaped the plantations were hunted down and strapped up to rafters and left there swinging, for birds to pluck. They never talked about how the Negro and white people looted and burned down their shops, heaped hostilities on them.

Yet as Lowe looked out at them, at their emaciated bodies, their shrunken and ugly cut faces, their bulbous eyes glowing with renewed hope, he found he could say nothing, either. He hadn't the courage to crush their expectations. The newcomers were too eager to start over again; he couldn't fail them. Couldn't tell them that yes, there were opportunities to be had if they persevered, but only at the expense of other people. They had been brought there only to supply cheap labor and keep down wages. They had been brought there only to keep the Negro population in check. As he looked out at them, bereft of speech with which to prepare them, he wondered bleakly if they would even be interested in his Pagoda. If, as Kywing suggested, it wasn't still too soon.

The din in the room roared up. The red disk of sun had sunk

behind mountains and the shadows of dusk had approached and the tilley lamps burned low on the huge table, throwing greenish light everywhere and deepening the bones on their faces so they looked old and mean and menacing. Sometimes the lamps flickered, other times they swelled in illumination, and the room stank of food and coconut oil and onion and garlic and pepper and sweat and kerosene smoke and burned wick and the roasted remains of the moths and fireflies that savagely flung themselves at the hot glass. They started to eat and drink and dance and gamble, and Lowe stumbled about with them in drunken merriment, singing different songs, while a hundred stories and quarrels ruffled the air and astonishing bundles of notes piled up on the creaking table.

Their voices grew loud and aggressive and rose up above the click of chopsticks and the snuffling of food from bowls. They became obsessed with their games and concentrated on their dice with attentive eyes. Their conversations grew heated, they drank heavily, they sweated, they groped at each other's groins and at their own, they exchanged soft laughs and knowing glances, they rained insults on one another in seven different dialects and in the next breath recited potent love verses. They played Chinese instruments and sang pieces of opera in untrained and tuneless voices, and though Lowe danced among them, drunk with the fervor of their concealed anguish, he knew he was not of them, that his life had taken a stranger path than theirs and they would never consider his plans, knew that they would only scoff at his dreams, which were so essential to him now that he had nothing, and the more his hopes burned in quiet diminishment, the more he shouted, drunk and dizzy with his own eternal grief.

It was close to midnight. Soon the men would disperse, their faces corroded by life and etched with fatigue, and Lowe would have to begin the six-hour journey back home to Miss Sylvie's sighs, her empty arms, the depressed house. He left the roaring din of the room and went outside, where the starry beams of lights pierced the blackened night. He sat down on the concrete steps of Kywing's house, and a great swirling sadness devoured him. He was afraid to leave; afraid to return to the people who had so violated him; afraid to be left alone with his tormented and misguided thoughts. Afraid to return to Miss Sylvie, who was brimming with need. Tomorrow was Monday, and he had nothing to look forward to. No shop to open. No concrete floor to sweep. No rum to serve to the people who'd come by and burst open their wounds. No sugar to wrap and weigh. No codfish to chop up. A cool wind blew through the leaves of trees, and he wrapped himself with spindly arms and rocked, his head folded between his knees, his ears humming with the frenzied dialects he could barely distinguish, his chest crowded with their lamentable stories.

And the shelves of his mind tumbled again, down into the rusty hull of Cecil's ship, and his ears were filled again with the cry of sails ripping to rags in big winds, with the churning belly of the vessel as it cut through black water, with the cymbal clash of waves and the clumsy scuttle of rats. There was the smell of grease and of smoke, of burning rubber, the smell of grain gone to rot, and then there had been the fever blazing through his limbs for days now, leaving him almost extinguished there on the planks of damp wood where he lay, too weak even to return to the fish barrel that had housed him.

How many days now, how many nights, had he lain there—the rats walking his face and teasing his veins, waiting; his trousers cruddy with stains and stinking; his tongue swollen with thirst and leathery in his mouth; his head in torment—before he heard the slogging footsteps through the gloom, the warbly whistling? How many days now? These were not the stupendous journeys his father had outlined. How had his people been swayed like this, fired up by this, when in truth the Chinese he had seen below, during his nocturnal stalkings, were there dying, were there starving and ill with diseases, were there chained to one another, chained to iron railings? Chained. An iron gang. In his village, there had been the stories of men who'd traveled abroad and who'd returned with their mouths full up of rare and exotic countries; men who, before they left, had been on the brink of starvation but had now returned in silken robes, with money to buy farms, send sons to become scholars. But there had been so many others, for whom they raised tablets once a year, in memory. This must have been their unfortunate fate. And his, Lowe worried, as the dark breathed slowly and the long awkward steps inched closer, as the warbly whistling grew louder.

The fear tapped him, and Lowe rose up covered with sweat. He peered out into the dank cold gray, at the swaying man moving toward him, sheathed in the fragrance of rum. On wobbly legs, Lowe edged, a giant crab. And burning with the last dregs of strength, trembling with the final gasp of potency, he swung, a lightning of steel drawn from his waist. The man ducked. Lowe swung again with all his might, out into the great undulating gray. The man sucked in air. Lowe's hand grew slick with blood. Lowe lunged again with the bleeding knife. The man knocked the fist; the knife disappeared without a thud. Lowe stormed again, his hands an iron clasp on the column of throat, across the pipe, wrenching the man backward, until feet crumpled, spine scalloping the floor. Lowe clamped his mouth to stifle screams, to ward off others. They lay there for minutes, maybe hours, just the two, like lovers entwined, Lowe's whistling chest, his roasting fever, his fading strength, his belabored breathing growing more and more faint, no light, just the undulating gray of the place and the groggy rats watching.

But all of a sudden the man was on his feet pulling at Lowe and lunging, hammering out madly into the undulating gray, pitching and swirling and swinging and swinging and floating as if in some frenzied minstrel. Lowe's jaws collected fist after fist, his head, blow after blow, and still he fought, with no strength behind the hands, bruised and wet and heavy on his wrists. Still he struck, steadily and against invisible surfaces, his teeth rattling, his nose pouring blood, until finally he buckled. And they tumbled down onto the hard damp floor, skittering the crates of shimmering silk, the chests of fine tea and spices, their limbs tangled and bloody.

Time passed. Lowe stepped from groggy place to groggy place. He tried to move his fingers, so fat now and slow-moving and without sensation. He tried to find his breath and heard instead a heave and a gasp. The gloom lay between them, long and deep. And outside there was the rush and roar of the sea.

The man lit a match. The light wavered. Leaving a white curl of smoke. The man lit another and another and another. Finally a blue flame, burning. Lowe tried not to bawl out, as the pads of fingers traveled the puffy contours of his bloody face, as the insides of his head drummed with the boom-boom of blood.

Then the clumsy fingers were busy at the humid throat, ripping open the padded jacket, groping for a thumping heart, searching for a slow-moving pulse along the hardened chest plate, the mass of ribs, only to wade into a banded chest, a banded chest and beneath that a ruffle of smooth lambskin and the dense weighty mounds of woman's flesh. Woman's flesh!

The match went out.

The man lit another and another and another.

There was somebody out there in the dark. Lowe made out the fiery tip of a coil of mosquito destroyer moving toward him. He heard the sweeping slippers, saw the majestic dignity in the shadowy figure. It was Sharmilla. She sat down next to him and he was at once comforted and disturbed by her presence. She smelled of crushed ginger and of roasted garlic. She smelled of yellow curry dust and of coconut soap, of polished leather and of violets. The night brought the distant croaking of frogs. It brought the call of an owl. A rooster responded. He expected

that she would want to talk, but she said nothing at all, and he
listened to her steady and deep breathing and imagined that she
must be thinking about her people back there in Demerara,
where Kywing had met her, or her people far away in India.
They too were arriving on the island by the boatloads and meeting a similar hell.

They had never been alone together like this, in the ten years
he had known her. All his feelings of self-consciousness returned.
Yet she didn't seem disturbed by any of it or even to notice
him. She seemed lost in meditation. He unwrapped his arms
and straightened his back. He was covered in patches of sweat,
and his breathing was still excited from the memories. He
searched in his pockets for the smooth square of handkerchief
and wiped his brows and the inside of his collar by his throat and
chest and returned it to the back pocket of his trousers, soiled
and crumpled and bunched into a ball. She hummed softly
under her breath and he thought that he liked the strange and
discordant melody of her voice. He couldn't begin to imagine
the kind of life she lived with Kywing, who struck Lowe as old-
fashioned and set in his ways. But Sharmilla, he knew, was not a
fickle woman; she had her own stall in the market, where she
sold pastry and cakes and candied fruits wrapped up in brown
paper, trays of square-shaped speckled eggs that originated from
the wombs of exotic birds, and perfect rows of plump pullets,
their feet tied up with English cord. The money she earned was
for her passage home, and she kept it tied up in a thread bag
close to her bosom.

The humming stopped in mid-note, and she cleared her throat
and paused as if about to tell him the gruesome details of her
life, which would color his image of Kywing forever, but then
the humming started again and his relief knew no bounds until
he realized that she had posed a question to him. When was he
going to patch up things with his daughter? And at first he was
just speechless with surprise at how knowingly she could read
him, then he swallowed and told her that he had been thinking

of writing her, and she said sometimes we expect too much from our children, expect them always to make the first move, expect them to apologize or to forgive. And he told her she was right, we expected too much. Then he was quiet, for suddenly the idea that they could run it together, the Pagoda, fired up into his chest and he was invigorated again with renewed enthusiasm.

Sharmilla coughed, and he told her he was going.

"Right away, Lowe?" There was alarm in her voice, and she grasped his arm closest to hers. "No, man, Lowe. Look how the night dark! Sleep here tonight and carry on daybreak."

He got up shakily and she stood with him, tugging at the material that had fastened itself in the deep crevice of her tremendous bottom. Lowe shook out his legs, and the deep green of his gabardine trousers trembled in the silvery speckled night. He was determined to see his daughter, whom he had neither seen nor spoken to in years, twenty to be exact. His voice was serious. He said, "I must go, so I can arrive tomorrow afternoon." He didn't tell her how he was afraid to travel the dark and winding roads so late at night and alone but how he had to overcome it, otherwise he would be as good as dead, there on the island. He didn't tell her how afraid he was to meet up with his daughter, who was a complete stranger to him and his life, this daughter to whom he owed a whole catalogue of information.

He was never a spontaneous person, but tonight was different. He bade farewell to Sharmilla, kissing both her cheeks, then went inside to say good-bye to Kywing and to his friends.

It was way past midnight and he hadn't slept in days, but his body quickly fell into the monotonous rhythm of the mule's trot, as the dark swiftly swallowed him. He didn't know exactly what he would say to the daughter or how. He didn't know how he would reveal his true identity or if he would. Maybe he would start off first by apologizing, though it wasn't entirely his fault, this estrangement, but he would take Sharmilla's advice, he wouldn't blame, and once she seemed more comfortable with him, he'd begin to tell her his dreams of the center, with the flame-breathing dragons embroidered in the concrete and wood; its double fringe of red roofs with swirling swallowtail ridges and leaping eave corners; the gigantic stone animals with fierce open jaws shielding the entrance; and beyond that the portico, with pillars wrapped round with dragons and illuminated by glowing lanterns.

In the yard he wanted a fountain surrounded by stone benches, pruned trees, plots of grass and rings of flowers. He wanted tiny streams pushing clear water over smooth stones, little footpaths bordered by chipped rocks, and he wanted just to sit in the courtyard, mesmerized by the murmuring, spraying fountain and the bellowing children rehearsing poems in Mandarin and practicing their calligraphy. He was barely fifty, but he wanted to relive his childhood in that hot small place on top of the hill overlooking the district.

And then he sighed out loud into the darkness, and the mule let out a long solemn wet wheeze as well, for there was so much to do and already his heart was starting to fail him, already he was losing his limbs to arthritis, his eyes to myopia, his memory to long, empty stretches of white even space, his stomach to frequent bouts of constipation that bloated and twisted the coils of his intestines. Then there was his daughter, a grown woman, who didn't speak one word in Hakka, who didn't understand him or know anything at all about his life, his past. Of course all of it was his fault, for he'd wanted so badly to fit in, for the two of them to succeed. Furthermore, what difference would it have made, when it was just the two of them alone there in the village, cut off from everything familiar, what was the use of his dialect there, and the stories of his family, and the songs of his people, when there was no war to fight, no family to inculcate with values, no power to preserve, it had been just the two of them, the two of them alone there among the Negro villagers. Of course, now it was different. Now he had nothing. Nothing at all. Not even the daughter on whom he'd bestowed no filial piety. He had to get Miss Sylvie to agree. He had to sell the plan to her. Figure out ways she would profit, for that would be the only way she would buy it. He needed her to clear the plan with the government, put it up in her name if need be. He had to save his daughter from the amnesia he had brought upon them both, save the other children as well, even if Kywing, if no one else, saw the use. He pressed the mule onward and rode without feeling exhaustion or hunger. Without feeling remorse or dread, though he stopped often to water the mule at standpipes and feed it with handfuls of the grain he had brought, and to let it graze in wild pastures.

He rode in the dark with the hooves of the mule snapping low branches that snagged the path and he passed the preposterous villas and gardens of the rich, silvery in the moonlit night, and when the moon slipped underneath a feather bed of cirrus clouds, he saw the dimly lit concrete and plaster hovels of the poor. He rode through the black thickets of parks, sometimes he stopped and dismounted and rested, other times he wandered on silently, and the mule, as if by instinct, ferreted out the route through the winding, serpentine path.

The sun had appeared by the time he turned east again, and it battered down on them and on the hilly and dry and hard red earth. The water in his canteen had grown warm, and the mule switched its tail though there were no flies. He passed people burdened with baskets on the way to market, overworked donkeys straining under impossible weights. The trees, foliage, and brush blanketed the roads in abundance, no sight of the shimmering glassy sea, just the blue-green mountains bristling with lush vegetation and fluttering butterflies, the meandering dirt paths broken up by ruts, the pure heat, the thatch-roof roadside stalls full of arguing women and girls and squealing babies, squatting and laughing and selling and buying and standing round and eating and philosophizing. Scrawny dogs and

peel-headed chickens rushed from the stalls to the road to yell at
the mule and then back again to the stalls, where they rooted
through the mound of rubbish in silence. He rode on, passing
stone buildings that separated into bank, infant school, drug-
store, hairdressing parlor, barber saloon, tailor shop, fish market, butcher shop, post office, church, rum bars, and grocers.

He slowly approached the center, where Queen and Princess
Streets intersected and where hundreds of handcart men sold ice
cream and snow cones and cool drinks and the brown and green
heads of coconuts. There was the high smell of meat and fish,
which rushed out of the nearby markets and into the streets,
where the haberdashers had spread out their wares on the
ground on colored cloths or in boxes. He heard the bells and
chants of blind beggars and seeing ones without legs, their trousers folded and hooked at the knees with shiny safety pins. Among
them too were the noisy children, busy at their complicated
games until they saw him, then they paused to stare at him and
to point and to shout out "Chink" before turning back to their
games. There were the musicians who sang in deep baritones
against the din of jangling banjo strings and stormy tom-toms.
The claws of hunger finally dug at him, and he stopped in the
center, removed his hat from his parched head, and staggered
past the mob of confusion, his legs wobbling from ill use. He
unsaddled the mule and looped the noose around the waist
of a sycamore and tucked his shirt neatly into the waist of
his trousers and checked if his mustache had escaped, and he
entered the square. He carried his hat in his hand and his
shadow lumbered ahead of him, mammoth-like and imposing.

There were men everywhere, some white, but mostly men of
a million assortments of brown, no two ever the same shade,
dressed in white shoes, some with string ties and felt hats and
bow ties and bowler hats and brightly colored short-sleeve
shirts. There were men who had faces broken up with laughter
and men with chattering mouths full of solid-gold bars of teeth
and men with smirking smiles and men with eyes that crouched
with anger. They stood in the entrances of bank and school and

post office and clinic and police station; in the entrances of the towering and Gothic government buildings. They stood in the entrances of bars holding glasses full of rum and bottles of beer and sticks of cigarette and rolls of tobacco. They talked and laughed and slammed dominoes on upturned crates. They stood with their legs wide apart, hugged their balls, and thought of their frustrated longings. They stood with their legs wide apart, a row of them, backs to the street, pissing and waving their blue cocks. They sat with their legs crossed at the knees and with their legs spread out in front of them and folded at the ankles and with their legs collapsed underneath them in a squat. They leaned against broken-down stone walls, against the wrought-iron gates that protected the colonial monuments; they wrapped themselves with frail, sinewy arms, they talked in loud voices, with wet eyes, about politics and the infertile land and the approaching drought and about their people back there. This they would say with their heads flung behind them, for the island, now erased of its original inhabitants, was composed of a transplanted citizenry. They talked about women and their pendulous breasts and swinging hips. They talked about women and their provocative and secret smiles, the drum roll of their tremendous bottoms. They talked about love.

With unhurried and precise steps, Lowe walked into one of the shops, and the smooth flow of conversation hushed. It was midday, and he carried his steaming sweat and the stink of the mule and his trembling radiance inside the shop. And they looked at him as if he were a rare bird indeed, with the sleeves of his shirt flapping round his gangly arms, with his voluminous trousers tucked into the mouth of knee-high boots with studded heels that resounded on the asphalt and concrete, with the bristling mustache that swallowed half his face. He nodded and they avoided his beaming eyes and he went up to the counter and saw the enormous crumbling wooden shelves tiered to the ceiling and stacked with tins of goods that winked in the glare of the afternoon.

He greeted the proprietor, who was an old Chinese man he

didn't recognize, and whose face was full of tufts of whiskers, and he ordered two tins of sardines in tomato sauce, half a loaf of hard-dough bread, one bottle of grape-flavored aerated water, a cut of cheese, and maybe one little red pepper if he had any growing in the back. He said all this in an English punctured with the few remnant pieces of Hakka he could recall, his face split up into a smile. He so badly wanted to feel close to this man, who reminded him of his father, he was so badly in need of community and of love all of a sudden and right at that moment inside the shop. Lowe watched as the proprietor's face tightened and folded and grew hard and lean and his eyes avoided Lowe's and stared out past him at the shopful of men who had been sitting there idle since morning. Lowe ordered again in English, his voice suddenly gone to rot, the muscles in his cheeks shuddering. This time the man brought a fat green and orange Scotch Bonnet pepper and a chipped enamel plate still dripping with water. He began to cut the bread, which Lowe noticed didn't look so fresh, and he arranged the slices nicely on the plate. But Lowe had lost his appetite. He sighed as he chewed, the food tasting like cement. He looked out at the road with bright eyes. Chickens and a few scrawny goats ran round confused in the heat, the dry earth, the fine red dust. A multitude of sand flies suddenly appeared and turned the world black. They disappeared. The world turned real again.

The shopkeeper tried to be friendly. He asked Lowe where he was traveling from and where he was going. He asked Lowe which part he lived in and if he had a woman and children. Lowe responded with words that were no longer than two syllables, bobbing his head up and down, grunting and gesturing with awkward arms that said nothing at all and everything. All of a sudden he was missing his shop and the spindly and rotund women with crocus-bag bundles on their heads who stepped in just to ease the load or to get some shade or to remove the thirst from their parched throats with a glass of rum or a bottle of Guinness. They would always talk and laugh in spirited voices and argue about the elections, the lying and thieving politicians, about education for their children, family planning, the women they loved on the side, about their wayward husbands.

They talked about the protest groups sprouting up all over the countryside intent on fighting the inhuman working conditions on the estates. They recounted again stories of Maroons who had lived in the crevices of mountains and had waged wars against white slave owners for over a hundred years. They clucked about their sons on scholarship in England, and those others gone to farmwork in Cuba and Costa Rica. They complained about the scarcity of goods and of work, the pittance they earned, the approaching war and the inequities of conquerors and empires. He liked it most when they lowered their voices and talked about their garish sexual lives and laughed deep, throttling laughs that revealed secrets and insatiable cravings. But the women would never linger long enough, though he opened up tins of sardines and offered them sandwiches made with fresh ginger buns, so they'd keep him company in the midday heat. Only the men with washed-out eyes stayed, telling him their broken dreams, their bottled-up fantasies, and asking about his life back there in that small village in Kwangtung. But now they were gone. Everything was gone. And inside his stomach he felt again the stirrings of a deep and incredible sadness.

He paid and wobbled out slowly, with no dignity at all in his steps, which moved clumsily one before the other, and into the blazing sun to collect his mule, and he took the reins and lurched on his journey to his daughter's house. He rode past a few more concrete buildings, then the foliage overtook the world again and there was only the one roadside stall here and there and the yellow sun coppering his face. He realized that maybe he was truly mad after all to be thinking of a benevolent society, especially when those white merchants beginning to harbor bad feelings against Chinese businesses had even gone as far as to enact bills now sitting in the legislature waiting for passage. Maybe he should just drop the idea at once and think of something else. Something more practical. But nothing came to mind, and a depression descended on him so profoundly he wanted only to throw himself off the mule, only to sharpen a stout piece of stick and run it through his chest, only to hack at his wrists with his knife sleeping there at his waist, anything, anything to relieve him of the abyss in his stomach.

And then he thought of Joyce, fabulous Joyce, who had been his friend all these years but whom he didn't see much anymore, though she had attended Cecil's funeral and had absorbed him with her hugs afterward. He remembered the shrill ring of her musical laughter, and the gorge in his stomach ebbed, and suddenly the journey to his daughter's house wasn't etched with as much torture. Joyce had been the only woman who often stayed at the shop to keep him company. She was married to Mr. Fine, who was a policeman and rode a shiny bicycle he imported from England. She used to come twice a week and at two in the afternoon, the hottest and stillest part of the day, when the zinc roof of the shop crackled and popped; when the tar on the asphalt bubbled and whirls of steam rose from the road; when the birds were still and the insects screeched a gruesome music and stray dogs and goats walked round dizzy.

This was when she would arrive, when Elizabeth, his daughter, was unconscious with sleep and he would be dozing off as well. She came always with new installments of stories about Mr. Fine and his warmongering relatives, about Mr. Fine and the corrupt policemen with whom he worked at the station, stories about her manic depression and anxiety, about the hideous details of their sex life and the incredible adventures of the three children she had for him. He looked forward to her moist eyes, which clamped shut when she sprang into laughter, the tiny rat teeth and purple gums. He diligently awaited her lunches of escovitched fish or curried crab or beef stews, always wrapped in white linen, starched and crisp. All those years she visited, he had never said much, just listened to her steaming chatter and laugh. Then one day he noticed that their interaction had changed. That she wore lower-cut dresses and more red on her full and heavy lips. That when she leaned over on the counter to tell him confessionals, though it was just the two alone in the shop, he was confronted with the great deluge of her breasts, with the poignant essences of her perfume and body lotions, with the gleaming dark of her velvet skin, which glistened in the unbearable humidity.

He noticed too that her dishes had become more exotic: croquettes made with codfish and béchamel, which she told him was Spanish; chunks of meats seasoned with Indian spices, pierced with a wooden skewer and left to roast submerged under warm ashes, which she said was kebob; and noodles tossed with fried eggs, golden squares of bean curd, and sprouts (he had no idea where she found those, for he was certain they didn't grow on the island), garnered with a rich and brown peanut sauce she said was Siamese. During all this, he noticed too that she touched him more when she spoke, and he saw that her fingers and hands were shapely. She talked and laughed less, though she asked more questions about Liz and Miss Sylvie, encouraging him to reveal secrets. Lowe noticed too and with much alarm that on Mondays and Thursdays he wore a cleaner shirt, spent more hours at his toilette, polishing his false mustache and sprinkling his throat with sandalwood, and that he had taken to saving the leaner, less bony and fatty, more tender pieces of codfish and salted pork and red herring for her, and that his hand on the scale was not as heavy when he weighed her rice and sugar and cornmeal, and that when goods were scarce he didn't marry them for her—a ball of blue with a cut of butter.

Then one day when she leaned over to indulge him in confidence, she clamped her wide-open mouth on his lips. At first he struggled, and the pressure of her hand on the back of his neck was strong and kind. His breathing by this time had stopped, his stomach turning into metal, and his tongue lay logged in the wide-open door of her mouth, while hers darted and burrowed, and slivered and cornered. He worried about Elizabeth, who

might awaken from the fuzzy edges of sleep, and about the villagers who might descend on the shop at any moment, herded
by Mr. Fine. He worried about the dribbles of saliva leaking
from either his mouth or hers, he couldn't quite tell, and he
opened his eyes slowly, peering out at the solemn world behind
her head.

He saw that the light had changed, that the sun was softening,
and that shadows were more diffused. He saw the quivering
edges of his mustache from the corners of his eyes. A black cat
crossed the deserted street and a purple-breasted robin flew
by. A mother walked by with six open-beaked and clucking yellow chicks. Her hand had tightened around his neck, and he
smelled the fragrances of cinnamon and oleander in her hair and
hibiscus on her skin, heard her galloping breaths and soft,
almost inaudible moans, but maybe those he had made up from
the sensational stories the drunken men told on the piazza each
night. He saw an enormous pimple on her cheek that he had
never noticed before, and an extraordinary long strand of hair
piping from the rounded tip of her small and flattened nose. He
thought she must have suffered much or was prone to deep
reflection, she had so many lines cornering her eyes and generous lips.

Then she pulled her mouth away, just as abruptly as she had
enforced it, fumbled in her handbag for the list of items she
intended to purchase, patted her straightened hair scraped away
from her forehead into a bun, though not one strand had come
undone, and began to read from the list. For many months she
did not return, only Mr. Fine came, accompanied by her children. He inquired once and was told that she was ill. He never
sent his regards, though he thought fondly of her, but he feared
that she might read more into his greetings and decide to pick
up from where she had left off. Several years later, she started
up again, this time without the dishes, and though they still
shared deep intimacies, it was with some formality. Lowe
remembered that she had hugged him at Cecil's funeral and he

had caught a glimpse of her watery eyes and a whiff of her perfume, the flavor of which was different, more fruity; the other
had been of spice.

He rode on, his heart graced with cheer, the journey filled
with much less foreboding. It was the middle of the afternoon,
and the world was silent, for even the insects were too miserable
to voice their despair.

When he arrived at his daughter's house, it was near evening.
He arrived with his skin scorched and brittle, his throat parched
dry as leather, and his eyes brown and muddy and full of dust. He
had never set foot in her house, but it had been described to him
so many times by Miss Sylvie and with such vividness and preci-
sion that he felt he knew each room by heart and the location of
all its contents. He tied the mule under a tree by the side of the
house and fetched water from the tank and corn from the buttery. He rinsed his face and smoothed down his hair and his eyebrows and adjusted the mustache. His fingers danced by his sides
and he put them into his pockets and tried to whistle. No sounds
came. A dog collapsed underneath the branches of a banana tree
opened one eye to glare at him, started to snarl, grew bored, and
stopped. Lowe walked on toward the house, passing a bicycle
leaned up against the wall outside the veranda. He had not prepared a script and was too exhausted now to compose one.

Swirls of music from the organ leapt out at him, notes
repeated over and over, then a pause, then repeated again. He
had not seen the daughter in years, and though a blurred image
of her still burned in his head, it was not what he expected when
he peered at them from the door of the veranda facing the road.
He did not know this woman who was tall and robust, with hair
that was a spiraling chamber of bronze curls that trembled
around her chiseled cheeks. He did not know this woman leaning over her student, pointing out notes with a ruler and explain-
ing bars and scales. She was tall and robust, with gray-speckled

eyes, and was tapping beats in her palm and counting them so he would learn.

The student was a youngish Negro man with a small head and a long thin spade of a goatee, and he sat on the stool, his feet on the pedals, cocking his head and admiring her face and darting furtive glances into the swelling breasts that crowned her chest. The house was quiet when the music stopped, and it smelled of boiled food. Cod especially. Lowe suspected that the husband was out working at his carpenter shop and that the son was asleep and the mother-in-law was attending to her grocery store, not far from the house. He hated to break up the intimacy between them, but he almost felt afraid for them and protective; it could've been anyone creeping up on them like this, watching.

He rapped on the door, and the columns of his stomach trembled. He had brought her nothing at all. No gift to give her as truce. No token prize of forgiveness. Nothing except his empty hands and his overflowing chest full of supreme joy, though there was the lurking fear that she'd pretend not to know him, that she'd curse him and turn him away. He could not find any traces of the girl he had raised. He saw that she was a mature woman; it was there in the sway of her hips, there in the foundation of makeup that masked her face, there in her lascivious laughter, which fondled the student's groin. They did not know each other. They were never friends. He had pushed her away, disclaimed her.

He remembered the letter and decided that since he was here now he would be frank with her. He would tell her the conditions under which he had lived in China and why he had left. He would tell her about the ship and about Cecil, and the reason for the life he had had to construct here with Miss Sylvie on the island. He'd tell her why he'd been so disappointed when she ran off with the Negro man, her husband. He'd wanted so much more for her, so much more than just mere marriage and the bearing of children. Maybe she could've run his shop after he passed, maybe they could've run it together and branched out, maybe she could've learned a skill and taught school. The island was growing, opportunities were opening up more and more for people of her complexion. Maybe she could've traveled. And at that he sighed and thought of his father. He would tell her that Miss Sylvie was not her mother, but that Cecil was indeed her true father and not him, Lowe. Not him, Lowe, as they'd believed all along. But he was afraid of the reel of questions that would come. Why the masquerade, she would ask, why the lies and the silences, and who was her real mother, then, and who the hell was Lowe? Maybe he would tell her nothing at all.

He rapped again and wondered if she was sleeping with the young man who was her student and whose brown eyes glowed as if with the fever of love. He didn't know anything at all about her or about her life down here with her husband, only the few details Miss Sylvie had given him, which had dimmed in his memory. She looked nothing at all like the woman he had seen in his dreams, and he worried at the huge gaps in his mind. Did she look a little like his mother? He could not remember what his mother looked like, he'd never spent time with her, yet there was something so familiar.

He rapped on the door and painfully watched her face jump from annoyance to fright to confusion and then to nothing at all. She had no eyebrows to speak of and had penciled in a narrow brown arch above her eyes that put her face in perpetual question. She smiled when she finally recognized him, and walked over slowly, knocking down a small table she must've forgotten about, which was in the way. A cat that had been curled up asleep underneath it sprang out of the way of the commotion. The student looked on, bemused by it all, and Lowe began to apologize. But she ignored him and brought him to the kitchen, where she helped him off with his boots, which had blistered his toes, poured him a tumbler of lemonade with ice swimming on the brim, laid out a plate of steaming-hot food, which he devoured at once, all the while attacking him with questions about Miss Sylvie: about her murmuring heart, her high blood pressure, her arthritic limbs, her prolonged headaches, the exquisite horses she bred, the choir in which she sang, the sonnets she wrote. She asked about Cecil and expressed regret at his untimely death, at the wicked nature of those people, his murderers. Had Cecil said anything before he died? Had he left any important messages? Had he seen it coming at all? She said nothing about him, Lowe, or the burning shop. About him, Lowe, she asked nothing. Nothing about his loss or of his health or of how he'd been keeping himself all these years. She wore the same smile that had greeted him at the door as if it were pasted onto her face, and it disconcerted him, for her eyes that were hard as stones didn't seem to fit into her face, and he saw now that beneath all her exuberance, her movements seemed stiff and stilted and her voice when she launched into her questions was teeming with hysteria.

He was adamant that she not dismiss the student, and after he had satiated his thirst and the balls of his eyes regained their gleaming white, he made his way slowly to the guest room at the back of the house, listening for some time to the tortured sonatas falling off black and white keys, refusing to think. He had not seen her in twenty years, and she had not inquired about his life. Not even one question. But maybe it wasn't so important, he decided; after all, here he was, able-bodied, he had not passed, they had not attacked him, Lowe, though they had killed the dogs. Plus here he was imposing himself upon her, for he had not sent word ahead of time.

He must have dozed off, for when he opened his eyes, the daughter was there at the side of the bed, watching him, and the boy, who looked like no one he'd ever seen, except that he carried Cecil's head of red corolla springs, was curled up next to him underneath the white sheets, watching him as well. He cupped his mouth and turned his head and made as if to cough and instead felt for his mustache and, upon finding it, straightened the edges. They studied one another quietly in the hot and silent house until his gaze slowly wandered away and he was assaulted with memories of those early years when he had just started the shop, those years before Miss Sylvie came, when he was mother and father to her, shopkeeper as well, telling the customers his wife had passed when their dark looks and prying eyes became unbearable. He used to walk ten miles in the blazing sun to buy goods for the shop, with Liz tied in a sling to his back.

How the schoolchildren ran behind them and jeered. How the women crossed the street just so they could tell him howdy-do, with curious laughing eyes, as if he were one of them. How, whenever Liz got sick, he had to lock shop and attend to her, morning, noon, and night, without sleep, just the two, and her roasting temperature and hacking cough, her body fuzzy with rash and patchy with fever. How he had to spend so much money on quack doctors' fees, squat silver bottles of medicine that only worsened her ailments. He alone in that place with her, and those suspicious people looking for every reason to rob and thieve him. To cut his throat and burn down the shop. He had just arrived. His English was spare. He couldn't read their furtive glances and secret smiles. He didn't understand their codes, their gestures of kindness. And then there were the days, too, when he just wanted her to die, when he willed her to die, so he could leave and not have to be indebted to Cecil and to this life. It wasn't what he'd imagined from his father's fictions and those of the men in his village who'd traveled overseas and returned with stories of wealth and good living though the work was hard. They had lied.

His daughter started to tell him about the book Miss Sylvie had sent her, and at first he was confused, and then she told him it was a journal, a travel journal Uncle Cecil had left there with accounts of some of his travels, a book with soft moldy boards, a flimsy binding, and humid pages that were loose, coming apart, sticking to her fingers and to each other, with pages that had been ripped out, reorganized, rewritten, still wet with ink that ran, smudged, leaked into sentences, that set the room awash with the humming, murmuring sea, the shrieking gulls, the clanging masts from the forests of boats.

Lowe was annoyed. He didn't know Cecil had left things and that Miss Sylvie had been sending them to her. He was annoyed at the prominence of the position both Miss Sylvie and Cecil had staked out in her life. Especially Cecil, whom she saw once or twice a year, for three days at most, when his ship full of stolen laborers docked and he collected his purseful of gold and he stopped by the shop to oversee his goods. Maybe he would bring her a trinket, a jade bracelet, a pair of red booties, and at night if he was sober he'd put her on his lap and sing to her all the bawdy songs they sang on the ship and he'd let her play with his beard, and maybe that was what she liked, what she remembered.

Lowe saw that her eyes were large and damp, and that her lips, pouted slightly like Cecil's, were trembling. He wondered what it'd be like to just pull her to his chest, just to hold her there. He missed her. He loved her. He hadn't done right by her. He'd abandoned her when she ran off, closed up his chest and locked her off. He wondered if she'd bristle under his touch, if she'd freeze up first, then pull away in a hurry. The gulf between them seemed so unbreachable. He stroked the sleeping boy's head, which was full of strange indentations and protrusions but was surprisingly comforting.

"You Uncle Cecil did love you a whole heap," he told her, trying with all his might to beat back a rush of feelings spoiling his voice, almost turning it rotten. For what else could he have said: that her father was a trickster, a rapist, a thief, a smuggler of illegal Chinese, a kidnapper, a madman, a demagogue? How could he tell her all that and still gain her confidence? Still gain her affection? "You finish read the book already?" he asked, slurping noisily from a tumbler on the night table by his bed. The room smelled of wood shavings and of dust and of fish glue and varnish and reminded him briefly of his father's shop and the rounded coffins and their lids propped up against the walls. Blue waves of nostalgia swirled around him.

"No," she told him. "Soon as I find time."

He saw deep lines by the corners of her mouth and even deeper ones that furrowed her forehead. He wanted to ask her if she was happy here with her husband, if she loved him, if she liked married life or was feeling asphyxiated. He had not seen her in so long. He wanted to ask her if she didn't think of him all these years, if she wasn't curious about his life there on the island, if she didn't think it strange that they hardly resembled each other at all, if the husband didn't ask. He thought again about the letter he'd been trying to write and wondered how the hell he was going to find words to say all that had happened on the ship, all those days and nights tied up, and who her real mother was. He saw her eyes again, large and soft and shiny and questioning, and he told her again that Uncle Cecil had loved her, almost like a daughter, then he was quiet. He worried about the contents of this book that Cecil had written.

Then she wanted to know more details about Cecil's life, so she'd have stories for him, she said, nodding toward the boy, who was awake again and who exchanged glances between his mother and Lowe with eyes that were equally skeptical and thoughtful. Lowe wet his lips and swallowed, his head suddenly crowded with a conglomerate of fantastical creations, and when he began, his voice was surprisingly clear and calm, though inside his chest his despair surged.

"At first you Uncle Cecil didn't know anything at all bout sailing or bout ships. It was his Uncle Rob who used to collect the African people and sell them, who give him the boat. And in two-twos he could read the sky like the belly of his hand, like a newspaper, he could keep watch and tiller the wheel and bow the compass. But since he was a man who like to watch his money, he hired captains to run things and he looked after the accounts. By the time he carry us here, the boat was old. In fact that was her last journey before he scrap it. His Uncle Rob had run it down almost to nothing with the trips back and forth from Africa. And then Cecil used to run her from India to Trinidad and British Guiana and Cuba, and from China. But that last trip, with us, she could barely make it. The mainmast had cracks and splinters everywhere, and it was wet and full up of all kinds of insects that had burrowed in there, the body needed a good coat of paint, the seams were ready to burst out, the fasteners and fittings on the keel, loose and ready to drop off, the bow of the boat use to dip instead of cutting the water; what he wanted was a new boat, one of those long lean sleek American clippers popular then, with nice masts and sails and bows and such and that can knife the water and chop up the waterways and can make the trip to the West Indies in half time."

Lowe paused to blink back wet patches of images that had suddenly broken his vision. He cleared his throat and glanced at the grandson, who had dozed off again. He marveled at his own inherent knowledge of boats and continued. "On that last trip there, on that nasty old boat, ready to turn over any second, ready to sink, he had eight hundred of us pack up down there. Eight hundred. And you should see how little the ship." Lowe's voice grew shaky. "Five hundred of them kidnap." Lowe paused. He wet his lips. "Yes. Kidnap. Drag out of bed deep into the night. Tie up and beat up and bundled off—"

He stopped when he saw that her eyes had turned into hard, deep, labyrinthine pools, that they had wandered off, and that the smile had reappeared by the sides of her lips. He sighed and began again. "Still, he wasn't a bad man. They had worse than him. He at least used to feed them, the coolies. Is that they call us. The same slur that they throw at the East Indians, but we one and the same. One and the same."

Lowe repeated it over and over, thinking first of Sharmilla before his mind slipped again, down into the mad frenzy of hull, down there among the rotten planks of wood crawling with cockroaches and rats and scorpions, that night Cecil had found him and they had exchanged blow after blow until he had fallen and Cecil had picked him up, swung Lowe neatly over his shoulders, and, stumbling blindly through the swelling gray of the heaving ship, had carried Lowe, who slipped in and out of consciousness, his mouth full now, so full with blood that he was afraid to cough, afraid to heave, just in case he choked right there, choked on the blood puffing up his cheeks.

Cecil must have moved swiftly and with cautious steps, as they passed behind the crowd of howling, crouching drunken sailors glued to a game of dominoes under a dull and wavering light, their roars breaking the sullen dark. What would they've done with this treasure, all of them at once and then individually, taking turns? Cecil must have staggered up the ladder, with unsteady legs at each narrow rung, sweat pouring from his face, blood gushing from the wound at his side.

Lowe woke up to the whistling of wind through the rigging. He woke up to the gentle undulation of the rising sea. To his right were the sounds of haggard breathing, the swig of whiskey from a bottle, the repeated scratches of matches on a box. He inhaled the smell of tobacco and another smell too, which soaked the room and reminded him of the coffin shop and his father's grave voice and the magnificent stories and the frozen dreams. Straight ahead in the dismal gray light he could make out the barricades of books, the sheets of paper and old maps dotted with ink spread out on the floor, tacked on the walls, and piled high on the great wide desk that dwarfed the room. Hanging off a hook on the wall was the dying light of a steaming lantern, and hung on pegs were hats and worn oilskins. On his forehead lay a cool rag. Across his throat lay a cool rag. His lips were hard and cracked, and he'd never known a more furious thirst.

Then the eyes fell on him. Fingers. Fondling the base of his slender throat, stroking the shelves of his jaws, rubbing the lobes of his ears. And his own eyes grew frantic, scrambling along the dusty carpeted floor for an exit, searching the dark wood panels for an opening, searching for a way to escape the awful silence. He raised his head just slightly, and the pain, as if crouched there waiting for him to move, sprang. He slid again into the furry edges of darkness.

He slept and woke and slept, and when he saw the world again he saw Cecil kneeling there, his face bathed in sweat and in fading light, his eyes sunken into enormous and deep caves as if they hadn't slept, as if they'd been in watchful attendance all day, all night, nursing Lowe back to life, cooling the forehead that rolled in delirium, wiping away froth that leaked from the sides of lips slightly bruised and swollen from the rag put there to suppress bites. Had he been biting? And Lowe buckled under again, into that secret fluid, and when he woke up he didn't know whether it was night or day, but he recognized the sea salt smell and the slow steady shudder of the ship as silent currents pressed up against her belly. He could hear, too, the low hum of voices, the harried steps of moving men, the crying timbers and the creaking mast, the loose cables splitting and lashing the sails. And always, Cecil was there, bathing the blue columns of his shackled feet in salt and vinegar water, so as to pull down the swelling, traveling the rag up and around the thin flabby calves, above the puffy kneecaps and further still, along the lean thighs and bony hips, parting the sooty down, parting and leaving the sodden rag there.

"Pa."

Lowe heard his daughter's voice as if from far away, and he felt the sturdy pressure of her hands on his shoulders, and he looked up again into her gray speckled eyes and remembered. "He try hard, Cecil. He wasn't like them others. He try to follow the government rules. But still. From a sensible point of view he had to separate the legal ones, the ones that sign contracts, from the ones they kidnap." Lowe hoped his voice was sincere enough, that his eyes would not betray him.

"He try hard, Cecil. He didn't leave them to die hungry. Four, five times a day, he hand out tea, hand out rice and salt fish, hand out water and allow them to blow and knock the instruments they carry, flute and cymbal and such. And he talk to them, for he was a traveler, he knew a few words here and there, he tell them bout Caribs and Arawaks, original inhabitants of the island they were going to, and about how the Spaniards came, raping and pillaging with guns and Bibles and the words of God. Two, three times a day he bring them out for air, walk them up and down on the deck, a chain gang of them clanking as they drag the iron. He hose them down with jaze and then water to kill crab lice and then leave them there little to dry off, to yabber at one another."

Lowe paused again to wet his lips, and then he told her about the ones flung off the boat and back onto the streets of Canton to die of starvation; how in that stifling heat of the ship's gut there was just the floating gabble of their voices, the slap-slap of their lips, which ate without tasting a thing, without even chewing, such an indifference they had. They'd been on the ship five months total. Half of them were already dead and thrown overboard or just leaning up next to one another, stiff with rigor mortis. The rest of them carried faces crumpled up from fear, faces with no life at all. They carried eyes with the lights extinguished. How they keeled over by the dozens, how they just dropped down dead from the homesickness, from the nasty food and dehydration and disease. They hung themselves with the imperial queues, a group of swinging men. Lowe's voice was bitter. He didn't care. If she didn't like it, she could get up off the bed and go her way. She could shut her ears. She could take the boy with her and go.

Behind his daughter's head, through the window, the sky was tinted pink by the dying rays of the sun and full of fast-moving cumulus clouds, and he saw the timidly approaching arch of dusk and the leaves of trees sheathed in amber light, and Lowe wondered where the hell was her husband and why was the bloody house so solemn and why were the walls bereft of mirrors and of pictures, of any vestiges of her identity?

That evening at dinner, Lowe saw Cecil in the wide gaps of his son-in-law's teeth; saw him in the hazy glow of the son-in-law's eyes; heard Cecil in his deep, throttling laughter; saw him again in the somber pathos of his son-in-law's gestures; and he asked himself with quiet alarm, had Miss Sylvie seen this grotesque manifestation? All through the meal, he observed them with vigilant eyes, though he was silent as a hawk and passive, for he had not come to gawk on the strangeness of their life, or on this decrepit old man whom she'd escaped the convent school to marry; he'd come only to reconnect with his daughter, who was a complete stranger to him, only to try and make amends. And if possible, to try to seduce her with his plans, which he had been carrying around now for so long he felt choked up with the information. But the old man was so slovenly and unshapely, though his voice was deep and kind. The man was so much older than Lowe, so much older, and didn't he look like Cecil!

Later, when they had retired to the drawing room for cordials, and the husband inquired what he was going to do, now that the shop was gone—was he going to take it easy, or try to build it back, was he going to rent out some of Miss Sylvie's land so his people could build houses on it, or start up farming?—it spilled out, and Lowe forgot entirely about Cecil's teeth in his son-in-law's mouth. He told them about the school and benevolent society, about the stone animals guarding the entrance doors, about the spraying water fountain, about the manicured lawns and picturesque gardens, the skills they would learn, language and clerking and more. He told them about the new jobs they would hold, teaching and doctoring and policing, the additional buildings that would come later on. During all this, the husband just smiled, nodding his head full of bushy white hair and crinkling his cheeks full of long tiny pleats. But when Lowe announced how he wanted his daughter to run the meetinghouse with him, the smile disappeared from the husband's wrinkled face and his eyes hardened, though his head, like a gecko's, kept nodding.

The husband's mother looked on with admiration gleaming in her eyes, cloudy brown from cataract, and the grandson, who had never heard anyone speak so passionately or eloquently about anything, and as if expecting something further to occur, leapt from his chair and went to put his head in his mother's lap. She stroked his head, which was a pillow of loose and large and rose-colored curls.

"At first is farming and such. Then next thing shop, and before you know, a little shop in every blasted corner you turn. Now is school and property. Soon you have my people working for you on the estates, cleaning for you in the big house. Calling you massa and such. Calling you . . ." He paused and then he smiled again, with the pleats foresting his face and the kind eyes twinkling. "What next, eh?"

He said it so quietly, so passively, and with the bushy head rolling, Lowe wasn't even certain the husband had said anything nasty at all, until he heard the gasp from the daughter and saw her face brightening, and the mother-in-law's eyes suddenly clasped onto her glass of port. The boy slipped from his mother's lap and onto the floor underneath her chair, where the cat sat. Outside, the fretting hens prepared to roost on the branches of a bamboo tree. Inside, the husband's mother's false teeth clacked as she worried them, the sagging jaws moving up and down. The husband inspected his tumbler of brandy, pouring into the deep-brown liquid, watching his distorted reflection glare back at him. Then the giggle started, a slow, shrill, rising, hysterical, and twisted noise that leapt from the daughter's throat. Lowe watched her mad eyes and freckled cheeks, the face marked with suffering. She laughed until his mouth corners trembled with ache. He watched her unable to stop, and she continued, until the insides of his stomach ached just from watching her beautiful and big teeth.

The husband roared at her to stop, and Lowe rushed at the husband, wanting to tell him to mind his blasted voice, who did he think he was barking at. But he did nothing at all. He remained seated in his chair with his eyes rooted to her face and watched his daughter's laughter come to a full stop, and a bundle of tears rushed out the corners of her eyes instead. She wept long and hard and deep right there in her seat across from the organ, which was closed up now and covered with an ornately designed antimacassar that he was certain the mother-in-law had knitted. She wept long and hard, with the tears falling into her glass of brandy, her shoulders shuddering and buckling, her nostrils clogged with green snot, and in a strange way he felt relieved just from watching. In some strange way he knew she was crying for her lost childhood with this old man, and for her Uncle Cecil and the bind she and her Chinese people were in, there on the island, caught up as she was between two estranged worlds and not wanting to choose sides, though it was growing harder and harder not to choose. At that moment he saw her bravery and her brilliance, and his love for her was without bounds.

She continued to weep as the mother-in-law cleared the table, and the boy stopped playing with the cat to put his head in her lap again, and the husband, pulling and scraping the chair and clearing his throat, stretched and made his way clumsily over to them. He was the spitting image of Cecil, Lowe thought, except for his dark skin and his hair and whiskers, which were so completely white, though he worried that exhaustion and the shadows from the candles and lamps might be playing havoc with his vision.

That night, crouched underneath the towering pillows, Lowe couldn't sleep; he stared into the darkness, watching his dreams defeat him, watching his yellow spirit swirl about him in delirium. He wanted to go and wake his daughter, to plead with her about the clubhouse he wanted to build, this Pagoda, to beg her to give him a chance to fulfill his one and only dream, but he lay there suffocating under the burdens of his rapidly failing attempts. And what would she have said? That a center like that wasn't really necessary. We didn't really need to preserve anything. After all, everyone on the island was mixed up. No one was pure anymore. Look at her. And at her son. So many schools now for everybody to learn whatever they'd like. There wouldn't be the need.

Plus was their Chinese history any different? she would've asked. Was it any different from that of the Negroes, who had arrived there in a similar fashion, kidnapped and sold and bundled off and beaten up and dead in hordes on ships. Was it any different from that of the Indians coming now, standing on those very same auction blocks, trying their best to blot out the memories of their own middle passage? Or maybe, she would've said, the benevolent society might make them too noticeable, might make them more of a target, especially when already there was so much turmoil and bad feelings; it might really show the Negro people that they planned to stay. Planned to take over. Why not leave things alone; they were business people, traders, they hadn't come to take sides, they were outsiders, they should keep their distance as such.

He realized that he didn't know anything about her. He didn't know in which direction her head spun. He saw again that they were strangers, that it would probably take years before they could get close, and he blamed himself bitterly, for he had never showered her with affection as a child, had only pushed her away.

He had never told her stories of his life in that river town on the Kwangtung border, of his tiny village on a peaceful green hillside that overlooked a river that was the commercial life of the town and was always clogged with houseboats and junks. He had never celebrated her birthdays or lunar new years and the other festivals of his birthplace. He had never instilled in her filial piety or ancestor worship, never acknowledged the elaborate rites and celebrations connected with marriage and death, with her very birth, her existence in the world. He had never told her of his father's fervid imagination and how he and his father had been bottom and bench, hand and glove, eye and socket, until he turned into an adolescent, his body changed, and the father, who had no spine to speak of, betrayed him. He had kowtowed to custom and given Lowe over to the cripple.

He had never said a word about his mother, whom he'd never known himself. She'd always seemed so distant. He had never taught his daughter any of the stories and poems and songs his father had told him, had never taught her the languages of his clan, which he had been masterfully trying to forget. He had taught her only those skills Cecil had taught him on the ship, to read and write English, to do simple arithmetic so she could in turn run a shop. He had tried to keep her away from the half-naked children that ran round the shop half-starved and lovingly called her red mongrel. He had tried to beat out the bad English that crowded her mouth, the break-up sentences she learned from the shop people. It was so impossible. And he'd been so full of alarm when her ability to speak the villagers' dialect grew to surpass his own, even to the point where he and she could hardly communicate, for Lowe was not as versed as she was, and he had not taught her one word of his own tongue. Now thinking back, it all just made him desperate, for he saw how clearly they needed each other. He had not been a good parent, and was this now the price? Was this the unfinished business, then, brought over from generation to generation? Was this it, then?

The miserable whining of an ill-tuned violin wafted through the open windows of his room, and he imagined that the husband was wide awake as well. He fought off his depression, pulled on his slippers, and went to the door. The moon shone thinly on the rusted zinc rooftops and turned the leaves of some trees silver. He heard the fluttering wings of bats. The lazy dog started to snarl.

"Who there?"

"Is me, Lowe."

He heard the instrument being lowered to the ground. He

heard slow approaching footsteps burrowing into gravel, the snap-snap of twigs. The snarl continued, and a voice gently told it to quiet. The night was cool with the crazy rustle of trees, and the sky gleamed with stars that gave off little illumination. There was the scent of jasmine.

"Look," Lowe started, as the steps neared and he could smell brandy and sweat and oil and sex. "I, we, not trying to take over." His voice started to tremble. "Jesus Christ, man, I just lose the shop." His voice started to break. "I just lose everything, and now I want a little place where we can have ceremonies and the like, a place so you little boy there won't forget, man, won't forget that he part of two, of three." Lowe cleared his throat and was surprised at himself. He had never yearned for anything quite so concrete in his life. "Just on the way here, yesterday, I pass five, six new building, schools. Why we can't have one too? I mean the government not going to do it for us. We have to do it for we." The husband was quiet, except for his labored breathing and a few tortured laments escaping his stomach, and Lowe was a little surprised too by the political nature of his discourse. He worried that the husband might be a member of the Native Defense Team, which was pressuring the government now not to sell land and give out loans to foreigners. Still the husband said nothing, and Lowe went back to his room and began to put on his trousers and boots, which were dusty and caked with old mud.

But immediately he was swinging back outside, with a heated face swelling with anger. This was the man who had taken his daughter; had seduced her away from him all these years, had turned her against her people and toward his own, this man to whom he was pleading, asking permission to have a damn meetinghouse for his people. And he didn't care anymore about this man who was his son-in-law, this man whose Negro people had worked hard to free themselves, only to see themselves replaced. This man was his enemy. This man's people had burned down his shop flat to the dirt, had taken everything he had, this man who was as old as he was, this man who could've been his daughter's father, this man who was the dead stamp of Cecil. And Lowe lurched at the husband's throat, out there in the rapacious dark. He lurched at the husband's throat and heard the astonished gasp, heard the growling dog slinking away in fear, felt the husband's slow staggering as he fought for air. He had done nothing to these people, nothing at all, except to live there next to them, provide for them the very things they needed, and now they had burned it down, now they were turning against him because he wanted to build a clubhouse, a meetinghouse, a Pagoda.

Lowe wrenched his fingers even tighter into the fleshy throat. He listened to the troubled breathing, to the thumping veins under his pincer clasp, and still he held on, until the husband recovered from surprise and flung Lowe to the ground. Lowe leapt up and lunged again, but the husband was quick and he grasped Lowe's fists in hands that were iron wrenches, and Lowe, packing his jaws with spit, lashed mouthful after mouthful of foam at the husband's face until the husband set him free, and the two were quiet except for their haggard breathing, their swirling emotions.

Lowe collected himself and straightened his shirt, tightened his trousers, and the husband said nothing, only coughed to clear his throat and to swag his neck and massage his throat, which still hurt like the dickens. They stood there sheepish in the moonlit night, neither one speaking or glancing at the other, until the husband broke the quiet.

"Who this man Cecil? That's all she talk about, morning, noon, and night. Ever since we get the telegram. Now she want the boy there to turn into sailor, to work on ship and travel. Now she want us to book passage on boat and travel. I mean who the hell this man, who the hell!"

Lowe walked away slowly and went back into the room. He ran his trembling hand over his face and found his mustache. He picked up his hat and his bag. He didn't say good-bye to his daughter, but he knew she must have watched the exchange from behind the curtained windows of her bedroom. He fetched the mule from the side of the house and didn't say good-bye to the husband, who he imagined had returned to his seat on the log underneath the tree, shaking his head. He had stopped coughing.

Lowe rode home to Miss Sylvie's house in the trembling dark. He rode home with the rude smell of the son-in-law's sweat furred in his throat, with the son-in-law's laments still singing in his head. He rode home with the shrill ring of his daughter's voice bubbling in his ears, with his chest full of regrets. He had accomplished nothing. Nothing whatsoever. Only shame and a hellish bruise on his thigh. And now here he was going home to Miss Sylvie's empty arms waiting for him, to the empty old house and to the razed building that was his shop. Here he was going back home to nothing whatsoever. And there was the gap in his stomach churning about again. There was the gap that tunneled away at him, that poked and fired at him.

Sometimes he rode with both legs dangling over one edge of the bloated belly of the mule, just gasping out into the hostile night. Other times he rode leaning low on the saddle, his body flung forward, his chin rustling into the wet withers of the heaving beast, just jabbering out into the black. Finally he fell asleep, dozing upright on top of the moving beast. And when he awoke it all began to unravel before him. He saw plain as day how he could get his meetinghouse, his Pagoda.

He would make love to her. He would kiss her face over and over so she felt the full softness of his wet lips. He had never in all their years together initiated lovemaking. But he would do it for the center. For wasn't this the way men got what they wanted? First by seduction and, if that didn't work, then by force. He would murmur things in her ears with his pointed and freckled tongue. He would kiss her roughly with the edge of teeth, tighten the rim of ear in his warm mouth, blow moist air into the solemn curve of her throat, the dip between her breasts. He would go further still. He would kiss her large and weighty breasts, nibbling the ruffle of purple skin around the knobby nipples before stuffing the whole delicious fruit into his mouth. He would go further still, and twice a day if need be, and certainly every night. He would nestle his nostrils into the fuzzy cups of her armpits, fuss with the straps of her nightdress, meddle with the hook and eye at the throat, the knot of string laces, fiddle with her soft white drawers. All this while he still wore his coarse green trousers and worn brown riding boots. All this while his shimmering silver buckle glimmered in the dark and rubbed up roughly against her soft skin.

Then he would lean into her stomach, breathing in her potent body smells, dissolve into her desires, drinking her sea-salt silkiness until her stomach heaved, her ragged breathing melted into moans and laughter, until her thighs buckled against him, until she was exhausted and glistening with sweat. Until she was feeling sweet and generous. Until she was loving him completely, loving him to death. Then he would lay down his plans. Outline his dreams. Tell her the amount of acres necessary, draw up the blueprint on a sheet of paper right there in the room with the lamp close by throwing off strange shadows against the walls.

By the time he rounded the aging cotton tree by the side of the blackened concrete columns that was the shop, the legs of his trousers drenched and the air stinking of a broken-down and destroyed foundation, dawn had announced its slow approach. Lowe sped up the hill, the hooves of the mule drumming the moist earth, his torso sweeping a parallel along the shaft of the beast's neck, his hair like shelves leaping on his head. He cornered the house and saw the brilliantly lit lamps in the steel-gray dawn; he saw the shadows swaying behind the embroidered lace curtains. The mule slowed, and Lowe felt the panic rising in his chest. The mule bucked with the front hoof and pawed at the ground. Lowe tugged at the rope, but the beast would not move. It foamed at the mouth and wheezed into the night. In a soft voice loaded down with disappointment, Lowe leaned into the musty ears. "Is just Whitley," he cried into the tunnel, wanting desperately to calm his jangling nerves. He was so completely weary. "Is just Whitley." And then he was quiet, for he knew it would be a good two weeks, running into a month, before Miss Sylvie would be available again.

He waited outside in the yard, yearning for the dogs to press their wet nostrils against his waist. Cool winds blew around him and demented fireflies sped by. In the distance he heard the miserable shrieks of a cat in heat, the monotonous howls of dogs. Around him the night hummed with the frenzied symphony of insects. He fed and watered the mule, patting and stroking its mane, and muttering praises that flowed ceaselessly from his lips. He inhaled the potent discharge of flowers that perfumed the night. Despondency weighed heavily on him. He raised his head again toward the curtains of the guest room, facing the water tank, and saw that the lights now were turned off, the house fused in black.

That night he prepared the bed in the room at the other side of the house, far from the clatter of their voices. That night he locked and bolted the door and hid the keys, struck by the savagery of his thoughts that implored him to wreak disaster on their love. That night he took off his boots, caked with mud, and the wet socks and left them outside the door. He hung his hat among others on the peg on the wall. He peeled away at the bristly mustache and vowed never to wear the disgusting thing again. He removed the bills and loose change from his pockets, dropped them on the dresser, unbuckled the belt, and removed his trousers. Piece by piece he undressed, with care and without haste, laying the accoutrements of his masquerade on the dresser, while the pictures on the wall, Miss Sylvie's still lifes, the one gilded mirror, and the remaining bare walls, full up of shadows from the lamp, watched him.

That night he carried the face of a person who had suffered a hundred indignities and betrayals. And indeed he had. For how could she bring in Whitley now when he needed her so badly? How could she, when he'd lost so much, suffered so much? And couldn't she have waited till Cecil's bones turned to dust before she was in someone else's arms? Couldn't she have waited! He paced the room, folding her white clothes wherever he found them, pressing them each to his nostrils, her corset soaked with the odor of her skin, which lingered in his mouth, her soiled drawers and sweaty slips, before tucking them away. On the mantel, his fingers were frantic, rummaging through her green medicine bottles, through brown envelopes of yellow pills, eyes pressed together deciphering the names and dosages scripted in capital letters. It was as if she were dead and he was left there lovestruck and smoldering, though she slept not so far away in another room, in the snug embrace of someone else.

That night he lowered himself in the depths of the bed, which was exceedingly large, lowered his head into his hands, and acknowledged that he didn't know anything at all about Miss Sylvie. He didn't know why she'd agreed to come to live this masquerade with him. He didn't know what she was running from or running toward. Sometimes she went away but never for long, and always she returned with her face haunted, as if there was the fear of being hunted. He didn't know what kind of agreement she had had with Cecil. He didn't know what she wanted or needed out of this entanglement. He didn't know who she was or how to please her. And maybe it was his fault, for in the same way he didn't know his daughter, in the same way he had neglected her, he had neglected Miss Sylvie as well. All these years he'd just clogged up his head and buried his mind with the rust of routine that was the shop, never giving himself the chance to feel, to acknowledge all that was going on around him.

There was Miss Sylvie and the old housekeeper, Dulcie, and Dulcie's son, Omar, and all those years living there with them and all those years his not seeing them, not getting to know them. All those years! Was that possible? Was it normal? The way he had locked up his chest, closed down his eyes, fused off his heart. All those years! Hearing only what suited him and shutting up his ears otherwise. Sinking his head underwater if it disturbed him. And so now he was not sure how Miss Sylvie felt about him, Lowe, and the sham of their marriage after all these years and whether or not he could even ask her to help him build up this Pagoda. He didn't know who Cecil was to her, how they had met, why she had agreed to become a mother to Liz, why she had agreed to come and live there, live with Lowe as man and wife, what she was running and hiding from, if she had loved Cecil. For why else would a woman still so young, still so beautiful and feverish with life, come and retire her life away there in that bush? She had nothing in common with the local people. She could marry anybody she set her eyes on. And still!

He had never seen her grieve his absence when Cecil left to travel for six months, close to a year; she had never seemed impatient for his return. When Cecil came, she entertained him in the same back room by the tank where she entertained Whitley when she came. Did she love them? He himself did not know the meaning of the word, he did not know who they were to her. He had never seen her misty eyes weep or grow faded and downcast when for that one full year Whitley ceased from calling; he had never seen her eyes blaze with rage or glow in exhilaration when Whitley arrived in a horse-drawn cart and spiraling clouds of yellow dust, laden with dazzling gifts and a bashful smile.

He imagined she must have confided in Dulcie, who had been her housekeeper back when she was married before. He decided that perhaps they shared secrets, though in public there was always the distance of class between them, the distance of color. They never walked two abreast, Dulcie always lingered a little ways behind, and it was not because of the slow leg she had to pull. And when Miss spoke to her in front of company—for it was never that way when the two were alone, as Lowe had noticed—it was always in a voice loud and precise and with the words carefully drawn out as if all of a sudden Dulcie was hard of hearing and slow.

If, from the train of men Miss Sylvie employed to till the land or oversee her animals, Dulcie had taken one on as a lover, he had never discerned it. Yet one had to admit it was strange. All those years they cohabited in that house, and he didn't know anything about Miss Sylvie, or she about him, except the details Cecil must have told her before the arrangement, and those things she had told him, Lowe, at the beginning, when her mouth was youthful and full of strange and beautiful dreams and visions.

One thing was certain, and that was she cared for Liz in the deepest, most profound way; she loved Liz. And as that had been the arrangement from the very beginning, that she serve as Liz's mother, he had to admit she played her part astonishingly well. Those early years, he had been jealous to see Liz so admiring of Miss Sylvie's porcelain skin, her precise speech, and the cloak of hair that fell heavily down her back. She mimicked the pendulous swing of Miss Sylvie's hips, the fantastic drumroll of her bottom, the shrill laughter that grew more pronounced, more frivolous, when her friends came to play bridge. Under Miss Sylvie's tutelage, she learned organ music and voice training, she watercolored enormous volumes of wandering animals and assorted birds, rode the horses in the stable and recited entire volumes of English poetry. It got to the point where Liz no longer visited him down at the shop, as if she were ashamed; he barely saw her, not even to cut her hair in the same bowl cut he had worn as a child though her hair was more unruly and refused to adhere to the style.

Over the years, he had watched her slip by him, ripen into a woman, and he planned in his mind how to get her away from the stares of the slovenly men at the shop, whose watchful eyes undressed her. He saw how she flirted with them, and in his fear of what they could do to her, in memory of what had already been done to him, he barked hard, short curses at her, and she cried out and told him so often how she hated him. And he, uncertain how to love her, or protect her, without feeling regret or loss or anger, without feeling jealous or anxious, had just stopped loving her altogether, growing distant from her instead, growing indifferent and uncaring. Little by little he must've destroyed his affection altogether, he was so loaded down by his fear, and she, sensing his withdrawal, must have pulled back as well, clinging to Miss Sylvie even more, and to Cecil, the few times he visited.

At Cecil's funeral she didn't weep, Miss Sylvie. She sent for the coroner, who came to inspect the body and to prepare the certificate. She sent for people to come and prepare the ground. They had come, entire families of them, and for three days straight, with powerful saws and axes, the men felled tree after tree, hauled away cords of timber and cleared the land of stones and grass, uprooted stumps and rocks, dug the hole, cemented its sides, smoothed the planks for the coffin, while the women cooked huge vats of food and topped glasses with more rum and stitched the red satin interior and wailed and wailed all day, all night, as if Cecil had been taken directly from them. They worked until late at night under the yellow glare of kerosene oil torches and started again early in the morning, with the first fingers of dawn. He didn't ask her why she hadn't sent word to Cecil's family; why none of his people were there. He didn't ask her the exact amount Cecil had given to her over the years to assist in Liz's upbringing, but he knew it was plenty, for gradually over the years she had pushed off the poor people from their scratch of land and slowly acquired hundreds of acres for close to nothing.

At the funeral, he had tried to avoid the dark smiling eyes of villagers, who turned to stare and to talk quietly among themselves. He had searched for Miss Sylvie in the black crowd of mourners, and when he picked her out, he had noticed for the first time that there were sprinklings of gray at the roots of her enormous hair and that the rounded shelves of her alabaster jaws trembled. Her eyes too had seemed wild and frightened, in a face that was a mask of seriousness. Had Cecil's death unhinged her in the same way it had unhinged him?

Maybe Miss Sylvie had expected more from the marriage Cecil had arranged. A more tender kind of intimacy? Cecil had arrived early that Sunday morning with a priest, a short broad-shouldered man with a great head and a dark beard. He had brought Lowe a solemn blue suit made of strong English cloth that made him itch and sweat, and a white, shiny frock made of Chinese silk for Miss Sylvie, who refused to wear the dress she had already worn to her first marriage. It had been a small ceremony. Just Dulcie and Omar and Cecil, the priest, Miss Sylvie, Lowe, and the daughter, who was two. Cecil had brought rings as well, flat bands of gold, and the priest, whom Cecil must've paid enormous sums of money, had blessed them right there in the drawing room and one month later had mailed the certificate, which was now rotting with mildew and yellow but still hanging above Miss Sylvie's organ in the drawing room, framed. She laughed loudly and gaily those first years, and though he saw her only late late at night when he locked shop, or in the twilight gray of morning when she was still drowsy with sleep, or on Sundays when the shop was locked all day and he caught glimpses of her between soaking his aching feet in steaming pails of Epsom salts and the throng of visitors from distant districts who came to talk politics or business or to play bridge with her, all along he had fixed it in his head that they were each just playing a role till it was no longer necessary. There wasn't supposed to be any greater intimacy.

He imagined that Whitley must have given her all the things he had deprived her of. That Whitley had loved and admired her shapely bow legs and muscled calves, had showered compliments on her waterfall of hair, had flooded her with expensive gifts. He hadn't invested anything in this relationship, and whatever she might have invested personally, aside from what was expected, he had never acknowledged. He saw very clearly, then, that there was no reason now for her to care about him, or about his plans. Cecil was dead, the shop was gone, and Liz was grown, though that morning when Miss Sylvie poled through the rubble of the burned shop, he had been struck by her glistening cheeks, struck by her silent weeping, and he had thought then that it was curious, especially when Cecil was lying in the orange grove not three feet away. She hadn't gone over to look at the body. She hadn't raged at the villagers for killing him. She only wrung her hands repeatedly and then touched her throat as if to check if her jewels were still there. Briefly, he had wondered how on earth she had ever become entangled with Cecil and why she had agreed to such a peculiar marriage and how much she was paid and if she too was running away from a past full of secrets and locked doors and was here now just biding her time. But just as immediately he had brushed the thoughts aside, not wanting to know if her dealings with Cecil had been as torturous as his.

But all those years he had had the shop. And Cecil. And Elizabeth, his daughter, whom he had named after the island's governor-general's wife. When Miss Sylvie's lover came, he didn't have to hear their laughter rippling throughout the house. When the last customer left, he bolted the door and slept on a bag of long-grain rice underneath the counter. Daybreak, he splashed water on his skin and wiped it down with a rag. The villagers gossiped, but he plugged up his ears and blinded his eyes. Now there was nothing. Nobody. Not even the daughter, who had foolishly given herself over to her husband's whims and desires, who had forgotten completely about her people, who had betrayed him with her silence, her inaction.

That night he did not wash, though Dulcie had left a goblet of warm and perfumed water on the stand, though he was tired and dirty. That night, as he blew out the lamp and eased underneath the cool sheets and pushed his head deep into the soft feathers of his pillow, trying to keep at bay the anger that rose in him, the temptations that flung themselves forward, he craved, as he'd never craved before, in the most virulent way, in the most visceral way, the prodigious noises and smells of Miss Sylvie's Sunday nighttime preparations: the unclasping of hooks; the stirring bed as she removed her corset and slip, then fumbled for the nightie folded underneath her pillow; her pleading undertones as she quarreled with God and with herself about the value of what she was about to undertake; the chokefuls of breaths as she swallowed, one after the other, thirteen fat brown pills; the intestines' fierce and immediate rebellion and the frequent ahems to clear her throat and mouth of their loathsome tang; the malodorous ointments used to ward off the throb of arthritis, hereditary in her family; and he would fall asleep to the movements of her full-body massage, which swayed the bed, to the warm sole of a callused foot shifting against his calf.

4

The next day, he awoke close to four and looked out the window by his bed and saw that the ground was damp, that it must've rained overnight, though the rosebush below and the green clusters of banana trees beyond looked more wilted and exhausted and depleted of sap. He awoke close to four and was alarmed at how easy it was to grow slothful; especially now that he no longer had the shop. Aging terrified him, and each morning, with microscopic eyes, he examined the obscene warts that were once sweet and innocent moles. With a thudding chest, he listened gravely to the gurgling juices fermenting in his system and knocked repeatedly on his wrists, measuring the deep pulsation of his heart. Grazing with two fingers and a simmering brow, he studied intently those joints that had a tendency to crick or tingle or twitch; bruises that had crystallized into festering cankers; pieces of his flesh that had either petrified or pulped.

And when there was nothing, he whistled as he washed and

sang in off-key notes and yawned with astonishing vigor that bespoke an interior calm. But if there was anything, as there had been several years ago, the lump that cemented his left breast, he plunged into a strange and complicated self that absorbed him completely. He stopped eating and talking. He suffered. He locked the shop, crept into bed, and drew the thick red curtains, blackening the room. He refused to see the quack doctors with their hard and battered black bags, allowing not even Miss Sylvie to breathe on him. And each morning, with cautious fingers, he nursed the lump, mollifying it with the exotic oils and herbal potions he had sent Dulcie all over the countryside to procure, which drenched the room with fetid odors. When the lump finally dissolved, the crumbling-alabaster look disappeared from his face and the crinkles round his eyes straightened and he regained his sprightly walk and boisterous laugh and he offered credit and free rum at the shop for one whole week straight.

That afternoon he snorted and splashed and whistled in the tub of tepid bathwater, sprinkled with perfumed leaves and the bark of great trees. He trimmed the sides of his head near his ears and blackened the tufts of gray. He waxed his false whiskers and curled the pointed edges thoughtfully. He oiled his hair and powdered his skin and perfumed his throat. Back in his room, in the open door of his wardrobe, he rummaged among the clothes Miss Sylvie had passed on to him from her first marriage but that he rarely wore: slinky and shimmering silk shirts, striped cottons and twilled linens. He parted sharp lines of gray and black suits, and one by one, in slow meditative gestures, turned over shiny pairs of shoes, tasseled brown loungers, inspecting their leather, the cushioned interior that wrapped the feet in velvet, bringing them slowly to his nostrils, then looking off with glass eyes as if seduced by the slender and straightforward curve of heel.

He tried on a gray checked suit, but the cloth scratched and he exchanged it. He tied his neck with a silk scarf and scowled at the profusion of colors that knotted his throat. As he walked toward the clatter of their voices, he caught glimpses of himself in the many gilded mirrors lining the walls. His forehead worried, and he straightened it at once, composing his face into an expression of calm, of steely determination. He fretted at the large slabs of orange in his suit and at the silk bordering his neck, which made him claustrophobic. He glanced in the open door of Miss Sylvie's guest room, his eyes settling on the half-empty glass of water on her night table and hardening at once at the sight of the indentations of their heads on the pillows, the tousled white sheets, bedraggled from their wild night of lovemaking, and he could still sniff the sweat and perfume that clung to the hot damp air. The closer he approached, the uglier he looked and the more he worried about the task he was to undertake.

They were there, the two, out on the veranda, sitting together on the couch with their backs to him. They drank tea, hot and sweet, that Dulcie had prepared, and he saw that the red outline of Whitley's lips still lingered on the sharp white rim of the cup. Miss Sylvie's eyes were closed, her head thrown back, the lighted pipe on her lips. Whitley's great white arm shouldered the couch, the fingers lost in the warm ringlets at the base of Miss Sylvie's neck. Not knowing how to chop up this closeness between them, this intimacy, Lowe paused in the entrance and listened to the low worried tones of Whitley's voice complain about the rioting and rebellious Negroes, the spontaneous acts of disorder and chaos and anarchy exploding all over the countryside, at the ineptness of the police to protect them, them, the porcelain alabaster people who for decades through marriage tried to bleach stains of black Africa from their skins. She talked about the severe shortages and soaring prices, the government-imposed rationing. She talked about injustices and of unfair imprisonment, which Lowe remembered had been a frequent topic of conversation on the lips of the men at the shop. Before they burned it down!

He hated how they ignored him, how they pretended not to

have heard his steps, not to have inhaled his persistent perfume. He coughed and cleared his throat, pulling up his trousers, which were tight and made it difficult for him to breathe deeply, difficult to move with ease, for the lack of room in the short crotch chafed him. Still no one moved. He shoved both hands in his pockets, intending to jingle the coins there, but there was nothing except his folded white handkerchief, bordered with his initials. He coughed again, blowing his nose furiously into the handkerchief, but as there was no phlegm, the noise was not impressive. He sounded only as if he were wheezing.

Finally Whitley looked up, and he saw irritation crouched there in her eyes, red and wrapped with kohl, and in the poise of her stiff white neck with the hair hanging loose and in supple waves on top of the square shoulders. Her eyes then lurched away, and he could tell she was thinking of what to order him to do, so he would disappear, but he was not dark-skinned, he was not of the African peoples, not mixed race, not Indian, not low-class white, he was Chinese, different altogether, his people were immigrant merchants, were threatening the economic stability of her own alabaster people, so she said nothing at all, and her irritated eyes climbed back up to his composed face and Lowe saw bitterness burnishing the horizons of her pupils, and he knew she was thinking of his relationship with Miss Sylvie and he wanted badly to smile, for suddenly he felt a rush of strength.

Whitley turned away with a shift of her black curls and lifted, with ringed fingers that slightly shook, another stick of cigarette from the pack lying there on the wide flat arms of the couch and brought it to her lips. With one quick scratch of match, Miss Sylvie lit the tip, and Lowe saw the misty outlines of somersaulting dogs, of flying snakes and swooping birds of assorted shapes swirling from her lips, rounded up and projected forward. He saw that her fingers no longer shook, that her eyes had taken on a glassy glare, that her jaws were no longer in tension, and even he relaxed just from watching.

He sank down into a nearby chair, defeated. Neither one

looked at him. He tried not to stare at their fused shoulders and hips and thighs sitting there on the couch, not to stare at the smoke coiling from Miss Sylvie's soft lips, at the blackened rims of her eyes, which were swollen and red. Whitley's face too was wet. Lowe squeezed the handkerchief in his pocket, uncertain if he should offer it. Maybe they had had a fight. Maybe he was mad to try to come between them, to try and ask for what he wanted, to establish his rightful position there with Miss Sylvie. They both looked drugged with love, and neither one paid him the smallest regard. Whitley stroked her right knee with circular gestures, and from his seat he saw the muscles rotating in her back and shifting against the stretched fabric of her tall white dress, which belled over the tops of her shoes. He saw the curve of her cream calf sheathed in silk stockings as the rustle of muslin rode up her legs. He had tried so hard never to let himself feel so much turmoil and confusion. He had tried so hard all these years to bay his emotions.

"Everything all right here." The squawk of his voice embarrassed him. Still no one glanced his way, and he saw now in their long tender gestures, just in the way their massive shoulders slightly brushed, just in the way their plumb and angular bodies tilted, both facing the hills and gray sky, away from him, but turning so attentive and tranquil and yielding an arch, he knew that this was different from what he lived with Miss Sylvie. He knew that what was displayed here in front of him was some hot deep dark searing thing. He knew that what was displayed here had nothing to do with how he awoke each morning to Miss Sylvie's humid palm on his throat, or her heavy hand thrown carelessly over his rounded stomach, the sole of a warm foot shifting restlessly in sleep on his calf. What was displayed here was sharper and wetter and hotter. He shuddered just from thinking of it.

Finally Miss Sylvie spoke into the quiet. It was late afternoon and hazy, as if making up to rain again, the sky an iron blanket and the air still, no movements except for the tortured flies and mosquitoes that approached them, the gray buzzing of bees, of droning beetles, the leathery lizards that slithered by his chair and stopped at the squared toes of his shoes and stuck out a fiery orange tongue and nodded and slithered off again. There was the clink of porcelain cups settling into the circular bases of the saucers. The scratch of cloth from the slight movement of their legs. "Whitley want more. She want me to move there and live with her. And maybe she right. Things here drawing to a close now."

Lowe glanced quickly at both of them and at the dark deep caves around their soft sad eyes and the green forlornness blowing around them. He saw the great oblong shadows cast by their stout figures extended across the polished tile of the veranda. From the opposite slope of valley, deep in the green mass of banana grove, came the short and sharp and shrill call of birds. He felt a great fluttering in his chest and thought he wanted to cry. "So what you asking me for then, if you mind already set, what you asking?" He was barking at her, and in his mind he saw the image of the center diminishing, heard the waning cries of schoolchildren, an orchestra silenced and without musicians.

"Well, you asked, eh, Lowe, you asked."

His lips trembled. He wanted so hard not to be possessive, not to seem so weak in front of Whitley, but there was such a turmoil in his gut, such a deep tunneling, and his chest was constricted and he felt as if he could barely breathe. He rose from his chair and faced Miss Sylvie's high and glistening forehead, faced the top of the head that was beginning to thin and feather. "Look, you place is here with me. You hear that." He banged his hand against his shallow chest. "Not with this woman. This . . ." He was out of breath. He was frightened at the hysteria in his voice, at the cords standing out in his flushed neck, at the false foolish quivering mustache he saw from the corners of his eyes. At his bared copper teeth that snapped up and down in his mouth. "Tell her to pack up and go now." He pointed at Whitley and took a step forward. "Tell her to go." A fugitive smile unsettled Whitley's face before it was immediately absorbed. Miss Sylvie didn't even blink. And Lowe, blushing all over and hot with shame, rushed almost tumbling to get away, his eyes full of tears, arms helpless by his sides, flailing around, searching for invisible exits, doors through which to escape. Inside the kitchen he brushed a stack of plates from a table with the sleeve of his hand. They crashed to the floor and he looked with surprised eyes at the destruction before him. Tears slid to his cheeks then, though he did not feel them at first. And that was when he thought of all those years between them.

How she arrived one morning with a colony of luminous gold butterflies frolicking round her head. It was late June, and the air vibrated with the odorous smells of blooming lignum vitae trees, and a horse-drawn cart rumbled to a halt at the mouth of the shop. It was still early, but the searing sun had already centered itself and was beginning to suck back early-morning moisture that had glistened the backs of leaves and stalks of grass, wet the legs of trousers or the heels of shoes, and had left sweat on the panels of glass and stone sidings. The shop was empty and Lowe was sweeping, cupping water from a chipped enamel dish perched on the counter and sprinkling the concrete, stifling the spiraling dust. Cecil leapt out, lean and angular in a frayed white frock coat and felt hat, and said, "Lowe, I bring a mother for the little girl." Then he disappeared underneath the canvas covering of the carriage.

Lowe swept, with trembling hands, sweat and dust clinging to his face and neck, the sun beating down on his temples and burning his white shirt. He worried. Admittedly, he was relieved. Finally the people would stop talking behind his back. Finally Liz would have decent company, and he would have help with her upbringing and with the shop that was slowly starting to prosper. But still he worried. For every time Cecil came, it disrupted the relationship he had built up with the villagers, who only came to distrust him again. Every time Cecil came, he was assaulted with the memories of the ship. The dank, dim quarters of Cecil's cabin with the cold white light pouring in through a porthole and the wooden panels glistening with charcoal sketches and watercolors, the loose, rough-cut sheets of brown paper scattered across the carpeted floor with illustrations, the scrawl of letters and words Cecil was teaching him.

He remembered rope wrenching into his narrow wrists, Cecil's footsteps hurrying with the enamel bowls of rice and the goblets of water for the baths. Cecil's frowsy smell filling up the room that was their home; his callused hands rough on Lowe's shoulders, his breathing quick and sharp in Lowe's ears; Cecil's face buried in the back of Lowe's head; Cecil's teeth tight on the tip of his earlobe; Cecil's fingers buckling and unbuckling, buckling and unbuckling, and Lowe lying there, no image behind the expressionless eyes, no movements from the taut and tightened limbs, from the soft, thin shell, no movements save for a soft and precise singing from paper-thin lips, nothing save for a face of indelible calm.

And still Lowe worried. For what would be the price of the mother Cecil had brought? He knew Cecil enough by now. There were always strings with him. Always. Just six months ago, when Cecil last visited, he had been furious that there was no decent food to eat, just dusty tins of sardines and bully beef on wooden shelves; no place to sleep except in squalor, underneath the counter, on top of an old rattan mattress full of chiggers. Lowe had continued to wait on customers, whose pricked ears and wandering eyes betrayed their curiosity. He had continued to tally up their purchases with a steady hand and a precise arithmetic. But the edges of his eyes strayed. They followed the abrupt movements of Cecil's frenzied gestures: the way his fingers hooked and unhooked like cripples, the way he ground his teeth, rotated his jaw, and blinked often. He stank of rum and of sweat and of old and unwashed clothes and of day-old cigars. He swayed from drunkenness and from fatigue.

After the shop closed and it was just the three, Cecil paced and fidgeted. And Lowe, completely absorbed by the riot of unrest, lurched with Cecil's short quick steps to the barred windows of the shop that looked out at the squalling rain, and back again to the locked door that faced the empty square, and back again to the barred windows that looked out at the silvery slant of persistent squalls. During all this, Cecil complained. He wanted to know where the profit was from the capital he'd given Lowe. One hundred pounds. If, like a damn fool, he was allowing those nigger people to eat him out and what kind of blasted Chinaman was he, anyway. What kind of blasted China businessman. This he said with laughter clacking through his false teeth.

Slowly, steadily, Lowe had begun to seethe. His eyes were muddy and his limbs blazed with the pounding fear. He opened his mouth and in an ostrich voice said, "Did you once ask me what I wanted, when you bring me here? Did you know anything at all bout me when you throw me the bag of money and the shop key and left? Left me with the baby so weak and sick?" Lowe's stomach hardened, redolent with memories, even though down there, down there, he was moist.

One day Lowe awoke to the awful singing of sailors; to a wind swiftly collecting and burying their music, then replaying it. One day he awoke to a blinding sunlight, to a gush of sea air blowing in through an open porthole, to a washing and whirring of silver water and tumbling black cliffs. One day he opened his eyes and found his queue chopped off and lying flat on the floor, and Cecil was there plucking lice big as beans from his hair, the sides of which had been evenly trimmed, a deep part in the middle of his forehead. He saw too that his clothes, the padded jacket and half trousers, had been replaced with Cecil's khaki trousers, his striped shirt and white merino and woolen cardigan, his leather belt with a gleaming silver buckle, his cotton drawers and woolen socks and a sturdy pair of boots that shimmered.

Scattered on the floor of the cabin were half-empty spools of thread and buttons of assorted colors, mounds of scraps left over from old trousers that had been gutted, then basted and stitched and hemmed and darted and reassembled. He saw fantastic slopes of wool and khaki and felt, saw the jagged jaws of scissors, and Cecil looking on with the frivolous fringes entangled in his red beard. With gesturing arms, he commanded Lowe to his feet, and Lowe picked himself up slowly, on creaking arms, on wobbly blue legs still slightly swollen, and he staggered round, his head spinning.

Lowe didn't recognize himself, this melody of pain gushing through his limbs. He didn't recognize the clothes that rubbed roughly against his skin, he felt naked without the coil of hair, and in the mirror hung there on the wall he saw the stranger peering back at him, with weary eyes, and in front of him was Cecil with the cords of thread in his fire hair, and lurking in the corners of Cecil's eyes a huge well of tenderness, which did not calm Lowe. He remembered a sharp curve of disappointment in his father's back when he turned thirteen and puberty struck. He remembered a weighed-down and weary neck hanging off his father's shoulders. He remembered a slope of resignation lurking there in the black hole of his face. And he looked again at the spotted-skinned man standing there, and he looked again at the trousers that veered over his legs and at the cardigan that draped along his shoulders, and he swung his head, which felt light without the cord of hair, and he knew he had crossed over again, that he had come to that place of uncertainty before and here he was again. But this time he wasn't sure of the outcome, he wasn't sure if he would make it to the island alive, or in one piece, whole. The stakes seemed greater somehow. The risks so much graver.

"Did you ask me if I wanted shop life?" Lowe yelled out into the darkened shop, nauseated with the memories. "Did you ask me if I wanted married life, wanted to have daughter?" His voice trembled, he held on to his stomach, which was extremely weak, and in his mind he located the metal bar leaning up against the counter by the trapdoor near the barred window. A metal bar he kept to wave dangerously at customers who got out of hand. "For who is to tell, maybe it wouldn't've turn like this," he cried. "Maybe it would've been different." He searched for possibilities and saw instead the old Chinese men with cracked faces and bleak glassy eyes working out themselves on the plantations; he saw them swinging from trees with the imperial queues at their throats, leaning over shop counters, drowsy with sleep and from fatigue yet weighing out the bags of sugar, serving the glasses of rum. He'd only known when he left China that he'd had to leave. There was the intuition driving him to live. Plus his father had betrayed him under the guise of tradition, though his one gift had been the dreams with which he infected Lowe so he could fly. But still!

Lowe said it again, in a thin, clenched whisper: "Why you couldn't so much as ask me what I want? Eh, why?" Nobody had ever asked him. He had just lived out all their fantasies. There was his father, who used to dress Lowe the same way he dressed himself. There was his father, who used to pile up in Lowe's head all his broken-down dreams, and then it was Cecil's fantasies and his grand plans for both Lowe and Miss Sylvie, and now all of a sudden Lowe had turned into a bad businessman, a useless Chinaman. After he had turned concubine to Cecil on board the ship. After he had raised Cecil's daughter. After he had been there, shackled to the shop. "Did you ever so much as ask me what I want?"

Cecil laughed, a harsh metallic din that revealed none of his teeth. "What you wanted, Lowe, to marry like a real woman and settle down. Is that?" He weaved closer and wavered there beneath Lowe's granite eyes. "You, the only Chinee woman on the island. Is that? What you think they would have done with you? Miss China Doll. Miss China Porcelain. You know what them do with the Chinee women in British Guinea. In Cuba. In Trinidad? Bring them to whorehouse. Is that you wanted?" Cecil laughed again. A stiff wooden laugh that betrayed no mirth, for it was bridled with so much bitterness, soaked with so much scorn. A laugh muddied with mockery. A laugh that clashed with the thin silver drops of rain pelting the zinc outside. "Is that you wanted, Lowe?" Cecil laughed again, and Lowe backed away, frightened by the smile in Cecil's teeth, the oily desire in Cecil's eyes, the rum on Cecil's breath, the trembling on Cecil's lips, Cecil's face shiny and bloated in the tilt of yellow glare from a fast-fading candle.

Lowe thought again of the cold, dark dank of the place, of the buckling fingers, and again of the metal bar behind the counter of the shop. Cecil's shop. But Cecil was quick, he lunged at Lowe, ripping open the front of his khaki shirt, tearing at the waist of the white band hiding Lowe's skinny woman's chest. "Is that you wanted? To live in house married like real woman? With husband and things? Servant and things? With five Chinee children running round? Petting the dog? Petting Blackie the dog?"

Lowe sprang, his fingers twisted on the pipe in Cecil's skinny throat, determined to unhook the Adam's apple, determined to tear the nasty grin from his face. Determined to shut him up forever. On the ship he'd been no match for Cecil. Not even after the fever had abated and he had regained strength, the rust had returned to his cheeks, the diarrhea had slowed, and he had been infected with the voracious appetite—the bowl after bowl of rice and stew and soup he devoured, stuffing his bloated cheeks, barely waiting even to swallow as grains fell from his oily lips back into the bowl on his chest, on the floor by his feet; the hunger that knew no bounds, had no stoppage, was insatiable. Even after his appetite was curbed he had been no match for Cecil, for there had always been the fear of the other men devouring him one by one, or in a pack, wolves. The fear of being thrown down below into that sewer of human waste with the other Chinese. And what if they discovered his differences—how they would've turned on him!

But now, now the fear was different, now the fear had turned, now he would kill Cecil and bury him there at the back of the shop. The villagers would help him, wouldn't they! They'd clear the site, they'd dig the hole, wouldn't they! After all, wasn't Cecil the common enemy?

Beneath Lowe's hands, Cecil battled for air. Beneath Lowe's hands, he struggled. But he was so light from fatigue, he was so unsteady from drunkenness. And against his thin angular frame, Lowe's nostrils were just calling up all kinds of smells from the cabin, all kinds of oil and fish and salt and rotting smells. The cry of terrified and shrieking Chinese, who went wild with the heat of fire that broke out on board. How they screamed and stampeded with the rattling chains clamping their feet, and there were the howling sailors hurrying to remove the stout iron bars that bolted them in, to open up the hatchways that had been barricaded. There were the bubbling and blistered and charred and hissing and smoking Chinese bodies thrown overboard into the wrinkled black brow of the sea, into the jagged jaws of swirling sharks. And then there was just the iron blanket again that was the smooth sea. No winds. Just a slow-moving boat, a twisted knot on inky waters. But those days were gone now, and sure as rain, he would kill Cecil. Sure as rain, he would blot out the images furred in his throat and tear out the tongue, pluck out the eyes. He would stifle him to death, choke back the laugh down the rusty throat, for there was no love between them, nothing at all between them, a daughter, yes, but no love.

Liz's shriek startled them.

With a trembling hand, Lowe slowly unlocked his fingers, slowly released the thimble of neck, slowly collected his wits about him, slowly collected his calm, and Cecil staggered away into the night, coughing and holding his throat, and Lowe heard the timorous taps of his shoes sluicing into wet mud. That was six months ago. Now he was here with a mother for Liz, and the fluttering and luminescent butterflies curved halos round the carriage.

In the room at the back of the shop Lowe had built on since, Liz slept on a four-poster canopied bed with a sturdy mattress, and Lowe's eyes, shifting with their movements, returned again and again to the door in the back where his daughter, Cecil's daughter, slept in the room. He hadn't taken tea yet, hadn't taken even a hunk of bread yet, and so mirages swam before him and he felt slightly faint. But still he swept, the bristles of his broom leveling the dirt pyramids of carpenter ants, crushing shiny white eggs that would later have emerged as nymphs. Still he swept, though the bristles of the broom traveled the same area over and over and dirtied again the neat spots he had just now cleared. Then Miss Sylvie alighted from the cart. A tall and stout and white-skinned woman, with a stole of fine yellow hair and a matching yellow skirt that swelled out from her tiny waist into a full-blown flower.

Cecil took her to the back of the shop and Lowe continued to sweep, nosing the bristles of the broom into corners long forgotten, turning it above his head, knocking down contortions of webbing that had formed in the corner of the roof. He tried not to listen to their mumbling, rumbling tones, and when the back door slammed shut, he stopped himself from wondering where they had gone. Several hours later they returned, neither spoke to him, and the carriage whisked them away again in a cloud of pebbles and dust.

The following weeks, cartloads of carpenters and masons and plumbers arrived daily. They felled trees, set fire to bush, and cleared the land of rocks, of broken bottles and garbage. They sawed and hammered and cut and laid pipes and gutters, and when midday approached, they laid down their tools and brushed the dirt from their dusty backsides and wiped their dripping faces with the loose tails of their shirts and slowly edged toward the shops, where business picked up. For as quickly as the crumbling shelves emptied, they were replenished. In the fire of the midday heat, the men crowded the shops and laughed and smoked and drank and ate with enormous vigor and dozed with their foaming mouths wide open on the upright wooden benches or outside underneath tight clusters of trees and awoke exactly one hour later to carry away wheelbarrows full of stones and mud and cement mix.

They lifted the trunks of trees and flung them on the columns of their shoulders, and the muscles in their forearms strained underneath the impossible weight, and the veins on the sides of their faces and in their necks reddened and bloated up into pipes. They paused often to wet their parched palates with the rotgut rum that they carried in flasks tucked safely away deep into boots and to roll and smoke the wet brown leaves of tobacco and other herbs growing wild in the fields, which turned their eyes wet and bloodied and glassy.

And still they worked with astonishing expedience. Holes were dug. Cement was poured to create a foundation. Wood poles were inserted. More cement. Concrete blocks. For weeks the district prospered. Contractors boarded with villagers, and the thin bellies of the underage girls swelled with pregnancy. Rum bars were packed Saturday nights, church pews on Sundays. The butcher slaughtered hogs and cows and goats. The price of eggs increased, and that of cow's milk. Several months later, the house stood grandly on the very pinnacle of the hill, its back nestled against a forest of rocks and trees and woods, while the veranda gazed down at the villagers' mud-and-wattle, thatch-roofed hovels and huts, and ambitious half-finished concrete houses lined up side by side amid hillside and empty swampland.

Late one evening, the thunder of hooves filling the entire valley finally separated into the harsh rising pitch of one lone rider, a speck of black on the rim of a purple horizon, before the figure gradually swelled and then dismounted in a cloud of spiraling dust at the shop piazza. It was dusk and the square was deserted and the craven dogs slept close by in the short thick grass across the road facing the shop.

Lowe and his daughter had just eaten, and he had nodded off on a stool behind the counter while Liz rattled to herself in a corner swarmed with the many wooden animals and assorted paper birds customers had given her over the years. He had already boarded up the windows to lock out the swelling night shadows. He awoke to clods of horse shit licking the pavement and saw the woman standing there at the counter, watching him with a ripple of a grin splitting her flushed copper face. Lowe coughed and straightened his shirt, brushing back his hair, which was recently trimmed, and swung his trousers off his hips and up to his navel and closed up his face and clashed his eyebrows together and tugged at the curling handles of his mustache.

She ordered a beer and he knocked off the foamy top and watched her lean the bottle to her head while her long sleepy eyelids locked and the corners of her mouth leaked. She burped long and deep, ordered another, and he wanted to laugh, for he had never seen a woman quite like this one. She was tall and robust, with full and heavy breasts that strained against the fabric of her jacket. She removed the hat tied underneath her chin with ribbons and rested it on the counter. A bundle of gold hair sprang out, and Lowe saw that the nape of her neck was damp and the sides of her face were deeply flushed from the hot winds that lashed her as she rode. Sweat had dampened parts of her back and blotched the underarms of her blouse.

Liz, by this time, had flown to the other side of the counter to inspect the quivering flanks of the foaming white beast that was her stallion and that was continuing to pile up loads of filth at the mouth of his shop. Lowe listened to her voice, rumpled with affection as she pressed Liz's hands against the slow-blinking eyes, the wide trembling jaws, the slender and handsome face. He saw the jutting blades of Miss Sylvie's wide shoulders, the large bones of her hands, lined with veins and scarred by rope burns, her cruel lips deep in flirtation, the strong even teeth, the jaw, big and brown with dust.

She had appeared right at that moment before nightfall, when the colors were both vibrant and pitted with melancholy. It was the moment, too, right before the forest released its symphony of sounds, before the night stalkers descended on the square with their beating pans and bellowing accordions, their appetites boundless for drink. In that hour, right before the dying rays of the sun disappeared, she was more handsome, the smell of her sweat more tart, the stench of the decayed and abscessed molars more fervent, her smile more haunting; her pupils were more distended and dark, her deep voice rumbled with more resonance, her lips brooded.

She returned to the counter, with Liz, his daughter, beside her in love, and ordered a third bottle. They stood in the shop, their faces bathed in the scanty light by the leaping shadows, the front door of the shop opened onto the deserted square. He had not lit the hissing lamps yet. There were the glass shades still to be rinsed off and dried with newspaper, the kerosene to be poured out from the oil drum and funneled into the spouting mouths of the lamps. Wicks to be trimmed. Still he did not move. And outside there was the swiftly approaching night, which carried the smell of storms. Through the glass doors of the display case, there was the silvery reflection of the slow-creeping moon grinning in the eyes of needles that sat in boxes on low shelves, glimmering on the piles of silk and cotton, embroidering the rings of ruffled white lace. There was the distant knot of stars, the echoing cry of a pack of swallows as they fluttered noisily in a circle over the darkening square.

She nursed the beer, straightening and folding her fingers, and talked quietly to Liz, and he saw the meandering movements of her fingers, some with flat broad ribbons of gold. He wondered if she had married before and if she'd given birth. She seemed so vigorous with strength, so bold and brassy in her gestures, yet her eyes carried a dullness so intense he tried not to meet them. He wondered what Cecil had told her about him, Lowe, and what had been her response. He wondered what the parenting arrangements would be exactly, what they would entail. And then he brushed the thoughts aside, for they troubled him too much. There seemed to be no ending whatsoever to the masquerade. The layers just seemed to pile up more or harden. Furthermore, there were still the glasses to be rinsed, the rum to be watered and measured out into flasks and half flasks, the jugs to be filled up with water and drops of lime juice, the caps and bottles of beers and stouts to be polished so they winked at customers from their shelves. Still he lingered.

"Is funny," she finally addressed Lowe, without a smile, and in a voice loaded down with despair. And her eyes, he noticed, without wanting to, seemed lost, and the corners were wrinkled with worry. "But I been dreaming bout you for years. You and me and Liz in that white house on top of the hill overlooking the district. Strange, ain't it? For two full years." Then she was gone, her bill left there on the counter, fluttering from the sudden onslaught of wind, and Liz jumping up and down on the pavement and crying and waving after the figure that had hoisted to the saddle and was galloping up the hill at a conquering pace. Lowe was irritated. The shop had plummeted into darkness, and he couldn't find matches to light the lamps. Plus there were the packs of cigarettes to be separated into sticks, tobacco to be cut up into feet and inches. There were the daytime accounts to be sorted and tallied and recorded and hidden away, and loose change put out in the till to assist in the night's transactions. There was the piazza to be swept clean of sweetie wrappers and the hardened black butts of cigarettes, and still there were thoughts lurking there and the worry of what would happen now, what would he have to pay out now, how much, now, to this woman whom Cecil had sent to mother Liz. And what was this nonsense about dreams!

He stormed outside to yell at Liz to get inside at once and stop acting the blasted fool and saw that the world was completely black and engulfed by the deafening racket of crickets. Inside, there were the counters still to be wiped down with soap and warm water, two- and three-pound bags of sugar and of rice to be weighed out and wrapped in brown paper, Liz to be tidied and bye-byed and put to bed, the firewood in the kitchen at the back to be doused with hot water, the dishes and pots scrubbed and turned down.

Every day for the next two months Miss Sylvie sent a note by way of either Dulcie, the housekeeper, a tall dark-skinned woman who carried a suffering face and dragged behind her one slow foot, or Dulcie's son, Omar, imploring Lowe to join them for dinner. And each day he crumpled the note and burned it in the fire that cooked his meals, cursing the audacity of these porcelain alabaster people to want to control his life so thoroughly and completely. Plus he didn't like the air about them. The son, Omar, was sullen and restless, and he paced the four corners of the shop and watched Lowe with hooded eyes. He made Lowe uneasy, as did the mother, who seemed resigned to some great tribulation that exhausted her and caused her to produce the longest and most profound sighs, which made even Lowe shudder. Omar made Lowe think of his father. But unlike his father, who had little by little and over the years neatly and tightly folded over his disappointments into tremendous fantasies and had molded Lowe as well into something both unrecognizable and foreign, Omar wore his disappointments unsheathed. The villagers called him hostile and cantankerous and they kept out of his way, claiming that he didn't smell good, he had blood on his hands and guilt written all over his forehead. About the old lady, Dulcie, though, they seemed more curious and cautious, almost more reverent, as if trying to discern who exactly she was, for in some way she seemed vaguely familiar.

But each time Lowe watched Miss Sylvie's invitation curling up into flames, he worried. For there was Liz going on three and he didn't know whom to ask about a decent school, just in case the villagers took it to mean their government schools and one-room classes weren't good enough. There was Liz going on three, with no real mother, just a woman who had given birth and was now playing at being a man, on a West Indian island full up of brown people swiftly growing more and more infuriated with their economic status and the snail's pace at which change seemed to be approaching and what they considered to be the opportunities the government was doling out to his Chinese people. There was Liz going on three, with no real family, no future, no guidance, no homeland, no country, no people, nothing.

Wednesday evening Lowe locked shop early, tidied Liz and himself, and meandered slowly up the hill, the chills of the evening falling briskly around them. There was no moon, no stars, and the zigzag path of dry grass, thick and straight, which had been trodden down by feet, stretched out ahead of them, a blue-black cape. There were dogs, but none of them barked. People passed in groups of twos and threes, but no one said hello. He had never seen the house, and he hissed his teeth at its glowing white splendor ahead, complained to himself at its excessiveness in that small hot district and worried at the leap he would have to make from shop life to that. For the people would never trust him now. Here he was Chinese, and here he was cohabiting with this white-skinned woman, Miss Sylvie, and here he was now living in the biggest house in the district with a dark-skinned maid and a dark-skinned yard boy. How to explain to the villagers when the very way he and Miss Sylvie lived up there in that house bore stark resemblance to a history and a way of life he did not live through but had heard as a story unfolding so many times at the shop he felt close to it. How to show them that he hadn't changed, wasn't changing, was still the Lowe they knew, he wasn't emulating the behavior of the ruling class even if it seemed that way, it was only that he wanted something better for Liz. And wouldn't any mother want the same for her child if she could?

Miss Sylvie, as if expecting them, was waiting at the head of the table with a smiling face that wrinkled up the corners of her eyes. They ate in silence, Dulcie wordlessly waiting on them with a stiff and wooden face, with a set of gestures precise and mechanical. Did they know everything? Lowe wondered. Had Cecil told them? And the arrangements, he worried, what would they be? Sitting stiffly at the other end of the table in a white shirt made even more gleaming by the single lamp illuminating the room, he watched Miss Sylvie fuss over Liz, cutting up her food into small neat squares, indulging her in extra portions of sweets, puckering up her lips and contorting her face into comical gestures so Liz would smile. And Liz did smile, and would sometimes even burst out into a laughter so gleeful it frightened Lowe, for she was always so solemn. Still, he kept his eyes flared on the pearls jumping about on Miss Sylvie's jutting collarbone and on the lamplit flashes of her teeth. He darted furtive glances at the tendrils loose from the upsweep of hair and falling into her forehead and along the temples and cheeks soaked in the diminishing light.

He listened to the tines of his fork scraping the plate, to the clanking knife sawing through meat, detaching flesh and bringing it to his trembling lips. He could not taste. He listened to his masticating teeth before the pink tongue rolled bolus back into the gaping hole of his throat. There was the gulping swallow of juice sliding into esophagus, the protesting gaggle of a distended stomach. He had left his body again. Still, he stared straight ahead, his eyes expressionless as they traveled up and down the weakly illuminated paintings that covered the walls, barely distinguishing the cylinder of shapes: the soft crisscross straw of hat, a pointed tip of a European nose, a white vertical line of ship, a square edge of canvas sail, gleaming enamel of eyes in black face, the blue-green oil of water, a yellow plume of foam.

Crouched on a couch in the solemn drawing room, he absorbed the slow steady swings of a pendulum clock and heard Miss Sylvie's and Liz's feverish exchange as they prepared for bed. He had never heard Liz so talkative. Always she was so sullen and pensive. He thought to get jealous, and then he stopped. A pair of white pajamas, starched and crisp, lay folded on top of the enormous pillows that crowded the great canopied bed of his room. But that night he did not wash, though Dulcie had left a goblet of warm water on the stand, though he was dirty and weary. He tripped over the rug at his feet and knocked off the night table a glass vase of white lilies, which crashed noisily to the floor, and he wrapped himself up at once and stood there cocked and waiting, but when the unending silence continued, he began to pick up the pieces, and they gashed and bloodied his hands. That night he blew out the lamp and eased underneath the cool sheets and pushed his head deep into the soft feathers of his pillow and slept soundly. All next day he was resolved never to return, but as evening fell and business ran slow, he locked up early again and he and Liz picked out their way slowly in the darkness up to the house, a flickering torch their only guide in that hot still black night with not even a breath of air, not even the rustling wings of bats.

One night he had a dream that Miss Sylvie had come to his bed, and when he woke up he was frightened to find her lying there next to him and even more alarmed to find that his spindly arm was trapped underneath her wide shoulders, and he tried to remove it at once, though stealthily so as not to wake her. It was impossible, though she slept without peace, with outstretched arms and churning fingers, with a face gashed by nightmares and a heaving chest that sometimes produced a deep rattle from her throat. Thin strands of yellow hair swiveled off her freckled cheeks and the fragile limb that was her brown throat. He had never seen a beauty quite like this and so close up to him and so overwhelmingly feminine and ripe and bursting it confused him. Frightened him, really. Even the way she smelled, as if frothing, and there was the taste of her sweat firing out from the barbs of bush that were her underarms.

It was early morning and streaks of light were already peering in through the chinks in the red velvet curtain and outside he could hear the stirring call of cocks and the response of other cocks from deep down in the valley on the other side of the rolling gray hill, and he heard too the warbling of swallows, the cooing of doves, the crying of chickadees, the whirring of hummingbirds, more cock calls. Slowly he turned his head so as to make out the location of his shoes on the rug near the door that would lead him down the hall, past the neighboring room, the gilded frames of handsome and romantic landscapes of regions he did not know, the low narrow chest of drawers, the well-made bed with unruffled sheets and balloon pillows, past the window that looked out at the kitchen, and then the door, finally the door that would bring him escape. It was too much, this . . . this . . . he didn't even know what to call it, his yearning was so furious.

She cleared her throat and Lowe saw that a rectangle of sun had hoisted across the room and leaned into her face and that she was wide awake and watching him with amused eyes still drugged by sleep, and he immediately freed his thin white arm that had long gone dead. He lurched toward his shoes, and she stopped him with the narrative of how she had been married since she was fifteen and within months after the dreams started coming her husband fell off his horse and broke his neck.

"But every night it was your face I keep seeing," she told Lowe, in a voice touched with tenderness. "How that to happen so?" she whispered, tracing the bones of his cheeks with the pads of her fingers, running them along the rugged lines of his lips, gently removing the black band of hair that lay there, circling the eyes and the curve of his nostrils, all the while singing the music of idle words, minuets about beauty. "Is the same round face with the one eye slightly bigger and the same mouth with the lips so full and pink and with the top one a little longer, the same teeth at the front caved in slightly. My husband used to travel, and I thought maybe it was his sketches that brought the dreams night after night. But it was you, you ownself. For two years."

Lowe fretted under her touch, his body stiff and unmoving, his breath barely able to escape his wildly beating heart, his roaring head. She knew! So then where the hell were the shoes! For if he could slip slightly to the right he would be free of her cream thigh sheathed in black garter that was the stumbling block in his path, he would be ready at the side of the bed and on the floor with the tap-tap of nimble feet down the darkened corridors with only creases of light to guide him through the maze of rooms, past the office with an untidy desk cluttered with papers, short squat chairs and a plush rug, the glimmering edges of a scrubbed floor. With her eyes closed, and with the steaming flesh, she straddled him. His great swooping copper bird with the dazzled gaze, the frenzied admiration, repeating her prosody of love.

Yet underneath her hands, plying his body, awakening it, her attentive fingers listening to it for harmony, there was only discord, for his body would not obey, would not dance, was not flexible and yielding, had no discipline. Above him, there was only the broiling cauldron of sky, a streak of light across a suction sea, a glittering dusk, an unreflecting mirror. Her butterfly kisses feathered his throat, and he was drenched in his own sweat and the fragrances of oils and perfumes, the harsh wet smell of tobacco, that clung to her skin. He felt her wet lips on his wide-open eye, on his sweep of lashes, on a perturbed forehead. A nibble on the lobe of an ear. A stab to the center of the throat with a pointed pink tongue. An ocean of moans. Hers? And then steps silent as a priest's on the rug and wood floors, to his little room at the back of the shop. The naked and unpainted concrete walls of his shop. The shimmering zinc roofs. The awful singing of men. The cracked laughter of men. Laughs deep with disappointments, muddied with mockery, bridled with bitterness. The wooden shelves tiered to the white ceiling with boxed and tinned goods.

There were her teeth tight on the buttons of his shirt, picking them off, one by one. From the hollow of his throat to the thimble of his navel, she roamed with the freckled tongue, with a bow and with a nod. She removed the strips of cloth that banded the chest and swallowed at once the knobby red nipples. She murmured into his chest. She knew! She murmured into his belly. She knew! He continued to lie there dead, columns of tears leaking out the wrinkled corners of his eyes. There were only teeth and hard bites and spread legs and splayed fingers and darting tongue, a valley of breasts, a whirlpool of desire, a feverish breathlessness, a profuse talk of love, words racing and running and leaping, tumbling overhead, there was the chaos of phrases, a dark loamy earth, and Miss Sylvie at his feet, picking off socks, a warm mouth, a gaping cave, swallowing one by one, then the whole bunch, crumpled up.

A gasp for air. His? Fingers on the cracked leather of belt, on the hook of trousers, then on the buttons, and frenzied fingers rummaging into the square white band of his drawers, and scrambling up again to wrestle with a wrinkled shirt the color of khaki, then down again, swimming into the white waist and plunging in, a pointed tip of European nose, a taste, finger by finger, then the whole fist crammed in. A ship. A square canvas edge of sail. A checkered oilcloth and the strange curve of flesh. Haggard breathing. Cecil's! The galloping rhythm of tongue, taste of brine on lips, a raised arm with torn wrist, a vague twilight and dreamy eyes gripped by the drug of sleep. A molten sky. An auspicious moon. A sweltering marketplace. A circling shark with a murderous tail. A leaning body full of erratic gestures, the undulation of limbs, the crunching of figures, the movement of light. Lowe could not retain the sequence from the chaos.

And so it continued for all those years, Miss Sylvie returning again and again to their room after spending weeks or months at a time with Whitley, who came to visit and who satiated the passion that she must have sought only in Lowe. And Lowe not moving, not rising to her touch or to touch her, not returning her kisses, her pronouncements of love, just lying there numb all those years, for each time, all he could think of was the dark dank of the place, a flash of bruised light, a pair of pliers, an unleashed fury, a strange curve of flesh, and those shoes, ripping through rooms, past the varnished wood of the table, the marbled chests. Secretly and in his heart he yearned for her embrace, and often he wished he could simply small himself up into her lap and sleep there. But always she wanted more. He heard it in her frenzied breathing, he could smell it like danger on her skin, he could taste it at the back of his throat, and it was always there in the pressure of her fingers kneading him. He didn't feel as if he had agency, as if he had voice. For who is to say she wouldn't fold up her fantasies into him and turn him further into something he wasn't, as his father had done and then Cecil? And who is to say she wouldn't abandon him once her mission was accomplished. Who is to say!

And so Lowe just lay there prostrate, so overwhelmed by his fear, allowing Miss Sylvie to love him, those nights after Cecil had come, and left again, those nights after Whitley had gone, those nights after Liz had gone to sleep, and later, after she had eloped with the carpenter and escaped the convent school, which only as an exception admitted the children of the Chinese and those of the porcelain alabasters, those nights after the store had prospered and he had expanded and met Kywing, those nights when it was just the two of them, just the two of them and the dark and impenetrable night.

And for all those years Lowe had never wanted to touch her in that way, never wanted to love her in that way, never wanted to stroke the lines on her forehead or the ones by the corners of her eyes and lips. For who is to say what he would have raised up in her! He had never wanted to touch the mole on her back or the one on the right side of her neck, never wanted to inspect the insides of her legs or thighs, never wanted to fondle her nipple, never wanted to possess her body or snatch her from the claws of that woman, never wanted to kiss her parted lips or the smooth column of throat, never wanted to smell her perfumed skin or to taste her sea-salt silkiness, never wanted to travel inside her, never wanted to crawl or push, never wanted, never wanted till that moment. For at that moment he was a child not so afraid of death, and of darkness and of solitude. At that moment he was a child full up of innocence, ebullient with faith.

5

Six weeks later and in the middle of the most fervid downpour, Whitley left. Omar saddled her bay horse first thing that grim and sodden Monday morning, and with a tilt of her head cloaked underneath a great black coat, she mounted up and disappeared into the hammering rain. But during those weeks she visited, Lowe was a person possessed. He had not known a rage so furious. He had not known a longing so persistent. All day all night, the feelings, as if long dormant, had now risen up finally, and they needled him. Unable to sleep, he awoke each morning in the moonlit dawn and fumbled into his breeches hung there at the foot of the bed and tucked in his netted merino and khaki shirt and drew on his thin socks and rubber boots and headed out into the dawn, where Omar, who must have been studying the weather of events, handed Lowe a mug and they slurped the steaming brew in silence until the first cock's crow.

At first there was just the swirling silence between them, just the smack of lips on the rim of their mugs, just their deep breathing in the slowly approaching dawn. He did not know Omar, he did not know what things to say to him. He thought to ask about the shop set ablaze, and the shudder in his gut stopped him. One morning Omar tapped him and beckoned Lowe to follow. And Lowe headed off deep into the winding forest with Omar, who was overseer and who knew by heart the endless boundaries of Miss Sylvie's land and who carried a machete to beat back the nettled bush that snagged the path and hacked at their skins and hummed around them. Lowe was comforted.

As if in preparation for the downpour that was later to flood streets and uproot thin, brittle trees and dismantle the mud-and-wattle houses crouched on the hillside and sail away with small, unsuspecting animals, the days now had grown dusky, as only a jagged and hazy light cracked through the clouds. Sprinkles of showers were expected now late in the evenings and a somber sky hung above, even at noon, a curtain of mist that was always just a few steps ahead. And each day they stepped with a quick loose gait, tunneling their way through bush, brambles cracking under boots, no words between them, just an easy silence and the screech of parakeets. Sometimes a sharp thin breeze sprang up and rustled Lowe's hair and bathed Omar's neck, and they shivered in the sudden turn of weather.

Then slowly, awkwardly, Omar began to talk. He knew the medicinal purposes of each bark and bush, each leaf and stem. And each tree and shrub they passed, he dwelled on their abilities to heal wounds and grow hair and pull down swellings and abort fetuses and beat back depression and cleanse blood and maintain sanity and regulate intestines and dissolve ulcers and ease murmuring hearts. Of the vermin and animals that scampered in the brush, he knew which one, if boiled for so many hours and left to sit for so many more hours, and the water poured off and drunk, could minimize the symptoms of chicken pox and mumps. He impressed in Lowe's memory ways to recognize roots—the bittersweet smell, the acrid odor, the jagged edge of leaf, the five-leaf cluster that looked like a clenched fist, the burnished Indian-orange color of the stem.

Lowe began to see Omar with renewed eyes. He saw that Omar was a grown man close to Lowe's own age who lived with his mother still, who had neither married nor fathered children and who did not sprout hairs on his chin or on his narrow and puffed-out bird chest, which was always exposed since he wore his shirt loose and unbuttoned. He saw that Omar no longer walked stiffly and with the disappointments dodging him as when he'd first arrived. Lowe saw that his blue-black skin was of the smoothest complexion and without the leathery seams that corroded Lowe's own face and that his eyes absorbed more than they let on. And so he felt safe enough to share with Omar those remedies he had learned too as a child, though of their effectiveness he was not certain. He told Omar how the venom of snake could heal syphilis, that the dried red-spotted liver of certain lizards cured asthma, that the gallbladder of bears eased aches and pain and the exuviae of the cicada stopped convulsions.

At midday they took lunch, lying in the tall grass, cocked on bony ashy elbows, watching the enormous fog hung silent over the slow-moving river that crossed Miss Sylvie's land, over the trees and stones and fields, over the rolling hills, and they listened to the stilted cry of birds traveling from tree to tree and that of the women they could not see but who washed clothes nearby and sometimes waded in the rapid rush of clear cool water. After lunch, Omar dozed to the lulling fall of water and Lowe wandered off softly into the woods to pass water, and when he returned, sometimes Omar would've rolled tobacco and silently they passed the cigar back and forth between them, fingers slightly brushing. And Lowe liked the easy silence between them, and the brooding, pouting lips of Omar, and often he felt the lazy glow of Omar's eyes traveling the contours of his figure, and at first the panic would rise in him, like a body memory, even after all these years, though there was nothing to betray him. For after forty years he wore his costume like a glove, a second skin. After forty years there was nothing womanly about him, not even his voice, which was a soft harsh bark, its octaves mellowing with time.

Sometimes he wished he didn't fidget so much, that like Omar he carried a sullen stillness. But instead he was always buttoning and unbuttoning his shirt, fondling his collar, drawing up his trousers way above his navel and tugging them down again to rest on his hips. He fingered his hair and ran his thumb through the part in the middle, which was impossible to maintain, and felt his face for the curling edges of the mustache that had a tendency to lean down into his throat or point up into his nostrils. He wiped his lips repeatedly with a handkerchief just in case he had left oil or crumbs there, just in case the corners were frothy with foam. The pockets of his shirt were always bulging and weighted down with the tiny notes he wrote to himself and the pieces of crackers or bread he intended to eat before he got distracted by customers and the numerous short sticks of pencil he kept for tallying and the leaves whose insistent odors he liked to inhale.

Among the villagers he was short for a man, but not among his people. And even if people were to grow suspicious, the virility trembling in his bristling mustache kept their thoughts at bay. He was thin and wiry and his sprightly step hinted at a swagger and he had kept up his figure over the years and the breasts that he still kept banded underneath his netted merino had remained the same rounded mounds since adolescence. Since his father turned against him. Nothing at all could betray him unless he removed his clothes, and over the years his instincts had grown keener and he could detect the precise moment at which innocent conversations verged on violence, when a demure innuendo could leap out of hand, when boundaries were crossed, and at that point he knew to remove himself as neatly as possible from the situation.

But perhaps with Omar he'd dropped his guard. With Omar he must've let himself grow vulnerable. Grow easy. He must've been manipulated by the curl of Omar's upper lip, which carried no trace of down, he must've been seduced by the smell of cigars he carried on his breath, the soft and crisscrossed pink palms of his feminine hands, which brushed against Lowe, by his dark shiny eyes, the serpentine movements of his muscled limbs, the tenseness of his chin with the hollow in the middle, the brooding, pouting lips, the vague laughter, the permanent scowl on his forehead.

For during those weeks he spent with Omar, he did not have to beat back the depression that hunted him, the gutting in his stomach abated. He did not have to think about Miss Sylvie back there in Whitley's arms and of his shame, the cuckoldry, his honor, the burned-down shop, his daughter who had betrayed him, and his deep disappointments. He did not have to think about Cecil and the fact that another chapter of his life had closed. He allowed Omar, who wore a blade of grass between his teeth, to lead him through the fields full of tall grass with fluffy heads, past the plantations of sugarcane, the neat rows of orange and lime and banana trees, through the dense yellow and green fields of corn, through hills of potato slips and of St. Vincent and Negro and Afu yams, through the creak and groan of bamboo trees swaying and rubbing. Temporarily his troubles dimmed in his mind.

"Two hundred and twenty-five and a half acres," Omar had told him with a florid sweep of his arm as they trudged through the dense vegetation, and Lowe thought he detected bitterness in Omar's voice, but he brushed it aside and whistled underneath his breath, for he knew that at least one half was for Elizabeth, Cecil's daughter, and all of a sudden his chest bloated up with renewed respect for Cecil's cunning and generosity and the way he'd thought through and arranged it for all of them so they could be comfortably tied there. He saw the way Miss Sylvie had turned the land into an empire, and it came home to him again that she was no fool, that she was indeed a shrewd business-woman, and that compared to her he had nothing at all, and he saw that with Whitley now in the picture and without the shop to use as leverage to get his Pagoda, he was relegated to the same position as Dulcie and Omar, dependent on her good graces. He saw that for anything he wanted now, he'd have to ask her permission. And he thought of the benevolent society again, and in his mind he drew up floor plans and calculated the amount of square footage necessary for each room and the shade of coloring that would best befit the walls and the specific kind of vegetation he imagined growing in the yard, and when he was done he drew up a likely budget for its completion and deduced from that figure the savings he had boarded up in a box underneath the house.

They passed the mile-long stables full of horses and brushed back flies that swarmed them and spat often to remove the loathsome tang of manure from their mouths. They passed the wired animal pens and dismissed the mournful lowing of cows, the disconcerting squeals of pigs, the maying of goats, and in the distance they could also hear the waning echo of voices, the workers' muted howls and chatter as they hacked away at the trunks of trees that were necessary as lumber, as they worked deep in the rocky ravine, preparing the ground for another planting.

During those first weeks, Omar steered clear of the stooped figures scaffolding the hillside in the roasting sun. And at first Lowe was relieved that he wouldn't have to face those thugs who had burned down his shop, the hypocrisy of their secret smiles and soft laughs. But as days grew into weeks, he began to notice another side of Omar softly emerging. He was not at all friendly with the workers, men and women alike who weeded and cleaned and planted and reaped and to whom he barked commands in a fierce and aggressive tone. If they were joking prior to his arrival, by the time Omar neared they were hard at work again with serious and sullen looks, addressing him with "yes, sirs" and "no, sirs," not meeting his eyes but keeping their heads lowered and their hands restless by their sides. One day Omar unbuckled his belt and flogged a man who quarreled with him about a damaged fence that should've been repaired some time ago, and his face, as he raised his arm repeatedly to strike the man's head with the buckle of his belt, a man who could've been his age or older, was tired and austere, his eyes unflinching, only his pressed lips trembled slightly and beads of perspiration gathered on the crown of his head.

The man did not storm back. The man yowled. The man's knees tottered and he slithered to the ground with only his hands stretched up, cradling his head. There was the sound too of iron cracking bone. How many strokes? The workers did not watch. They slunk off back to their patches of ground, but the cables in their necks throbbed like fuses. Afterward Lowe carried a fear too deep even to speak. He had just stood there nailed to the ground, with the fear steep in him. And by not acting, just allowing the spectacle to unfold, it was as though his hands too had been dipped in blood. He saw that he did not know Omar, nor did he understand the dynamics of his power. It was as if Omar hated them. Hated their helplessness. Their false groveling and subservience; he hated their poverty. So quickly could he turn into one of them if Miss Sylvie should turn him out of her house and put him off her land. So quickly could they turn against him if he had nothing at all. Omar must have sensed too how much they loathed him, how much they laughed at his supreme blackness, his ugliness. Yet envied him and his relation to Miss Sylvie, and to the land, his relation to Lowe, the Chinaman. How they sniggered behind his back and scorned him. The abusive names they called him.

Children on the way to school, stoning the mango and star apple trees, fled as if with terror when they saw him approach. Women nodded respectfully in passing, "Missa Omar," but at them he barely glanced. And Lowe noticed too, with much perturbation, that the children who had once called him "Godfather" and "Uncle" when he used to have a shop now avoided his eyes, and the women, many of whom still owed him money, said nothing at all to him. As if he were not there with Omar! As if by being seen with Omar he had doubly become their enemy. He did not know this Omar. He did not know him at all. One day when he could no longer stand the tension, when people who he thought were his friends, people who had sat long hours at the shop with him, men who brought him food those days after the fire and during his convalescence, when he saw those very same men who had told him secrets of their impotence and tumors, of their betrayals and breaches of trust, when he saw how those men took off their hats to Omar and pretended that he, Lowe, wasn't there, or they spat when they saw him, he opened his mouth to speak. But Omar, who had been studying Lowe with his intense eyes, suddenly asked, "And back there, Mr. Lowe, what was you profession again?"

They had taken the donkeys now, for it squalled nonstop and the mosquitoes were ferocious and enormous puddles of water engulfed the muddy path, making it impossible to walk, and the wet branches lashed their faces and the warm silvery rain pelted off their black oilskin cloaks and rolled down into the matted hair of the beasts' bloated bellies.

"Shoemaking," Lowe said, in a quiet trembling voice, as if he had been suddenly struck. As if he'd been backed up into a corner and silenced. He wasn't supposed to interfere with things that didn't concern him.

"Shoemaking," Omar repeated, and glanced down at his huge and ashen and cracked feet dangling over the swollen belly of the beast. He wore shoes only on Fridays, when the laborers lined up at the back of the house near the latrine to draw their pay, which he slighted. "Shoemaking." He looked again into the rain and studied the steel-gray sky for some time, and then Lowe, nodding, began to fill up the silence with the same story he had given the men at the shop, the story he had invented of his life back there, his mind swelling and racing ahead with the tumbled images. They had to shout, for the oilskin hoods encumbered their lips and the whirring wind whisked away sounds.

"It was just a little shopfront." Lowe outlined with awkward arms. "Not too far from the port. All sort of people stop in. Sailors from distant places with strange languages. Some who wouldn't speak at all. They just show me the broke heel, the sole walk down, the wear-out leather that need patching—"

"What about a wife, Mr. Lowe, is that I want know bout, this wife you tell everybody bout."

Lowe nodded and moistened his lips with his tongue, not liking at all the tone in Omar's voice, not liking at all the pressure he felt beating in his own chest, not liking at all his pulsing heart. He didn't like the sudden shift in the air between them. He touched the rubber handle of the knife resting there by his waist and measured with precise eyes the distance between them.

"Was she good-looking, Mr. Lowe? Was she nice? Plump and round with big thighs?" His lips curled. "Nice big titties?"

Lowe coughed to clear his throat, and in a tired voice he told Omar, "She was pretty, pretty like money, with a round button nose and a nice dimple when she smile, but timid. She wouldn't speak loud at all, you had to bend or move up close to listen, and when she laugh her eyes just shut up tight."

"Like yours."

Lowe said nothing. Their donkeys had stopped to nibble. The rain had stopped as well. The sun peeked out, weak rays. Loads of mist rolled away. There was the bleak outline of circling hawks. They could hear the whoop and call of workers, taste the tang of manure. Thin layers of smoke drifted from the roofs of housetops, crept along the highest branches of trees, and disappeared. Ahead of them, lightning flared. Lowe turned and brought his hands to his eyes and found that they were suddenly wet. He brought out his handkerchief from his pocket and coughed into it to calm his fluttering chest. "She was flat," he said into the dark, shiny, and unblinking eyes. "She was flat and thin," he said softly into the cement face with the curled lips. "With nice long shapely legs, curve slight." He looked down at Omar's feet, bereft of shoes, a pair of ashy boats with cracked bark. "She didn't want to get married; she was close to her father. But he betray her. He give her away." In his hands, the rope felt rough and heavy, and he remembered again a tiny village crouched on a hillside and a murky river pulsing with abandoned children, girls, and the steel braces of junks and an old man with a flowing white beard and an old man full of fantasies.

"Well, every girl must marry. Is tradition."

"But it was so different from the life the old man plan with her. He had plenty dreams. All he want was to travel."

"So he infuse her with them. Fill her up with highfalutin ideas so she turn independent. Hard to manage. The wife must hate him, spoiling her daughter like that. Was she the washbelly?"

The donkeys had begun wandering again and they tightened the reins and told them softly to heel and the donkeys obeyed and started to bray and Lowe hoped that his hammering heart would not betray him. "Yes, she was the last one. But nothing was on purpose. He felt cut off from his wife, his sons, she was everything to him, he bring her everywhere. Put her on his shoulders. Carry her to all the bars in Canton. She sit there with him and the men and the whores and watch them polish off bowl after bowl of wine. At the edge of the water, he would plan trips, expeditions—"

"All this with a baby girl."

"Well, you couldn't exactly tell. He used to steal her away and dress her up."

"But you can always tell those things, Mr. Lowe, if you want people to know, that is. But if you cover up things like that, that's another thing. Like the mustache, for example."

The mustache. Lowe's hand rushed to his bare mouth.

"You look much better without it. You don't need it. Look at me. Nothing at all. Definitely more attractive. So how you manage with this girl? You did love her? She must be hard as hell to handle."

All of a sudden Lowe felt exhausted. All of a sudden he felt burdened by his costumes, loaded down by his masquerade, by the labyrinth of lies, the excessiveness of his imagination, that self that no longer had inherent meaning and instead was just a compilation of fiction. Sometimes he knew not where one thing began and another ended. He no longer knew whether or not his stories matched up, if people realized the gaps in connections, the holes he was always digging. Of course there had been no wife, just a betrayal. A girl cut off from her father the moment puberty appeared and thrust into marriage.

A girl with bottled-up fantasies, a girl with broken-down dreams, a girl with a head full of expeditions by sea, a girl with a wandering eye, a girl given over to an old man so as to repay a debt, a girl turned into a wife overnight; a wife weighted down by tradition, a brooding sullen wife, a restless wife with wanderlust, a runaway wife with a shaved head and a queue, a runaway wife with the long easy strides of a father, a wife lurking on the piers of Canton, a wife dwarfed by the towering buildings of Canton, by the forest of ships and boats, by the simmering heat and dregs of the city, by the thick throng of foreigners, a runaway wife

"What happen, Mr. Lowe, you forgot?"

Lowe watched him. The granite face that betrayed no emotions. The curling lips. The black curve of his skin. The burning glass eyes. The vileness in his voice. The nastiness that had been turned away from the villagers and was now projected onto him. The vileness. "What you want, Omar? What you want from me?" His hands trembled on the bridle, and the tears in his chest surged.

"You've small hands for a man, Mr. Lowe. Small feet." Omar spat.

"And what of it, Omar, what of it?" His own voice had hardened, and the animals as if absorbing the tension picked up a slow disdainful trot, and Lowe's donkey shot up ahead, and Omar's tarried behind, and Lowe felt like a prisoner clanking with chains. And he felt the rub of the rubber on his waist and the sharp dig of the metal. And in the back of his neck he felt Omar's smirking smile and the piercing eyes. He saw the big coarse hands.

"These eyes don't miss anything at all, Mr. Lowe. I see everything. I know what go on in that house. I know the show."

"And so now what it is that you want?" Lowe asked him in a tired voice. "What it is that you want?"

"Land, Mr. Lowe. Land." He swept out his arm with a flourishing sweep. "You see all this!"

And they trotted on through the thrashing weeds with the gold sky above and the cruel silence between them and the dense forest full of twisting vines that lay ahead.

The next morning, he did not go to the woods but stooped down in the doorway of the smoky kitchen with Dulcie and looked out at the silvery slant of the squalling rain and listened to the pattering on the roof and Dulcie did not disturb him. She nosed the bristles of her broom around the edges of his shoes and the billowing bottom of her floral skirts lashed his cheeks and he inhaled her perfume and the odor of her sweat and he studied her frequent sighs, which sounded to him like screams, and tried to decode the moods betrayed by her sordid murmuring, the messages hidden in her solid back, in the hump of shoulders, in the sturdy neck. He glanced at her unreadable brown eye when she handed him his meals, and worried that he'd stumbled into more of the murky secrets of the family. He felt trapped in the middle of things, and Omar's blackmail, he was certain, was just the beginning. He wondered if Dulcie was entrenched in this plan with Omar, if she too had her eyes on Miss Sylvie's land, if she too had her ax to grind. He did not know these people with whom he had lived all these years. He did not know them. They were an armored gang.

He wondered if what the villagers had said about Dulcie was

true. For after all these years the people in the shop had never stopped speculating about her past. And as she was never one to come down to the shop and sit out on the piazza and labrish with other women who had a scrap of time to spare, as she was never one to reveal much of herself, just so, they didn't know how to read her. But they speculated nonetheless. She was from Trinidad, that they knew, for it was there in the song of her speech, and like them she had worked out herself on the estates as a girl, picking crocus bags of lime and peanut and orange, carrying cane. They knew. They heard the rattle of dust in her voice. They saw the line-striped face that symbolized suffering, they saw the muscle-bound arms that had known the weight of cane loads. But more important, they wondered if she was that same Dulcemeena that years ago had a bounty out on her head, starting at seventy-five pounds and rising. News had it that on one of the estates she had organized workers to protest the pittance that was their wages and for which they worked eighteen and twenty hours a day. News had it that she had begged the poor people to band their bellies and so for weeks and weeks workers did not show up and the canefields lay rutted with the abandoned and rotting bundles of cane.

News had it that she and her people had set fire to buildings and to fields, that they had sabotaged the factory equipment and had marched in front of estates with their signs and burning eyes, with their rage pouring in song. News had it that the protesters had been shot down by the hundreds and by the thousands, by police in cold blood, and that several more hundred had been beaten and left to rot out their time in jail. News had it that Dulcie and others had escaped and that the countryside had been scoured for their whereabouts. That bounties were posted. And at a price so high her own people had captured her and turned her in. News had it that she had been beaten almost to death and left in the prison to die. That she had been paraded naked through the streets, her skin gutted by whiplash. But somehow money had been put up for her trial. Humanitarian efforts and rich English people had rallied round her cause, it seemed. They put up the money, news had it, and set defense lawyers on the case to save her.

Was it the same Dulcie? they wondered. For she had the left eye that barely opened, the broken nose that lay like a fist on her face, the split top lip that had grown slightly curled, the missing fingers on her left hand that had dropped off from gangrene, the broken foot that had never properly healed so she always had to pull it when she walked and whenever a cold front struck had to wrap it up and keep indoors to her bed for the sake of the searing, profound pain. Was it the same Dulcie? Dulcemeena Maitland!

Lowe had never engaged her in a serious and deep conversation, and so he did not know. He thought once to ask her, but there was nothing at all about her demeanor that invited his questions. Indeed she had always seemed remote, but that wasn't a bad streak in a person, he decided. She seemed completely devoted to Miss Sylvie and to Omar, and when her duties were done she sat by herself, smoking her clay pipe and looking out at the world from her roost in the kitchen with just the one shimmering eye like a bullet. It was as if she had been terribly burned. As if the light or the fire that once charged her had run its course and now, years later, had left her extinguished. But wasn't that the nature of fire, he decided, once its fuel was done—to leave just the exhausted frame? She barely smiled, he had never heard her laugh. But then again, given the kind of world it was, what was there to laugh at! He knew she combed the same newspaper daily, poring over the same article, reading and rereading and grunting the same profound grunt, though, as far as he knew, she couldn't as much as spell her name. Was it the announcement with word of the bounty? he wondered. He did not know these people and their designs. He did not know. He did not know.

Lowe kept his eyes on the lookout for Miss Sylvie, but of her there was no sign. She left early in the wagon with Whitley each morning and did not return till nightfall. He had no idea where they went and he was too humiliated to ask. But he was worried, for clearly it was blackmail, clearly Omar would talk, would tell people. He did not know if Omar was bluffing or if he in fact knew. And knew what! And what exactly would he tell people? And the villagers, after he told them, would they just descend on the house with their tins of kerosene and catch them on fire? Would they parade both him and Miss Sylvie through the road, stoning them with rocks and lashing them with insults? Would they tie them to posts and leave them there in the scorching sun to die? He did not know. He did not know. The land was his daughter's, the land was to build his Pagoda, the land was there so they could live comfortably till they died. He had lived in that house all those years, but he still did not know why Sylvie was there and what her relationship was to Cecil. He did not know Omar or Dulcie, and in the short time he tried to get close to Omar he had already been burned. He didn't know anything about the land. He didn't understand Omar's intent. He didn't know what bones they all had to pick with Miss Sylvie. He did not know. He did not know.

To distract himself, now, he dabbled with the colors of Miss Sylvie's paints and discovered new variations of shades. He scrawled out, on enormous white sheets of paper, elaborate landscapes dotted with swamps, the crumbling stone houses, the jagged razor hills. He produced vague and distorted portraits of people he remembered in his village and the turgid serpentine flow of rivers. He painted colorful wildflowers that grew along a tiny stream that wound its way around ruinous wooden houses, he painted workers thigh-deep in mud-red fields, he painted their hats with the pointed peaks, he filled up enormous sheets with black lacquer coffins and their red satin interiors. When the colors no longer held his interest, he sat on the low narrow stool by the organ and plunked out tunes on the black keys, songs his father had taught him.

In the evenings, he inspected the solemn leather-bound

volumes that sat in Miss Sylvie's study, and in a white wicker chair near the window he started innumerable novels and biographies of great men, none of which he had the patience to finish, for he was plagued with worry. He could not wait for Omar to strike. He did not like the tension in the house. He did not like his placelessness in the house. He did not know how to enjoy leisure, and the enormous amounts of time on his hands made him worthless.

At night he could not sleep, and he missed his sweaty and itchy skin that was scorched and cut by the tall sharp grass and the dust that crept underneath his nails and the insects that burrowed holes in his flesh, for at least he felt alive then. He no longer savored his steaming baths, he chewed his meals without relish, the songs he whistled under his breath carried no tunes. And every night he lay awake listening to the howling silence of the house, for his dreams refused to take him, and it was just he alone with an unraveling of thoughts, with the weighted-down feelings of desperation, the uncertainty of the life ahead of him.

One night he approached the desk with the smoking lamp and crouched over the sheets of white paper that lay there and thought again that he should at least let the daughter know before word got to her, the same daughter that had betrayed him, that had taken the side of the husband over him, the same daughter that was the stranger to him. He had no rhyme or reason to his thoughts, there was no specific form or style to his execution of language, there was no specific past or present place to start, there was just a hovering of thoughts, a head crowded with images, a chest throbbing with distress, and a cocked hand with a pen.

This then is the terrain: mountainous coastlines brimming with butterflies, an arid countryside assaulted by famine, a town swarming with clans and secret societies, an anti-Manchu resistance, a coastal town full of fishermen, and junks bobbing on a shimmering glassy sea, an ancestral temple bristling with spirit tablets, a thin grove of trees, a muddy climb from the town, a village full of hunger and destitution, a poor and overcrowded village, a village full of Hakka speakers, traveling gypsies, a China war with Britain, a great war over territory, a war of opium, a South China Sea clogged with foreign vessels, a shimmering sunlit sea loaded with emigrant ships, North America, Australia, Singapore, a credit ticket system, the hordes of Chinese leaving, villages bereft of young men, the empire ravaged too by a Hakka sect, a revolution at Taiping, a backdrop of death and destruction, and hunger and debts, a faltering of authority, people leaving in batches, streams of refugees leaving in droves. To Malay, Panama, Africa, to the deserted West Indian plantations . . .

One night, when there was no sleep to be had, no dreams to disguise his despair or diminish the restlessness that demonized his limbs, no dreams to ease the whirlpool of thoughts, to relieve his fear of the horror that was to unfold when Omar decided to reveal his plan to get the land, he leapt out of bed and hauled on his clothes and shoes parked at the door and was swinging down the steep stone steps of the veranda and into the blinding dark, picking out his way past the burned-out ruins of his shop, where he had not been since he returned home from his travels to Westmoreland, where he had not been since the devastation.

The rain squalled into his hat and the light breeze rustled the fuzz on his neck and he stepped quickly, wanting only to reach in time, before the men returned to their homes and the comfort of their wives and lovers, before there was no one with whom he could share his solitude, his distress, before it would be him alone again with the repetition of images, with the circle of words, with the galloping fantasies of Whitley nestled in Miss Sylvie's arms, with nothing but the roaring silence and the sleepless night. Part of the way he ran, hoping not to fall, and the smell of fallow fields and the moist loamy earth suffused still with the burning remains of his shop rushed out at him, and the cave of his stomach trembled again, just remembering. The night was black and the pupils of his eyes picked out needles of light spiraling from Miss Cora's shop, and he could hear bursts of laughter. He walked slowly again to ease the boom-boom of his chest, to remove the flush from his cheeks, to calm the flutter of his eyelids, the chattering teeth, and he hoped with all his might that Omar had not gotten there ahead of him.

It was the shop belonging to his main competitor, Miss Cora, who was a shrewd businesswoman and not so prone to trusting goods on credit. He had never set foot in her shop, but it was in her little stone church, hot and choked with people, that Liz was christened, with the pastor sprinkling water on her face and muttering a few words over her head. He paused in the entrance of her shop, adjusting his eyes to the yellow beams of light glowing from the lamps. It was a Tuesday night and Miss Cora was there, leaned up at the counter cradling her jaw and peering into the glittery darkness, an enormous rusty scale blocking half her face. Inching closer, he could separate the cry of insects from the timbre of voices, and he could recognize the bursts of laughter, and he realized now that he had heard these very same jokes before, with the same interjections and snorts, he knew exactly what Mass Wally would say next, and that Raygun wouldn't respond to the jab until he'd asked for another shot of rum. He knew that Sprat's bitterness over the woman that had run off would erupt soon. He swallowed bitterly.

To them, nothing had happened. Their lives had not come to a complete standstill, with the ground rotting away underfoot. The disruption had not eaten away at them and left them with wretched nights. The proof was here in the circular lines of stories that were the same, the same he had heard every night for thirty years. For him, though, it had stopped. Now he had nothing. They had burned it down. Left him with nothing. But their lives, their lives had . . . Suddenly he was enraged, suddenly he shook with the feelings, suddenly his chest burned with the fever of his hate, and he turned on his heels, except that one of the men must have seen him, for someone grabbed his arm, and another a fist of shirt, another fingered the waist of belt. "Is that you, Mr. Lowe?"

"Is the Chinaman that? My God! Mr. Lowe!" He heard the surprise in their voices, the pause in their frenzied breathing.

"Bring him come, bring him come." That was Miss Cora, in a loud and commanding tone of voice.

"Come, come, clear the counter. Bring him come." Miss Cora again.

"Lowe, my God, man." Jake. That was Jake, with no teeth at all in his mouth so his words whistled. Two days ago Jake spat when he saw Lowe with Omar.

"Mr. Lowe!"

They held on to him. They pulled him to their chests. His nostrils brushed up against the stink of their armpits, rubbed up against the sharp cloth of their starched shirts, rubbed up against the soft sagging stomachs, their tight wiry limbs, their shiny faces stiff with beard, locked up into their sweat smells.

"My God, Mr. Lowe!" He felt their arms around his neck, wrapping his shoulders and chest, beating against his back, smoothing his cheeks, and he knew Omar had not struck yet.

"Bring him!" Miss Cora again, with a sharp voice. "And enough of this blasted hug hug. Bring the man!"

He heard the clink clink of glasses on counter, heard the rip and twist and break of new bottle cap, heard the pouring measure of liquid into glasses, smelled the razor cut of rum.

"Come, come!" Miss Cora again.

They must've lifted him off his feet, for he was suspended, there was no ground and he was face-to-face with the cobwebs in the corner of the wall, face-to-face with the dusty tops of glass case, oil drum, the thinning shiny middle of heads, he was deafened by the thunderous roar of men, and he was face-to-face with Miss Cora at the counter, and she grinned and he saw that the tiny squint of her brown eyes behind the thick black glasses was kind and that her wig of straight and fine yellow hair lightly dusted with flour was crooked on her head and so he could see the spiraling cottony curls of her own hair creeping out near her ears, and he saw the golden flash of diamond-studded teeth in the lamplight, saw her shuddering chins, saw her gesturing arms swinging with pendules of brown flesh, saw her fingers twinkling with jewels, smelled again the horse sweat of the men that had burned down his shop, the semen smell, rum smell, carbolic soap smell of the men, the smell of manure and of wood shaving, the smell of cut grass and of fish, the smell of cane juice and of unwashed skin, the smell of blood on the men who were arsonists, the smell of wood smoke, Limocal, the smell of bay rum and sulfur and tobacco and pea soup, the smell of cod and corned beef, of red herring.

"Drink up now!" Miss Cora again, with a mouth full of grinning gaudy teeth.

And suddenly the shop was crowded with toasting men, men with firm brown arms holding up in the air glasses of rum, men who had burned down his shop, men who still owed him thirty, forty pounds, though once in a while a wife came up to the house on a Sunday evening to drop off a few shillings. Men with mirth. Men with merriment. Men who beat their wives and fucked their daughters. Men with good intentions. Generous and kind men. Men who loved him and other men.

They dropped him to his feet. Lowe put the glass to his lips, and the fire bloodied his face at once and smarted his eyes and pounded so hard in his belly he felt his knees go wobbly, and Miss Cora burst out into a loud spiraling laughter that chopped up the night. "Drink up, man, Lowe." And she polished off two more glasses and was pouring a fourth round again for herself and the others, and Lowe said to them in a fragile voice, in a voice cracked with forgiveness, in a voice mantled with sadness, in a voice riddled with love, moist with confusion, for maybe it wasn't them after all, maybe it wasn't them: "Drink up, eh. All you, eh. Thanks." And he saw the shuddering brown sea of faces, the black gaping holes of mouths, and he was deafened again by the muffled roar of men who had burned down his shop, and there was no solid ground again, just the rotting and rusty tops of abandoned oil drums, just the deep, spiraling zigzag crack of unpainted and soot-covered walls, just the forgotten objects of art and crumpled pieces of old letters and yellowing IOUs sheathed in dust.

Each night now he spent at Miss Cora's shop was a celebration. Each night now someone brought him a hand of ripe Gros Michel banana, a head of St. Vincent or Renta yam, a foot of tobacco for Miss Sylvie, a string of perch, a cake of handmade soap. Each night now there was the rip and twist of new bottles of rum. Each night now they recalled again and again events that had occurred when Lowe's shop was still standing, and they shook again with laughter. And every night now they drank and swore and cursed and threatened each other with murder and boasted and made bets and inched closer toward Miss Cora's glass case, which caused her to scale the counter and fly at them with a broom, her voice echoing out over the great pandemonium, "Mind the glass, you know, brother, for is hundreds of pounds, that, mind the glass."

Each night now the shop piazza bristled with the political and social news of the country. They complained of the laws that had been passed to deter people from working away from the estates, the high taxes that had been instituted to prevent them from starting their own landholding business, from opening up shops. They talked of the closing of estates, which was putting people out of work, but the potential for other work as the government was building more and more schools and hospitals, more almshouses and prisons and lunatic asylums and police stations. More roads. They talked of the spread of cholera, how many they had already lost to the epidemic, the need for better water supplies, for medical and sanitary facilities, the conditions on estates where friends had had entire body parts ground up in machines. They talked of word they'd received from family members who had gone to other islands to seek work, and how there was plenty of farmwork to be had in Costa Rica, railroad building in Panama. They talked of the death camps in Cuba, where not so long ago Negroes got their freedom.

And at first Lowe listened and then he began to wonder again at the extent of their hypocrisy and hate, for who else would've burned it down if it wasn't them, but now here they were celebrating. Talking story as if nothing had happened. Here they were! As if it was essential that there be no barriers between him and them. No shop counters. For all of a sudden they were openly discussing their political plans in front of him, as if without the shop he had become one of them.

And when he could stand it no longer, in a loud sharp voice he asked them, in a voice burnished with bitterness, in a voice moist with confusion, he asked them: "So why the hell you burn it down, why the hell?" The conversations hissed to a stop. The piazza grew silent. The men pulled the screen over their eyes and looked out into the darkness.

"Jesus Christ, every night gift, every night present, but the shop . . . the shop . . ." His voice cracked, he started to weep. It sounded awful in his ears, it sounded babyish and unmanly. He sounded terrible. Like a woman.

"But, Mr. Lowe, it wasn't we." That was Jake, holding Lowe's leg with an iron hand and whistling through his gums into Lowe's neck. "Time will point out the culprit, Mr. Lowe. But it wasn't we, sir, it wasn't we."

Someone handed Lowe a glass of rum and he boxed it away and the glass exploded on the concrete not too far from his feet. "So now you hiding him," Lowe cried out, desperately wanting to believe them. "Is that. Now you taking up for him! Taking up for each other!" He remembered the night they celebrated his return, and the tears rushed him again.

"Mr. Lowe, man." That was Jake again, whistling in his neck. "Mr. Lowe, calm down now, sir, calm down. Is not we. It wasn't we, sir." And he offered Lowe his handkerchief and Lowe blew fiercely into it and returned it.

"Mr. Lowe, man, is all right. Is all right." Jake again, with the
iron hand on his kneecap. And Lowe calmed down with just the
pressure of the hand on his knee and the whistling in his neck
and thought maybe it wasn't them at all, maybe it wasn't them at
all, maybe it was more organized than that. Maybe it was the
Native Defense people. Maybe it was just criminal elements
stalking the countryside. For it wasn't usual. And he loved them
again, these men who were his friends and had kept him company over the years, though he wasn't completely sure that they
hadn't burned down the shop, wasn't completely sure they
would still love him like this when Omar stripped him naked for
all to look at in order to get the land. And there was a needling in
his stomach that wouldn't go away. Some old wound, some old
sore. A needling.

Then one morning, when he was about to set off for the
woods—for now he no longer accompanied Omar but set off on
his own in the opposite direction—one morning when he was
still on the veranda tugging on his boots, he smelled strongly the
odor of coffee and then again of the lavender Whitley used in
her hair, and he looked up and saw Miss Sylvie standing there
with two mugs. It was later than usual, he'd overslept; the rains
that had been coming for sixteen days had suddenly ceased and
the sun had already burned off the mist but still had not reached
too high in the sky and had already touched the whitewashed
stones that bordered the garden and was striping the yard with
vertical columns. And it was just he alone with Miss Sylvie and
the history between them, the memory of the humiliation of
that Sunday afternoon and the yearning for a meeting place that
would replace his shop and give his daughter a sense of her history and give the Chinese people a place just to be, in that hot
and hostile place.

She handed him the cup and he took it with a trembling
hand, and the brown juice splashed and burned his skin and he
winced and slurped and avoided her face and sat down on the

step of the veranda and looked across the hills at the banana trees and even further east to the red berries glistening with moisture in the coffee plantation. He slurped again and she sat down next to him and he heard her steady breathing and smelled the hibiscus and lavender on her skin and in her hair, and she said to him, "I don't think Whitley'll come back," and without even realizing he'd stopped breathing, he exhaled heavily and replayed again the few words she'd just said, and he realized he hadn't heard the tone and timbre of her voice, he didn't know if she spoke out of gladness or out of sadness, still he said nothing at all and he waited and the silence weighed heavily between them, but he was afraid to glance at her face, just in case she was looking at him, just in case she was weeping, and he slurped quietly so as not to break up the silence so cruelly and it loaded them down and he decided that maybe he should speak, but say what, he wondered, for the idea that she'd sent Whitley away just for him, that he somehow still mattered to her, even after all these years, all these events . . . "I sorry," he croaked, and from the periphery of his vision he saw that she had not touched her coffee, that she was merely looking out at the clusters of banana trees with a slow nodding head, with pursed lips and a tight sad face, and to the left he saw the criss-crossing of the neat rows of Ortanique trees and even closer still saw the paint-flaked posts that shouldered the gutters that carried the rainwater into drums and into the well at the side of the house.

"It's just us now," she told him, still looking at the hills with faraway eyes, and he repeated the word "us" to himself and thought what a strange, solemn, unmusical, disinterested, sudden, stiff word that was, "us," but of course it meant the two of them, he reminded himself, and then he thought of the strange combination they were, he and Miss Sylvie, but found he had no idea exactly what she meant by that "It's just us now," and he asked her, suddenly terrified by the possibility of more dreams, more fantasies, "What you mean, exactly?"

She didn't answer at once. There was the slow-breathing silence between them.

"Well, what is it you'd like, Lowe?" She turned to him finally. "Cecil gone on. Whitley probably won't come back. Is just us now. Omar is there, he can look after things, Dulcie too."

Was she suggesting that they move, that they go off somewhere together, was she suggesting that he move away, from the only place he knew, the only safe thing that was home? And what about the Pagoda, he began to worry again, as the fate of the other immigrant Chinese unraveled again before him. And he thought of his father.

A man with too many visions. A man full up of fantasies. A man who infused fantasy into a girl. A girl full up of filial piety. A girl wanting to remove the screen of shame from a father's face. Screen of hopelessness. A girl wanting her father's affection forever. A girl full up of her father's fantasy. A girl pregnant with her father's dreams. A girl with a bloated head full of dreams. A restless girl thinking of expeditions.

"Lowe, what is it you'd like?"

He outlined it for her, all the things he intended to build, the length and breadth of the place, the stone animals with the gaping and powerful jaws, the fountains with the murmuring spray, the green tiles on the curled roof, the groups, the various subdivisions, the funds necessary. He watched her face as he sped along with his dreams. It betrayed no emotion. And when he had exhausted himself, he stopped and pulled out his handkerchief and mopped his face, which was wet and hot and slightly ruddy.

"It sound ambitious, Lowe."

He noted the skepticism in her voice, and he felt a burning spread from a small deep wound in his stomach.

"But you don't want something for both of us? You don't want just to go to another island and start over, fresh? Where nobody know us. Where is just us. A fresh history. Maybe you wouldn't even have to be like this anymore." She looked up at him and stretched her lips.

Was that a grin? A grimace? "Like what?" he cried, though the burning was spreading out from the hole and enveloping the caves of his stomach. An old scab, it felt like, being slowly peeled away, and the old canker sore inside, the one that had never completely healed, was starting to fester again and fill up with pus.

She stretched her face even wider and he dropped his hand across his navel and left it there. He watched her face, slightly flushed, and the hair by the sides of her ears curling up. He watched her eyes of sulfur, and inside his chest, his heart clanged.

"Like your clothes. Like your . . . ," and she fumbled with her hands, and the gaudy rings on her snake fingers glittered. And the copper bangles on her thick wrists jangled. "You wouldn't have to dress up like that, you wouldn't have to look like a . . ." She fumbled again. "I mean unless you want to. But we could start over. We could . . ."

He was trembling, his hands were shaking, and he pressed them against the shifting soil in his stomach. Like a man! On the floor, his legs were like shuffling pegs until he folded them together and they ceased their disturbing knock. "Is that what you want, then, for me to look like that old whore, that nasty whore? You not interested in the meetinghouse, you not interested in me, what I want, you just interested in you. What you want!" His voice sounded old, even to his own ears, and far away. He thought of snakes slithering in the tall grass.

"Lowe."

"I don't have anything anymore. I just want the meeting-house. Just wanted a place. My daughter, Liz, don't know anything bout her people, don't know. The people." And then he remembered again the walk in the woods with Omar and his great shame when Omar laughed at his small hands, roved his doggish eyes over Lowe's slight frame. He thought of Omar shaming him down at the shop in front of the men. And he was exhausted. Crushed. And all of a sudden he didn't like his clothes, all of a sudden the trousers seemed gray and ugly to him, all of a sudden he felt unclean. And he heard in his head the clanging laughter of men crowding round to gawk at his skinny woman's chest, the children squeezing between legs to catch a better glimpse.

"Lowe." Her hand was heavy on his shoulders. The fingers clawed into his shirt. The snake fingers boned against the tangled cords in his throat. "Lowe, we can start the clubhouse elsewhere. We can still build it. But maybe another island."

"And what bout the land?" He lifted his arm to mimic Omar's florid sweep and hated the sight of his blackened broken nails. "You just going give it to Omar? Give him everything? You just going give?" He was feeling rootless.

"Lowe." She started to cry slowly, silently; her stomach trembled; there were no sounds, but her face was wet and he felt tremendous pity all of a sudden and he took her hands that were warm with humidity, her gentle hands that had never known hard work, never known labor, he took her hands ever so lightly and brought them to his cheeks and he saw that he didn't know anything at all about her, nothing at all, and when the trembling had subsided and her eyes had grown solid and clear again, had turned to ash again, he told her the conversation he had had in the woods with Omar and how he claimed to have seen them, how he claimed to have known. And how the land was what he wanted, otherwise he would tell.

She raised up her head and blew her nostrils tremendously into the tail of her dress and cemented her face and asked him quietly, "Is that all he said, Lowe?"

And he outlined again all he had lived with Omar and he told her piece by piece and she listened solemnly, all the while nodding and watching his face with intent.

"We have to move, Lowe, we have to move." She wrung her

hands over and over, and he saw that he didn't know her at all. He didn't know the people with whom he lived.

"But how you know he not just bluffing?" He was desperate. "I mean what exactly is it he has seen?"

"He know enough, Lowe. He know enough."

"Enough of what, though, Sylvie? I mean you can give him some of the land, work it out with him. But move? Jesus Christ, where? We belong here, this where we live, this . . ." He saw the cracked leather of his boots from the corners of his eyes and tucked them out of sight.

"You not afraid of what he could tell people, Lowe, how he could expose us, expose you? Cecil gone now. What to protect us? Don't you see we just have to move, Lowe, we just have to?"

"But why now, Sylvie, why now?" He hated the scratching khaki on his skin, the loathsome mustache he had taken to wearing again. "Plus you think the people here would believe him, though, Sylvie. I mean they know us for over thirty years. I mean who going to just turn round now and believe Omar?" Doubt was killing his voice.

"I kill a man, Lowe." Her voice was low and cutting, with a razor edge. "I kill a man, a white man. My husband."

And Lowe said nothing at all, nothing at all, for what could he have said? The saliva had left his mouth and it felt full of ashes, full of sawdust, full of straw and hay and manure. The saliva had left his mouth and his lips were white and dry, his lips trembled. Close by the house corner the donkey still waited for him, and Lowe heard the animal's slow wheeze and the rip of grass in its teeth.

"I choke him to death and I didn't think anyone would realize, but Cecil was his friend and Cecil found out."

"But, Sylvie, you tell me he fall off horse . . . you tell me the dreams . . . you told me . . ." This he said when he suddenly found words. When the enormous silence between them had finally rolled away. For what else could he have said but to go back to something old to hold on to, more of the fictions and fantasies, some old safe thing.

"I know, Lowe, I know. We made a deal, me and Cecil. He wanted a mother for Liz and a way to protect you, Lowe, for when you came it was just you alone on the island, you the only woman, and God knows what could've happen."

"But you told me he fall off horse." He had lost the hysteria, and now his voice was plain and flat. A plateau. "You told me . . ." He wanted to believe the horse story; it was so much cleaner, so much safer.

"I know, Lowe, I know."

"But why, Sylvie, why?" He was almost weeping; it was just too much, too much unraveling.

"I had to give away my children, Lowe, three of them." The blood had left her face and it was white with exhaustion and blue circles caved round her eyes. "They were too brown."

"Too brown!" The thing in his stomach flowered open again. "Too brown? How you mean, too brown?"

"Brown like my people, Lowe. Not as dark as Dulcie, but brown. Way too . . ."

Now *his* face had lost the color. Now *his* face had turned a chalky white.

"Octoroon," she said.

"Oh God," Lowe growled, and there was the silence between them and the screeching of nearby parakeets and twittering of nearby crickets and the trembling streams of air that stoked his chest and throat. She looked away with an indifferent face.

"They turn out too brown and my husband was a big government man with money and clout and a face to hold up and a lot of people working for him and capturing black people and still selling them. Dulcie deliver them. All three. We had to tell him they stillborn. We had quick ceremonies with nothing at all in the coffins. Omar built them. Dulcie give them away to church, to the orphanage. Left them in baskets on doorsteps. I don't know. I never ask."

Suddenly Lowe remembered the hands hanging limp inside his own and thought how much they felt now like weapons, the fingers hard and cold and artfully carved. He lived in a house full of murderers and blackmailers. "And where the children them now, Sylvie?" His voice croaked. "You know them? Them alive?"

She didn't answer. Her hooded eyes seemed far away. Her jaws worked a seesaw movement, and an overwhelming sadness brooded between them, enormous and infectious. And he understood now her indebtedness to Cecil all these years. He realized again that Cecil wasn't the kind of man one could easily box up into a category. He saw his goodness and his kindness and his ruthlessness and his cunning all in one. Was he the one who had put up money for Dulcie's release? It wouldn't surprise him. He understood as well Miss Sylvie's complete adoration of Liz and the emptiness his daughter must have filled. How Liz must have made Miss Sylvie's arms feel weighty again, how her cherubic smile must've stopped Miss Sylvie's mind from racing. He understood the suffering guilt that must've plagued her all these years, and he understood as well her silences and her double life, and he saw that their fates were linked together, and he saw that together they were badly wounded people. And he saw now how Omar was going to betray them. Cecil was dead. Cecil was out of the way. Now Omar could run things. Could even run them off the land if he had a mind.

"Don't you see now, Lowe, that we have to go? Don't you see how Omar getting more and more restless? He want the land. Don't you see how?" She stopped and looked at him.

And Lowe said nothing. He looked at the ugly bark of his hands and saw the depths of Omar's treacherousness.

"But didn't you try to find them, the babies, I mean? Why kill the husband, I mean, why?"

They spent the evenings now poring over the maps in Miss Sylvie's study. And each evening now he listened to Miss Sylvie's plans, her fantasies, the small wooden house on a cliff by the sea, just the two of them and a housekeeper that came daily. A picnic every day at lunchtime, a white-checkered cloth spread out on the ground, the housekeeper holding up the umbrella, the spray of the water, the wash and rinse of the sea. And every evening her fantasies grew more lavish. A small red house with yellow windows and a white door. A house with all the windows facing the sea. A house with a rose garden and a veranda. And more and more he thought of his father and more and more he felt enraged and more and more he felt like a louse. He didn't know how to tell her he didn't want to live out anybody else's fantasy. He didn't know how to tell her. He didn't want to go anywhere isolated. He wanted to have the Pagoda right here on the island, for the Chinese with whom he had grown close. He resented how she wanted him isolated, how she wanted him now to change, to look now like a woman, to wear a frock now and a corset and grow out his hair now way past his shoulders, and walk and wind his hips now like a whore, like that Whitley, and how the hell did she think he was going to run meetinghouse looking like that, who did she think would attend, would even as much as respect him? And Omar, who was to say Omar wouldn't hunt them down again, hunt them down and trap them in their frocks? Who was to say? Resentment was a hell of a thing! Resentment and blackmail!

She put down her pencil and looked at him. She removed her silver pince-nez, which made her eyes seem even more cloudy and bulbous, and looked at him. The room smelled of camphor balls, of mildew, of humid books and aging leather, of incense, of cigars, of the dust that had settled permanently into the grain of wood.

"One night we start to fight." Her voice was gravelly, and in the lamplit silence she seemed older, more exhausted. She seemed burdened and the air around her was dense and weighty. "Must be somebody tell him something; he used to make fun of my widow's peak when friends visit, he said maybe I was a witch. He said maybe I was killing them. I mean for how long?" She looked at Lowe with deep penetrating eyes. "I mean for how long can you listen to a thing as that? One night we start to fight and he said it, he said he heard I was a nigger and was killing the nigger children and he was going to kill me for shaming him like that. It was either him or me, Lowe."

"But why'd you marry him, then. I mean you must did know it could happen, eventually. I mean why put yourself through all that, why?"

"He like me. He pursue me. And I could pass. The entire family, two generations back, could pass. He buy me nice gifts." She stretched out her fingers that were slightly curled with arthritis, and the flat bands of gold shimmered. "A powerful man as that? Is every girl's wish. I mean what women have, Lowe, if it ain't what the father give them, what the husband give them? We passed. But we were just getting by."

Her eyes had grown restless now and were searching the room. "Maman was the only one nervous. We were three generations removed. But she worry all the same. And then it happened. And it's freakish when it happen. And they were brown, Lowe, browner than you can ever imagine, as if Egbert wasn't the father but someone else." She spoke in hushed tones as though the idea of it still frightened her, still perturbed her, these freakish occurrences of nature.

"And Dulcie," Lowe wanted to know. "She keep in touch with them?"

She shrugged. "I never ask, Lowe, I never ask. What behind me now behind me. How to go now and dig up the past? Why to go now and stir up old things? What the sense? No sense in that at all." She had found her tobacco and she rolled two cigars swiftly and deftly and she sucked on one as if it were life itself and her shoulders got more limp and rounded, the creases in her forehead and between the eyes ironed out, and her eyes grew fluid again and soft. She turned to the maps. "Barbados, Lowe, how bout Barbados? Panama?"

6

Each and every night now he lay awake listening to footsteps creaking on the veranda, he heard the traffic of people prowling through the house. He saw the huddled-up shadows of women in tall skirts, heard their soft conspiratory whispers. He heard the sharpening of long rusty knives on grindstones, saw the lightning flash of silver, saw faces smeared with sweat and blood. Blood. Dark thongs of it everywhere. Pools guttered between the floorboards, splashed on the walls, stained to the white sheets and tall curtains. And bodies. Charred and black and smoldering Chinese bodies.

They stared at him with eyes cooked in their sockets. They grinned at him out of a black hole of chattering white bones. He didn't understand how Miss Sylvie could sleep through all this commotion, and he drew the curtains and peered at her face by the slow moving light of the moon as it pushed through the tops of trees. The silvery flesh between the eyes was puckered. The slightly bluish face was tense and drawn taut over the bones. The thin-lipped mouth corners were turned down. There was fierce rapid movement across the eyelids. There were the quivering nostrils in the long slim nose. She was white as snow, yet underneath all that milk covering she was octoroon, had given birth to babies and abandoned them on church steps, had murdered a man with the hands, so peaceful, so soft and feminine, lying there. Then outside and up the steep stone steps and inside the low doorway of the buttery was Omar, sitting on the upturned mortar with his face black and ugly and watchful, waiting for the opportune moment to strike. And Dulcie. Was he to find out that she was the high priestess of it all? He did not know. He did not know.

He decided he would go and see his friend Joyce. He had not seen her since Cecil's funeral, months now. He did not know what he would tell her, how much he could tell, but he needed to talk, to feel safe somewhere. To think all these years he had been sleeping next to a murderer, to think all these years she was there supposedly protecting him, and now even she was wanting to expose him. To think even she was wanting to trap him into her foolish fantasy. It was late, tennish, the wrongest time to appear at a married woman's yard, but he was desperate. He hooked a lantern onto the silver bar of Omar's bicycle and stole away into the moonlit dark. He kept his eyes on the light snaking its way along the winding path. He listened to the whirring wheels and tried to keep the smell of charred bodies out of his teeth. He heard the crickets' slow soft music and way yonder saw the flaring lightning that lit up the thin spine of a mountain. He did not want to worry about whether or not Mr. Fine, her husband, was there, or her three children. What if she was away visiting relatives? He remembered again her shrill laughter, the throbbing organ swelling his mouth in the midday heat, the smell of patchouli that marked her slender throat.

He arrived at the gate of her house, set apart from others and shrouded in darkness. He took affront at the gleaming silver chains meant to keep him out and at the restless pacing dogs on the veranda, who showed their snarling teeth. It was late. He saw the foolishness in his plans. He thought to turn back, but the rusted-iron smell of blood nudged him onward. He rattled the gate timidly, the dogs hurled themselves at him and he lost balance of his bicycle and fell over into the bed of long-stemmed yellow roses that lined her compound. He howled out first in surprise as the spikes snagged his shirt and needled his arms and face. He cried out again, for there was nothing to rescue him and he just sank lower into the thicket of thorns. He suffered. He welcomed the studded pain. The dogs howled and there was light in the house. A curtain was drawn. As were others, in neighboring houses. He tried to pull himself up. He screamed again. He heard the unlocking of a door, someone came out with a lantern. She told the dogs to quiet. They obeyed and slunk away. Joyce called out. He answered back weakly.

"Oh, it's you, Mr. Lowe." There was no surprise at all in her voice, and that annoyed him. It was as if she was expecting his arrival, and just in this sort of way. He hated her.

She unlocked the gate with a terrific banging and helped him and the bicycle and the twisted tin lantern out of the bush with her strong arms. He felt the blood moving on his skin. He followed behind her slowly and stiffly and limping, pain everywhere. He moaned in his belly. He moaned in his throat. Joyce led him into the house and removed the plaid cloth from the couch and told him to sit. He did so gingerly. Then she disappeared and seconds later returned with some ointment for his cuts, which she applied with such tenderness he winced even in places where he was not hurt just so she would linger longer over his wounds. She covered his shoulders with a shawl to beat back chills and gave him a warm toddy to drink. He wanted to weep. She put the hassock by his feet and unlaced his shoes and then sat there looking at him. There was the silent melancholy between them and the glow of admiration in her brown eyes.

He started to weep—not at her generosity, or maybe it was,

he wasn't sure; still, he wept, for he could see now the kind of woman Miss Sylvie wanted him to be. Someone attentive like this, gentle like this, someone who knew how to soothe him even before he asked, someone who knew the precise locations of his ailments even before he opened his mouth to point them out. The house was quiet and she was sitting there before him massaging his feet and there were colored sketches of Mr. Fine and colored sketches of her grown children all over the papered walls patterned with flowers he had never seen. There were no pictures of her. Light from the lamp popped and glinted on the buttons and badges of Mr. Fine's helmet and police shirt. Lowe inhaled the talcum that powdered her skin and the coconut oil that massaged her hair, and he spoke into the quiet to chop up the intimacy between them.

"Sorry I bother you like this."

She silenced him with a finger on his lips and then leaned over to ruffle the cushions at his back. His chin sank into the soft fullness of her chest, and for a second he allowed himself not to smell her smell of sleep. She disappeared again behind the floral curtains, only to appear again with another glass of toddy. He didn't realize he had polished off the first. Exactly what part of it could he tell her? He didn't know. There was so much. So many secrets. So many lies. So many murderers. So many . . .

"You feel better?" She smiled. He liked the shape of her mouth. He grew calm again. He thought of Sharmilla. She reminded him of Sharmilla. She sat next to him and took his hands into her own. She studied his face. "You look better without the mustache."

Oh God! He started to cough. She knocked his back gently and rubbed it with circular gestures. He wondered if she was alone.

"The maid is here," she said as if reading his thoughts, or maybe he had said it out loud. He did not know.

And Mr. Fine, he worried.

"Fine down at the station," she said into the quiet. "He sleep there most nights."

So now was he to take that as an invitation to stay?

"You can stay if you like."

Oh God! He tried to relax, to breathe deeply from the shallow cave of his stomach. They were old people now, all of them, he and Miss Sylvie and Joyce. With the accumulation of lines on their faces, with the swinging skin, no longer taut, with the precise vision now given over to cataract and glaucoma. She was still circling his back; he worried about the swaddling band she could feel. He was thankful not to have to return to that horrid house right away. He was thankful not to have to listen to Miss Sylvie's mouthful of fantasies or how she wanted him now to turn into a woman. His head felt heavy. His limbs felt heavy. His eyes closed.

He fell asleep there in her arms, and when he awoke he'd never felt so rested. The sleep, completely devoid of dreams, had been long and deep and sweet, and he felt a little groggy still. He nestled his face deeper into the soft warm pillows, slightly damp from his leaking mouth, and took his time to open his eyes, which were glazed. He lay immobile for some time, listening to the mewling cats, the cantankerous roosters, the swarm of flies buzzing by the window, the ticking clock on the dresser by her bed. He yawned with astonishing vigor and dug himself deeper into the sun-drenched sheets that sheathed his skin.

Then he shot up and with a thumping chest peered halfheartedly underneath the sheets. Oh God! Then his eyes were furious, searching for clothes on the trunk by the foot of the bed, searching for clothes on the writing desk near the window, on the floor by the bed, on the dresser. His wounds from last night had gushed open again, and there was only sheer agony. He remembered the warm toddy and was positive she had drugged it.

There was a knock on the door, and before he could respond, she brought in a tray. She was wearing her nightgown, a see-through white thing that revealed her plump brown muscled legs and her plump brown muscled arms, and she set down the tray on the mantel by the bed. He tried not to look at her face and he waited for her voice to betray her. She told him to ease over, and he found that he obeyed, and she nestled in closer to him, and he found that her perfume was pleasing. She first gave him the mug of tea and ensured that his trembling fingers were safe round the handle, and then she took her own mug, blew into the steam that immediately sweated her face, and slurped noisily. Even her slurp had pleasant acoustics. He could not find words and maybe he should not ask, he should just wait. He glanced around her wide solid back at the dresser, and the clock showed late morning. She slurped again, and it was good to be distracted by the noise. Below his chest, his legs felt wooden; his whole lower half was without feeling.

"You sleep well, Mr. Lowe." She handed him toast dripping with butter and marmalade and he stretched out a weak hand to accept it and found that her mocking voice did not startle him, did not grate on his nerves; it was a soft trickling murmur, like water. How was that possible! His eyes darted again round the room and finally he saw them, folded neatly in a pile on the chair. The band was at the very top. On top of his merino which was on top of his shirt which was on top of his drawers which was on top of his trousers. Did she like how manly he looked? he wondered. Did he look manly to her?

She saw he could not eat, she took back the bread from his trembling hand, she took back the mug that was lying on the bed between them. She put aside her own mug. Ripples of furrow had appeared on her severely lined face. They were old people now.

"So you know, then," he said, with no life at all in his voice. He sighed. He waited.

"I always knew," she said.

He grew still. He remembered the kiss in the shop so long ago, her firm hand on the back of his neck, the solid heat in his chest. "How'd you know?" he croaked.

"I could just tell," she said.

"First thing?"

"First thing," she said.

And his fears, like sharpened knives, fell on him again. For everybody else probably knew as well and was just forming the fool with him. How they must have laughed behind his back, how they must have. . . . Oh God! No wonder Omar had said what he said, no wonder Miss Sylvie wanted him now to change, no wonder.

"But most people would never notice a thing as that," she said.

"No?" He so badly wanted to believe her.

"No," she said, and touched him again with the soft hands. He relaxed. "It was because of the way you laugh," she said.

"Laugh," he cried, covering his mouth and making a mental note never to laugh again.

"It was such a beautiful shy undercover laugh," she said. "As if you holding something back." She was massaging him again. "And I thought, What could Mr. Lowe be holding back? And I just decided it was that. It wasn't anything in you clothes or you gestures."

Thank God.

"Yes," she said, "it was just in your laugh."

He wondered what it sounded like.

"But what if I wasn't that way?" Lowe started again. "I mean what if, suppose I didn't like it, suppose . . . ?"

"I never been wrong yet," she said, and smiled. "Forty years now." Lowe shifted uneasily. "Sometimes is a walk, a look, sometimes is a silence, a dis-ease. But you know, Lowe, everybody seduceable. Man or woman." And she sprang into laughter, showing all her teeth and the purple gums.

"How the cuts?" she said, sweeping her perturbed eyes across the lacerations on his face and neck and arms, on his throat. Her eyes lingered on his breasts, and the nipples grew. He stared again in front of him, uncertain how to respond. All of a sudden he felt self-conscious. He wanted to ask her how he looked to her, if he looked like the kind of man she could go out with in public, like she went out with Mr. Fine. But he said nothing at all.

She uncorked the vial again and began to spread ointment on the cuts one by one; he savored again the gentle touch. She leaned over him and her breasts rested on his chin, sometimes on his neck; he pretended he was not enjoying each touch, but he could not fool her; she pressed even deeper in those places that produced the sweetest pleasure.

He returned after two days and Miss Sylvie did not speak to him. The first day, he ignored her, but by the second day it bothered him. She did not sit at the dining table with him to eat her meals, and whenever he went close to her she got up, made a disgusting noise with her teeth, and left. In bed she tried not to let their bodies touch, she sighed often, and when he caught glimpses of her face, he saw the depression hunting her. The third day, he did not knock but stepped right into her study. She was sitting on the rug, poring over her maps.

"You're a damn dog," she growled.

He said nothing. Was this betrayal? He thought of Whitley's white throat like a snake. And he saw the hardness around Miss Sylvie's lips, and the firm square jaw. She was not a soft, kind woman, he decided. She was not attentive, was not generous, was not loving. Or maybe she was. Then he was ashamed. Maybe it *was* betrayal. He stepped closer. Maybe he wanted to embrace her. She too had suffered. He had not gone to Joyce's hunting for love, but he had had a sense of her kindness. Furthermore he was so lonely. And there had been the knives. The taste in his teeth. He rested a hand on her shoulder. She shook it off. Did she desire him still, he wondered, or did he have to change now and look completely like Whitley? Was that the only way she would desire him now? After all those years of wanting him and all those years he had retreated, and she'd taken his rejections bravely, or so he thought, for she kept coming back year after year, trying to figure out ways to love him that wouldn't send him running.

"Go and bathe. You smell of the black woman."

He felt terrible. For he saw now how he'd abandoned her, in her most vulnerable moment. After she'd shared so much with him. He brought his hands to his face, and the lingering odor swelled his lungs.

"Look," he said, "is not as you think." His voice was kind. She had sent away Whitley so there'd just be the two of them. And now he'd run off, had slept elsewhere. As if afraid of what Miss Sylvie was asking, this closeness. But he'd been so terrified with the fur in his teeth, the charred effigies.

"Look, Sylvie, I just had to get away little. You can't imagine what these days been like." He remembered again the whispers of conspiracy, the sounds of sharpening knives, the flashes of silver. His shop. "Plus it was nothing. Her husband was there."

"The husband sleep at the station."

"Well, yes, but he come by first. I mean we talk. I know them from the shop."

She said nothing for a while and he sighed. Maybe she'd just given up. They were quiet for some time. He sat across from the desk cluttered with decaying maps, in a white wicker lounge chair. The evening was cool and now and again he heard the long deep sigh of the trees, the dry scrabble of hooves in the cobbled streets down the road, the high-pitched cries coming from neighboring shops. Barking dogs. A mosquito sang by his ears and he clapped out into the air with a vague sense of direction. He got up and knelt on the rug beside her. He felt foolish and clumsy in his clothes. He sniffed the oleander in her hair streaked with white, which hung off her face. Her lashes cast hopeless shadows against the wall. He put his arms around her shoulders and they hung off her neck like rails. She felt fragile now. Or was he just imagining it? Was it betrayal! She allowed him to hold her, to bring her to his chest, to cradle her in his arms, and that was when he saw the letter on the desk, and the flutter in his chest erupted again.

"Liz write!" he cried, uncertain what to do with the dead weight in his arms. Wasn't she going to tell him?

"Yes," she said, looking up and pulling away. She pushed back the hair and clashed up her eyebrows. "You didn't tell me you did go to see them."

"I didn't have time," he said, "everything all at once. Plus Whitley was here." And what the hell was that in her voice, anyway! "She said anything?" He stared again at the tumble of graying hair bent over the map. What the hell was that in her voice! He nursed his hurt all over again.

"She pregnant again."

"Ah." He waited. Wagging his head up and down. "That's all." His voice was low and gray. He tried to beat back a slow-rising hysteria. "I mean she didn't ask bout the clubhouse, bout . . ." Suddenly he grew quiet, the sore wide open, the memory of his fight with her husband stalking him.

"You told her, then?"

He saw that she had grown still. She sucked on her cigar and waited. He searched for words. This wasn't any of her blasted business. This was between him and his daughter. This was . . .

"Lowe?"

"Yes, well, I mean no, I mean I couldn't tell her there, I couldn't tell her everything but I start a letter. I mean." He searched for more words.

"You look better without the mustache."

Suddenly he was enraged and his hands trembled in his lap. "You listening to me or not? Instead of paying attention to what I look like, how I must dress now like a woman, how I must change so I look like . . . so I look like that whore!"

"Sorry." Her voice was kind and he saw the smile that snaked its way around her lips. "Go on."

"Don't bother." He got up to go, his ears humming with the sharpening knives.

"Lowe." Her hand was on his legs. "Sorry." Her voice was kind, and underneath he heard the rattle.

"Well, she didn't care bout me or the clubhouse, bout the burning shop. She only ask bout you, bout your life, bout you and Cecil. She . . ." His pain deepened.

"She don't know you, Lowe."

"Here I lose everything. Every blessed thing, and not a word. Not even 'How you feel.' All she tell me bout was this book you send her. This book."

"She don't know you. You should go back and see her. Send things for them."

"And she look so much like Cecil. Jesus Christ, it was like on the ship again and up close with Cecil. She don't look anything like me, like my people, no resemblance, as if we complete strangers, I mean how the hell can that sort of thing happen? I mean how the hell, we could pass one another there on the street and not know." He stopped and he remembered again Miss Sylvie's three and he saw there the naked pain on her face and he remembered again how after Liz was born he took one look at her and was relieved that she did not have his cap of shiny blue-black hair, she did not have his sleepy Chinese eyes, her cheeks were not high and pointy like his, because then it was easier to thrust her away from him. Easier to not claim her.

"We old people now, Lowe. You have to tell her before it late, before we move."

"Before we move," Lowe cried, suddenly frightened at this running here, this running there, this life full of crime and fantasy. "I not going anywhere at all."

"You not moving, Lowe?"

"Not even one inch." His voice was firm, and he had absolutely no idea where the strength came from. "I want the Pagoda here. If not where the shop was, then somewhere else, but here, here on the island." He was shouting now, and his voice was determined.

"Even with all that Omar do to you? Even with all he did with the shop?" She sounded exhausted again, disappointed.

"What he did with the shop?" Lowe's voice grew sober.

"Nothing," she said, frightened, and the cigar trembled in her hand.

"What happen with the shop?" he asked again, down on the floor with her, his voice gone to rot. "Is Omar burn it down?"

She said nothing, just looked at him.

"Is Omar!" There was no sound at all to his voice. Oh God! And his stomach swelled again. And he felt the searing pain again. "Is Omar. And all along you knew, all along." Traitors! He leapt up and brushed all the maps from the desk. They scattered in a cloud of brown dust to the floor. Knives sharpened in his ears and he tore all the curtains from the windows. Murderers! Dusk, brown and vast, gushed in.

And now it was Miss Sylvie's turn to cradle his hands. And he pulled them away and staggered round the trashed study, holding his smiting stomach and weeping.

"He'd been threatening me with blackmail for years. I never think he'd take it out on you."

He remembered again the people dousing the fire in the rust of the morning. He remembered again the venomous words he'd overheard. He remembered again the missing dogs, and his howling started up afresh. And there was absolutely no consolation, none whatsoever.

"Why didn't you let them lock him up?"

"So he'd squeal on me, Lowe? So that black dog would squeal?"

"Maybe I should go," he said, though he knew not where. Back to Kywing's, back to the safety of his people, and then what? Tell them how he'd been betrayed, how he'd been set upon by murderers and blackmailers! He thought of Joyce's arms soothing his wounds. "Maybe I should just go," he said, and began to put on the boots he had taken off, began to push the lace through the holes, but his hands were trembling and his head hurt like the dickens, and he saw he was not safe at all, not safe among them. Not safe anywhere.

Night had come. Out the bare windows, the night was without stars and the black throng of leaves on the trees waved. He heard the flutter of nearby bats, the chorus of their slow songs. Saw the fast-moving clouds.

"I'll sell some of the land, Lowe, sell it back cheap to the Negro people and give the rest to Omar. Then we can leave somewhere, we can start over fresh, where nobody know us. Maybe we can go to Belize City or to Trinidad; my own people come from Panama, but we can go elsewhere. Maybe even Australia." A gleam appeared in her eyes.

He gave up on the boots, Miss Sylvie's hands on the back of his neck, on his shoulders, Miss Sylvie's hands. Rocking him like crazy. Omar had killed Cecil, had burned him up in the shop. Oh God! A house full of murderers! A houseful! Miss Sylvie's chaotic hands again and her murmuring voice, her warm breath in his neck, her silken voice, his swooping copper bird.

Each night now he prepared. Each night now he sharpened the knife and strummed his thumb across the blade until it sang, then he hid it in the soft feathers of his pillow and savored its smoky smell. Each night now he prepared the same bundle of clothes, which he folded neatly at the foot of the bed. And each night now he lay awake, biding his time, listening to the howling silence of the house, the slow steady swings of the pendulum clock, the singing mosquitoes, the miserable fretting hens, the barking dogs in the distance, the muffled chatter of villagers passing down below on the main road, the twittering birds long before light appeared, the first crowing rooster.

Each night now he prepared over and over again in his head how he'd do it. He had no remorse. The bitterness that had been deep inside his gut had risen up into his mouth and it just hung there like stalks. He sloshed the stalks back and forth with his tongue. He swung them to the roof of his mouth and sometimes lolled them to the back of his throat, and sometimes they just rested there, globbing the back of his teeth. He had never known a greater furor. A greater rage. He was red with anger. And he was going to wipe off the neck clean clean and drop it on his lap, leaving just the stumps of his blood jutting out of his throat. He had done nothing to him. Nothing at all. And if bad feelings erupted as a result of something he'd done accidentally . . . it was simply that. Accident. He had done nothing to him. Nothing at all.

And so one morning when the first rooster crowed from way down deep in the valley, Lowe rose, quietly pressing down the mattress with both hands so as not to wake Miss Sylvie. His limbs jerked with the poison. His jaws were bloated with bile. He picked up the clothes and his shoes and tipped out of the room, though the creaking floorboards betrayed him.

"Lowe."

"Shh," he barked into the darkness. "Go back to sleep."

"Lowe."

"Sleep!" he lashed out again, and inside the passageway he dressed himself and then slipped out into the cool mist, closing the door gently behind him. The sharpening of knives stumbled behind and he smelled the great dark pools of blood, like rusted iron, rotting zinc. There were no dogs to betray his movements, and he crept up the stone steps and into the kitchen. A thin drizzle was falling. He cursed at the silvery slants, and his tongue, that great pink slovenly muscle, worked industriously at the bile in his mouth. He stood quietly in the doorway with his foot cocked. He waited. He had done nothing to anyone. He did not deserve this. He had the knife ready in his hand, and his chest plate rattled into his shirt.

A door scraped open. The deep convulsing yawn. The click-click of stretching muscles, a great shuffling off of sleep. A great yawn again. Then a soft walking. The hawk and fire of spit. A heaving, shuddering hull.

Lowe waited in the predawn dark, crouching by the wood-stove. He hoped the blasted phlegmatic rattle would not awaken Dulcie. There was the thick smell of seawater, the scuttle of rats.

The footsteps leapt away. Lowe's heart sank a little. Still he waited. He heard more hawking and firing of spit, he heard the bucket clanging against the sides of the tank as it was lowered. He heard the soft *pash* as the bottom of the bucket hit the water. A rooster startled Lowe with its blasted crowing. He heard a long gargling and then a *whoosh* as a mouth expelled the water. He heard a loud steaming piss darting into the wet grass. A flurry of farts. He waited and in his mouth was the restless organ, washing, whirling, tumbling. Footsteps again and a soft whistle. The clumsy scuttle of rats. Mist was rapidly peeling away, a finger of light crept in. Lowe backed up further into the kitchen, his foot still outstretched in the doorway. And then Omar was on the crumbling stone steps and then he paused again to hawk and fire phlegm and when he moved again there was just the flash of movements and his quick short cry of surprise before he lurched and tumbled flat on his back in the kitchen and on the stone ground. Lowe sat on his chest with the glittering knife plumb at his throat.

"Move and see what happen this morning." His voice was sharp and gray. "Move and see whose blood run this morning." Behind him were the thongs of jutting blood and quivering muscles where the neck once stood. Behind him was the head with the surprised eyes and the wide-open mouth rolling and rolling down the stone steps, behind him was the dry husk of a coconut. The horrible rats. The great undulating vessel.

Omar said nothing at all, and the whites of his eyes rolled in the darkened kitchen and his breath was just tumbling from him, the face shining, the fear breaking him.

"What I do to you, man?" He pressed the point deeper into the soft hollow at the base of Omar's throat. "What I do to you? The food you eat come from the shop there. And you burn it down. Burn it flat down. Kill Cecil. How Cecil bother you? You so full of grudge and hate, you burn it down. Flat flat. Just now I should just cut off you blasted head and lean it up by the pot there. Just now I should just slice off you blasted balls and feed them to the hogs. Just now. If you move, you blood run like river this morning. Run like river."

Water leaked. Omar started to cry. No sounds at all, just the trembling stomach underneath Lowe's rump.

"Shut you blasted mouth unless you want me to give you something to cry bout." He pressed at an angle so the sharp point would not slip into the fleshy throat and finish him off quick. And Omar was still again, though down below, underneath Lowe's rump, his stomach chopped. And the heart battered against his shirt.

"What I ever done to you?" Lowe cried, plucking the blade into the warm soft skin, picking away at flesh. A jigger of blood spurted into his hands and wound into Omar's chest. "What?" Lowe pressed. "What?" His voice faint and gray in the solid steel dawn, and he smelled the sleep on Omar's breath, smelled the froth of fear on Omar's breath. And Omar whimpered and Lowe remembered how he barked at the workers and he remembered again the plumes of smoke, the skins of rust in the approaching dawn, and he pressed the point even further in, and the blasted rooster crowed again and he remembered Miss Sylvie's brown babies and the empty makeshift coffins Omar had built to hide her secret, and he saw how they all were in this together, how Cecil had thrown them all in together, some innocent, some not so innocent, and maybe it wasn't even Omar so much he was angry at, but Miss Sylvie, Cecil, his father who had abandoned him. And now here they were killing and killing and killing to cover up more deceptions, more lies. Here he was with blood on his hands for no good reason at all. Here he was fighting Omar for land and for property that didn't even belong to them, that was still damp from prior bloodshed. Hadn't they plundered the Arawaks, the Caribs? Yet here they were like hungry dogs, setting upon each other and biting over the one little dry bone Cecil had flung them.

Lowe lifted his weight and released him. He wiped the wet knife on Omar's shirtfront and stepped away from him, pushing back images that fell upon him as if he'd betrayed them. Lowe slipped out of the kitchen, and at the house corner he stopped to retch. He retched for a long time, though there was nothing. Just the rude taste on his tongue of flesh caught afire on a burning ship. Then he wiped his mouth with his shirttail and went inside and bolted the door behind him. He undressed quietly in the dark and drew on his robe. He fingered the part in his hair and paced the rooms in the dark, his arms outstretched, waiting till his heaving chest settled, waiting till his roaring head ceased. He slipped back into the steam of Miss Sylvie's embrace that did not console him these days. He slept.

7

One by one, the bright hot days and empty tin-gray afternoons turned over slowly and with tremendous indifference. And each evening, in the stale dust, Miss Sylvie still studied with vigilant eyes the dusty sheaves of decayed maps that she scattered now all over the house so that at any moment the fancy took her she could lay her hands on them. During all this she darted furtive glances in Lowe's direction, but he pretended not to notice; he was not interested. Still, her restlessness disturbed him. And the way she watched him in his clothes distressed him. He could not sleep when next to him in the bed he heard her pacing mind leaping through the house, felt her churning ankles, her fingers wandering in violent activity. And in the mornings, when she stumbled from slumber, he could tell she was feverish with travel, that her dreams had given birth to entire worlds, that cities and islands and foreign universes had sprung up in her head and they bore no resemblance to how or what they lived now. It brought home to him again and again his own precarious position there in the house and on the island. It terrified him. His shop was gone. As were Cecil and his daughter. He did not know these people with whom he lived. The idea of Miss Sylvie leaving was too much, and he felt his shell dropping away.

He desperately wanted to see Joyce again but could not think of a way to get to her without injuring Miss Sylvie, further pushing her away, and so he relived in his mind her large body with the big bones, her heavy brown muscled arms, her strong neck, her vigorous embrace, her teeth on his nipples, the long spasms that ran through his limbs. The more he thought of Joyce, the more he worried about his appearance, as if the two were inextricably linked. He spent more time inspecting in the glass his long thin face, and he saw that his brows, which were once neat strips of down, were now almost gone and his lips, now without the badge of hair and with the top one slightly longer and heavier than the bottom, resembled his mother's. He saw that the particular way in which his top row of teeth caved in was his completely. He grimaced at the sharp curve of his nose, at the indentation in his cheeks as they grew more sunken with age. He scrutinized the tiny gutters by his mouth corners and those by his eyes and decided that he should laugh less, though he liked the deep spirals that crisscrossed his forehead and the space between his brows, for they reminded him of his father.

He couldn't pinpoint exactly when he began to discover that he liked things of flowing silk and neat lines, when his appreciation for subtle colors instead of dark solemn ones crept up on him. He did not know when he began growing fussy over the quality and tone of cloth, about the cut of trousers, the cascade of their fall on his thin limbs. He did not know when his search to find constant reassurance from the mirror began, and then from Miss Sylvie, which came with only a pleasant and lingering gaze. The black felt hat he wore in the evenings to prevent cold from seeping into his head and giving him pneumonia was now exchanged for a wide-brimmed straw with a blue ribbon. He decided that he liked the touch of color, that it added an air of distinction to his plain sallow face. He no longer soaked his neck with sandalwood, for all of a sudden its pungent bite was no longer odorous, and so he daubed drops of oleander and hibiscus and other scents he'd remembered from Joyce's embrace. He did not know if this was his slow and subtle way of trying to hold Miss Sylvie there, trying to entice her not to leave.

He found he was no longer comfortable in his netted merino. His skin roasted now behind the swaddling band, and so he had taken to removing more frequently the cloth from his chest and to inspecting more carefully his bosom, and not just when he was taking his baths. Each time he unpinned the hooks and the cloth unraveled, he was always surprised to see that they were still there, shiny pink apricots showing their red-stained nipples, which he circled slightly until they were hard, then he swirled even larger circles into the patches of velvet surrounding them, and those puckered as well, and he lifted one tiny breast delicately and savored the warm pulp on its underside. He took to doing this each morning in the privacy of their room, until one day when he heard steps approaching the door and he banded himself at once and hauled on his merino and stood at the mirror with the comb in his hand.

Miss Sylvie came in, and from the mirror he watched her rounded figure shifting inside the long pink gown and her face still flushed from the warmth of her bathwater and her still wet hair sucked to her scalp so her face looked more drawn and mildly innocent. He watched her slow serpentine movements approach him, and she grinned into his neck.

"You smell good," she said, holding him at the waist. "I could almost eat you up."

And at first he liked it and he began to smile. Then he grew frightened. Then he was angry as hell and he tore himself away roughly. "Like Whitley, eh. Like Whitley. That whore!" And he slammed the door hard behind him, trembling the mirror, and her soft chuckle followed him down the long dark hallway until he saw that he'd forgotten his shirt and the blue-ribboned hat.

In the evenings now after he ate, he wended his way slowly down to the burned-out foundation that was his shop with his head bowed to his chest and his hands clasped behind him, and little by little he shoveled up the garbage and piled it into a wheelbarrow and pushed it for some time until he arrived at a clearing, and there he finally heaved the garbage over into a heap and then he returned again to reload the barrow. The villagers had turned the ruined shop into a dump where they dashed their refuse, and he had to dig up filth and the peelings of fruit and food and the wrapping paper from their goods and the broken remains of old chairs, the rotting debris of shoes and clothes, pieces of pottery, rusted tins, charred pieces of firewood, ashes that had now hardened into concrete, defunct sewing machines, discarded pots, the iron and spokes and wheels from their abandoned wagons.

The work was especially strenuous, and beads of sweat quickly gathered on his forehead and upper lip, and he paused often to calm his fluttering heart and lean his aching arms on the handle of the shovel, but he looked forward to it in the evenings now as a way to escape Miss Sylvie's restless cogitations and digest Dulcie's meals, which were excessively heavy, and as a way to think about neither Joyce nor the treachery of his daughter, who preferred to write to Miss Sylvie instead of him. After he had gone to see her! After he had humiliated himself in front of her and her foolish husband! He did not have to think about the set of murderers to whom Cecil had entrusted him, though he knew that at least for now Omar would lie low. The fatigue relaxed his muscles and helped him to sleep peacefully again despite Miss Sylvie's wanderings, and without the tormented dreams that rode him throughout the night.

For weeks he worked alone until one and two of the men

started stopping by en route to Miss Cora's shop. They did not offer to help him, but they squatted down next to him as he struggled to fill the wheelbarrow with the foul-smelling ashes that had hardened from the rains, and they smoked the stinking tobacco that seeped into his skin, they hawked often and spat their gurgly pneumatic phlegm and clapped at invisible mosquitoes. Sometimes they would walk alongside him as he pushed the wheelbarrow to the clearing where he emptied it, all the while updating him on the women they had impregnated, their children that had dropped down dead from diphtheria, crops that had either failed or prospered, strikes that had flared up suddenly on faraway plantations and just as quickly had been snuffed out by the government, protests in which they were involved, the formation of new groups to organize workers, America's growing involvement in the region, the money they won at gambling, and the increasing unemployment as more and more estates lay idle since cane sugar had lost its foothold to beet sugar, which was cheaper now to produce.

One evening while he was filling up the wheelbarrow, Jake turned up. He was a carpenter by trade, a mason and plumber as well, and was responsible for most of the half-finished mud-and-wattle and stone houses crouched on the hillside. He watched Lowe for some time, with face washed clean of expression, and chewed absently on moist tobacco, twisting his head to spit out the slimy brown juice and to wipe his mouth on the back of his hand.

"You going build it back, Mr. Lowe?" His quiet voice whistled in the hazy light of the evening, and Lowe lifted himself to his full frame to stretch out his back and to hold his waist with one hand. He belched and remembered again the fervent hate of his daughter's husband, and he said, "No, man, I thinking of building a little ceremony hall instead. Maybe." His voice was squeezed dry of yearning, of enthusiasm; in fact he said it as if he was annoyed not to be building something much more ostentatious.

There was the deep silence between them, and Jake surveyed

the rubble of destruction with his hand over his forehead and chewed the tobacco in his mouth thoughtfully, and Lowe watched him from the corners of his eyes. He was tall and wiry, with a closed-up short thin face, grooved by knife wounds, and a hint of Arawak in his close-cropped gray hair and long sweep of black thick lashes. It had indeed occurred to Lowe to ask Jake, but he'd been waiting for the appropriate moment. One could never tell, with these people, the exact moment their jealousy would flare up. He knew better than to tell Jake all of what he intended, though the image of the stone lions stood up with great prominence in his mind.

"Like a benevolent society kind of thing"—that was Jake again, whistling through his brown gums—"like they have up in Troy, with maybe like a nice little garden and things that grow roses and hibiscus and bougainvillea and marigold." Jake paused and Lowe was suddenly frightened. He pressed his hat firmer onto the crown of his head and fondled his throat. He turned to look at Jake, who was still inspecting the land and who was still chewing thoughtfully, and the fright overcame him again and he said, nodding and shaking his head, "Well, we'll see, Jake, we'll see."

Above them birds veered dangerously into treetops, then vanished into the darkening mist. Jake spat and continued, his lips now full and filmy with the brown juice. "Maybe even a few wood benches and things where one could just sit out and read a book or hold hands with a girl." He chuckled softly and Lowe brightened. Then Jake took out a flask hidden inside his Wellingtons and uncorked the top and turned the bottle to his head and sucked for some time, staggering the Adam's apple. The veins stood out big on his forehead and like thongs in his neck. He finished the flask and flung it far over their heads and into the distance, and some time later they heard it splinter against stones and he wiped his dripping mouth with the back of his hand.

"The society at Troy too have some nice big columns out front painted a nice ocher and the floors have nice cool tiles and tall rectangle windows with stain glass of Madonna and things. But yours don't have to have Madonna, it could be landscapes, or Buddha, or whatever you fancy. I know a wholesale place where they sell those." He paused again and, ignoring Lowe completely, looked off into the distance, where the sun still bloodied the sky in patches. He scratched at his balls and at his dusty backside. He belched the awful-smelling rum and cried excuse.

"Well, we'll see," Lowe said again, "we'll see." He could not believe what his ears were telling him, but still he had misgivings, still he was mistrustful and afraid of their jealousy, and so he turned to his task again and pressed into the shovel with his foot and began filling up the wheelbarrow. But he did not turn his back on Jake; he did not want to give the impression that the conversation had ended. He paused often to grope at his hat and to fondle his throat, to worry at the direction of the thoughts he was accommodating in his head.

"And maybe even some carved animals too." That was Jake again. "Maybe some stone ones at the front. A nice spiral staircase leading up into the main parlor. Even an indoor latrine with nice wide windows so you could look out at the woods and listen to the birds while you on the throne." He chuckled, and there was nothing but the open black cave of his mouth.

"Well, we'll see, Jake, man, just an idea, you know, just an idea. And maybe it isn't the right kind of thing for the village, you know. It might be too different, if you know what I mean. Still is just an idea."

"I understand, Mr. Lowe, I understand. I mean all these things depend on other things. They all depend." He rubbed his pointed chin, stubbled with hair, and his rat eyes ran wild again, surveying the destruction.

Around them was the rapidly falling blackness and the pinkish blush from lamps just now lit and flickering from behind curtains of nearby houses. Domino playing had started up at Miss Cora's shop. They heard the crack of bone on solid wood tables, the clicking tiles as they shuffled. "Well, I could come by tomorrow morning and measure out things. We could draw up a floor plan and see where it take us; of course it all depends if other things work out." He paused to look at his ashy bony fingers. "But you know, a plan with four, five rooms, a general dining area for ceremonies and speeches and the like, an office to do the bookkeeping, one or two other rooms." He paused again, this time to wet his lips. "But of course it all depends." His voice sounded matter-of-fact, and his face and eyes seemed dull and disinterested, and Lowe, in order to conceal his jubilation, his supreme joy, shoveled deeper into the thick mound of filth, and his loud haggard breathing disrupted the balmy wheeze of Jake's voice.

After Jake left, he washed his hands and face carefully at the standpipe, dried up with his handkerchief, and cut swiftly through the woods and headed over to the shop owned by the Heysongs. He had to tell someone, and his stomach was trembling from the sheer pleasure of it. He walked half the way and ran the other half, he ducked behind trees and hid from the eyes of the winking shop lights; he didn't want the villagers to see him, to suddenly think he was abandoning them now that the Chinese couple had opened up a shop. They had moved in now a whole month. But he had to tell someone. He had to dream out loud, so the images could expand and deepen and become real. Still, it was with very mixed feelings that he was going to the Heysongs'. He didn't like the eagerness with which they had opened up a shop so soon after he had lost his. As if they were there just waiting for him to drop so they could quickly fill the gap. He had become so expendable. Tonight, though, he wanted to share the news with someone who mightn't be so threatened by the idea of his Pagoda.

He felt especially naked without the mustache and vulnerable, and he wondered if it had been such a good idea to abandon it. At the shop now, as there was no counter between him and the men, no boundary, no threat of Omar to keep their comments at bay, the terrain of his body, long off bounds to them, had suddenly become a familiar source of commentary. The piazza of Miss Cora's shop had become the great stabilizer. To them, he had nothing, had become nothing. He could no longer lord it over them. And so they commented on what they called his smooth and unblemished skin, his childish baby face now that he no longer wore the mustache, and one of them, an effeminate one they called Pretty, who had a penchant for impregnating young girls, then always crying that they just wanted to saddle him with bastards, for none of them was his, even went as far as to say Lowe looked like a woman he used to know. And at that they stormed into laughter, hammering their feet on the pavement, and Lowe's distress had deepened when he realized that even Miss Cora, cocked at the counter with her shimmering gold teeth, was smiling. Did they know? he had wondered. And if so, was it that it didn't matter to them? He had noticed that even with all their comments, they seemed not to harbor any bad feelings against him. Had he become laughing stock?

The Heysongs' shop was deserted and smelled of dirt and stale rum and sweat, and the lone lamp limping from a hook in the ceiling gave off diffused gray light that made the gloom more ghastly, and he glanced quickly at the half-empty shelves and went over to the side counter to greet Mrs. Heysong, who was broad and round, with dimpled cheeks, and who was singing in a thin soft sweet voice to a thin-limbed baby with a protruding stomach and a white and delicate and enormous moon face.

Lowe recognized the song and was immediately returned to his village and to the memories of his father and all those poems by Lu Yu and Su Shi and To Fu he had recited to Lowe and those other ones he'd set to tunes, though each time it was with a different melody, for he was old and prone to forgetfulness. They all came back to Lowe now in spotty patches and with entire lines missing, the song of "The Lady of the Xiang River" and "Crossing the Ancient Barrier Pass in the Rain," quotations from the Analects of Confucius, stories of legendary heroes who had fought gallantly in wars and of foolish men who had married ghosts thinking them beautiful women and those soliloquies from dramatic romances his father would act out, his face powdered and painted, his shifting image adorned with costumes made from bundled cloth and strips of bark to fit the numerous characters and their intricate plots.

All these he had refused to teach his daughter, for the words did not fit here in this place full up of brown people, and the melody was all wrong here against the jolting clangor of this new speech with its crushed-bottle sounds, this new terrain and this rhythm of life loaded up with hostilities and opportunities. And so he greeted Mrs. Heysong in a very loud and precise and formal English to break up the intimacy that her soft singing had invited.

"A very good evening to you," he had cried upon entering, and she had disappeared into the darkness behind a curtain with the big-headed baby and he heard her back there, muttering anxiously to someone.

He had been hearing now that Chinese officials had had to slacken laws and that more and more women were leaving China and traveling to countries all over the world. She was the first Chinese woman he had seen in the village, though he imagined there were many more in the larger cities, and her face seemed hardened and square, as if she had suffered much, though her eyes, partly hidden by the shock of hair, were kind.

The husband hurried out, his face oily as if he'd been eating, and Lowe apologized, bowing his head and stretching out his hand over the counter. "I just come now to say welcome," Lowe said, and the man bawled out a stream of phrases to the woman, and she came now promptly smiling at Lowe, which instantly lightened up her face and made her look younger, and she placed on the counter two glasses of boiling green tea and he heard the baby squealing in the back and she rushed out again.

"How business?" Lowe cried, with a jubilance he did not feel, and the man, who was round and sullen and seemed unhappy to be disrupted in just such a fashion, shrugged his shoulders up and down and sighed wistfully into the deserted shop with its half-empty shelves. He scrutinized Lowe with watchful eyes, and to break up the silence Lowe told him about the center. The man said nothing, he only wheezed into the gloom and jerked up his head now and again as if wondering what the hell all of this was about. Lowe was crushed. It was not what he expected, though in truth he knew not what he'd expected. Still, the man could have been more forthcoming. They were, after all, compatriots. He felt self-conscious and foolish all of a sudden and wished he had worn the mustache, and not this flowery hat but the solemn black felt. Did the man know they had just burned down his shop? That he had nothing now, just pure dreams? Did this man know that he no longer felt comfortable in his clothes, in his skin, that the persona that had once clothed him, shielded him, had come undone and there he was now, just unraveling?

In the back Mrs. Heysong was still singing the nursing songs of his childhood that he had never taught his daughter, and to ease his despairing chest he pulled from his pocket a sheet of paper and a stick of lead pencil and outlined for the man the layout of the rooms and garden, and exactly which courses would be taught and where. "Is not so much for us," Lowe cried, pointing back and forth between his chest and the man's, in one final effort to reach him, "but for the baby there coming up who'll forget. We can't let them forget." This he said with tremendous regret, for he had willed himself to forget just so his heart wouldn't break with the memories, and where had it gotten him; there he was a complete stranger to himself and there was his daughter, a stranger to him, and here they all were strangers in this place.

The man seemed finally moved and he managed to crack a smile and he pored over the scrawls on the sheets and nodded and grunted and massaged his rounded belly underneath the white merino, and Lowe felt his despondency nudging him in the humid shop and he hated this man and hated the smell mingled in the air, the smell of rum mixed with salted cod, and he was glad when the woman appeared again with the baby to distract them, and Lowe made gurgling noises at the baby and fluttered his fingers at the baby, who pulled at Lowe's nose and punched at Lowe's cheeks, and Lowe felt lucky he had not worn the mustache, for the baby no doubt would've tugged it off.

Every day now he and Jake talked. On the veranda, huddled over pieces of brown paper, Lowe outlined the curling five-tiered roof and ridges made of wood. He told Jake he wanted the interior walls to be of a burnished gold color, the floors and columns a polished ebony, the windows covered with a decorative screen made of rice paper, the door to be engraved with tortured carving that bespoke good workmanship. And Jake agreed that this pagoda was indeed a very noble and dignified architecture. "A study in curves," he told Lowe, beaming with his brown gums.

And each time Lowe allowed his dreams to sail away with him—the hand-woven straw mats to carpet the floor, the silk cushions to kneel on, the lamps with rice paper screens, the small lacquered tables for serving food, the standing mirrors of burnished steel, the dishes of lacquer and porcelain—Jake only wheezed, calculating again and again the cost of the raw material, the cost of the labor, the cost of each individual vase, before handing it to Lowe, who immediately grew calm. They talked about the hiring of people to clear the land and to lay out the foundation. They discussed the putting up of posts and the buying of lumber and brick, the payment of laborers and the purchase of other equipment Jake needed for the construction. And Lowe became obsessed with eaves and cornices and spent indeterminable hours studying the molded crowns and spiraling projections of the Corinthian columns that flanked Miss Sylvie's house.

Lowe was feverish. He smiled with everyone he passed and

whistled complicated tunes as he walked. He paid Dulcie compliments on her meals and had even started now to sit with her in the kitchen while she washed the dishes, though they said nothing at all to each other. Often he felt as if he was a nuisance in her way, for her hooded eyes only told him she was walking over old memories, but of what he would never ask. Her silence had always felt wooden to him, not something he could easily push up against or move through. He had forgiven his daughter and her husband and had even gone as far as to ask Dulcie to help him pack a box of food to send to them when she had time.

Day after day his spirits soared and day after day Miss Sylvie sank lower and lower into herself, though there was no precise illness. She rose early each morning and disappeared into her study to suffer over her accounts and fight with innumerable invisible characters and did not emerge again until evening, walking round the house with a distracted face and summoning Dulcie to bring her poultices of assorted types. Sometimes she called Omar and quarreled with him about the accounts, and then the two of them, with sullen faces, rode off deep into the forest beneath a spiraling cloud of dust. She no longer colored her hair, and the streaks of gray grew more pronounced. She wrung her hands as if washing off stains, until the skin reddened and chafed. While he slept peacefully at night and chuckled at jokes that amused his dreams, Lowe always had the feeling next morning that she had lain awake all night, watching him.

As the days turned over, she no longer read or painted, nothing was of interest. Even the accounts lay there abandoned. She no longer left to play bridge and take tea and crumpets with the high-class mixed breeds who had a tendency to ignore Lowe, and they no longer visited her. She just brooded about the house, dragging her slippers, cheep-cheep, on the polished floors. She grew more gaunt, sinks appeared in her cheeks, which had always been rosy and plump, her dresses swung off her hips, which were no longer round, her eyes ached, as did her throat, her stomach was delicate, her head had to be bandaged with medicinal leaves, her nerves jangled, her voice took on the lilt of near hysteria, and one morning he pulled her into his arms and cuddled her and pushed back her white hair from her face, which was swollen and slightly yellow. She started to weep.

He did not know how to infect her with his happiness. His life was finally starting to pick up. The one thing left now was to settle things with his daughter; the last thing now he wanted was for Miss Sylvie to fall sick on him. These days she coughed incessantly, though it produced no phlegm, and the thought that she might die, leaving him there with the hostile and warmongering villagers, was unbearable. The thought of being left there alone with the poles rushing out of the dirt, left there lonely with the unfinished building, his dreams disrupted midway. Left there with no protection whatsoever. Left there! Just so. Oh! It would kill him. He leaned over his side and pulled her closer into his arms, and the body inside the gown was warmer and lighter than he had expected. It was late morning, the sun had broken clear of trees and the sky was white with clouds tumbling quickly across, and outside in the hovering heat the cackling hens proclaimed eggs. He felt a slow-rising fire center itself around his lower belly.

A person who had never known how to encourage people to look on the brighter side, as he was so often tortured by the darkness of his own existence, found himself offering Miss Sylvie pieces of dreams. "Look, Sylvie," he told her, cradling her head comfortably in his arms, "we can travel." The idea had only just now occurred to him. And she wept harder and blew her nose deeper into his shirt. "Yes," Lowe said, building fierceness and determination into his voice, as he wiped her tears with his hand and pushed back the swiveling strands of hair from her face and closed up the collar of her nightgown so her shrunken breasts wouldn't come spilling out. "We can take a ship," he said, "and we can order the very best bunk and we can visit some of the other islands. You can bring you colors," he said, "and you could paint, and when you grow tired with that we could hire a wagon and take a tour.

"You could write a book," he continued, blanching at the

memory of the one she had sent his daughter. "You could write a book," he said again, "about you travels round the West Indies. You could even entitle it 'Sylvie's Travels Around the British Isles with her Chinese Companion, Lowe.'" He paused to find his breath, for he was suddenly exhausted, and he found that Miss Sylvie was no longer weeping, that her shuddering chest had subsided, that a flicker of light had touched the stones of her eyes. He pressed on, sweating inside his khaki shirt.

The sun was in full force, and he shoved off the blanket hovering by their legs and kissed her softly on her chin. She was like a child lying there in his arms. She was like a broken toy lying there in his arms. He had never held her like this before. He had never seen her so fragile before. He massaged her neck, which smelled of talcum, and the incessant coughing started and he raised her and held her shuddering body in his arms until it had ceased and he hoped to God it wasn't tuberculosis or pneumonia. She asked him to wet her head with bay rum and then to wrap it with the bandage Dulcie had prepared full of medicinal leaves. He did so, cradling her even deeper into his chest. "I love you," he said, and though the words sounded foreign, he was certain that was how he was feeling at that precise moment, with her lying so frail and broken down in his arms, with all those years between them, though some part of him burned with anger at how she had made him feel so self-conscious now.

"Kiss me," she said, and her voice startled him and broke the mood, and the warmth disappeared from his groin and he hovered over her face with the fear of the wiggling fish in his mouth pressing him down, and her eyes were closed as if waiting, and he kissed her forehead instead and pressed down on her. He wanted to take his own time, go at his own slow pace, he did not know this woman who had borne three children and given them away, this woman who had murdered a man and was living her life in hiding, this woman who had passed through one lover to another, wanting so badly to fill up her arms with those bodies that had been taken away, this woman who like him had passed and had been found out, this woman who like him had had fantasies. And then of course there was the warm wiggling fish that would absorb him completely.

The incessant cough started up again and when it passed he brought one by one her murderous fingers to his lips. And then held both warm soft weapons by their wrists and pressed them against his face.

A girl betrayed by a father and handed over to an old man, a cripple, he owed a debt to. A girl with a sweet soft face. A girl with a roaring head full of fantasies. A girl with a pocket full of itineraries, the routes they'd explore; a girl with her ringing ears full of clanging masts, the wet call of birds, the warble horns of ships; a girl who used to be a father's pet, a father's eye, a father's middle finger; a girl betrayed by her father and turned into a wife overnight; a girl whose last image of a father before she turned into a wife was of a cocked head, a lowered pair of eyes, the shuffle of feet, the muffled tones of voice; a girl on a cart en route to becoming a wife; a girl with a solid firm face, no longer soft; a girl with an enormous chest full of despair, a frozen heart; a girl en route to becoming a wife; a wife who dreams all day at the barred windows of a house . . .

"You never told me you love me before," Miss Sylvie said. Lowe said nothing. He rolled off her stomach and leaned by her side and pressed his chin into the dent by her breasts.

"Maybe I just feeling it now," he said into her skin.

"After all these years?"

Was she accusing him now! Was nothing enough for her! And after all, didn't love have everything to do with timing? He couldn't have loved earlier, not when his life was on such an edge, everyone else having claims to his body. Didn't you have to throw your whole self into it, and what did he have to throw? Plus how was he to have loved somebody so shut down, so locked up, as Miss Sylvie, with her million secrets, her mouth full of lies?

"And you?" he asked.

"I've loved you."

"All these years?"

"Every one of them." Then she looked away and her eyes glazed. "I've loved you too much," she said, "too much for my own good."

What the hell was that supposed to mean!

"What bout Joyce?" she asked.

"Oh, that is nothing." He colored up. "We just friends now," he said.

"Ah," she said. And was silent.

His daughter sent a telegram to say she was coming, and for the entire time before her arrival, Miss Sylvie's ailments retreated, but Lowe's stomach bloated up so profoundly he could drink only broth for supper and steamed bush the remainder of the time to ease the gurgle of gastric juices. Miss Sylvie hired people to come, the grass in front of the house was cut, the hedges were pruned, walls whose paint had grown faded and was peeling were whitewashed. In preparation, a calf was killed, two piglets were disemboweled, three rabbits lay quartered in a bowl of seasoning, and Lowe had to keep out of the house so the young village girls could polish the wood floors and tile.

At nights, with the candle at his elbow bathing the room in a pink glow, with the looming shadows peering over his shoulders, he reread the unfinished letters and wondered if he shouldn't just give them to his daughter. If he shouldn't just sit her down and tell her. But the magnitude of all that had to be said and explained overwhelmed him so completely he simply stared listlessly at the sheets. One night, though, a thought he'd never permitted himself to think nudged at him. He batted it away but it only began to flourish in his mind with greater relish. Perhaps she knew. Perhaps she had always known. Ever since she was a girl. Perhaps she had noticed something. Perhaps. And no wonder she had hated him so. No wonder she had clutched so tightly to Miss Sylvie and to her memories of Cecil. No wonder she ran off with the old man. No wonder she had kept away all these years, not one word from her. No wonder! The blood was pounding in his neck, the heart was banging into his shirt, and the tunneling in his gut had simply exploded. He pulled himself to the floor, where he stretched out prostrate, defeated by the onslaught.

She arrived late in the afternoon, when the sun no longer wove patterns on the rustling leaves, when the branches had grown darker, their shadows longer. She arrived much rounder and with several more chins than when he'd seen her last. He noticed again her unsettling beauty and his chest filled up with love. He had forgotten his fright. She clucked incessantly over her thin-limbed baby, which was brown like the husband. The boy was there as well, he had shot up a few more inches, and the husband, whom neither Dulcie nor Omar had ever seen, looked terribly decrepit in a dark suit that was so heavy and solemn that he seemed weighted down by it. He favored Cecil even more.

Lowe watched the spectacle from the slightly drawn curtain of the window of his room. He watched them alight slowly from the wagon. Miss Sylvie, who was remarkably better, rushed out to greet them, with wide-stretched arms and a tremendous outcry. Dulcie followed behind and he saw Omar lurking there behind his mother. Lowe's stomach ached, and he loosened his belt and massaged the distressed mound. He saw the small bundle of them edge toward the house, and he was suddenly barricaded by the turbulent laughter. He heard the wailing cries of exclamation as secrets were unmasked, the long braids of conversation. He heard them purring over the baby, and its shrill shriek and sometimes relentless gurgle, he heard the husband's nervous laughter, which sounded like Cecil's. It was his first time there, and Lowe felt sorry for him.

Lowe weaved toward them, his head bowed slightly, his hands wringing behind him, his stomach pounding at him. The little boy rushed over and held on to his legs. "Grandpa," he cried out. Lowe was touched. He tousled the boy's head, which reminded him briefly of Joyce's. The husband was beaming—he was an old man now—and Lowe pumped his hand, wondering if this wasn't in fact Cecil.

"Welcome! Welcome!" Lowe did not recognize the trumpet of his own voice, meant to block out his shame at his behavior at the man's house. Dulcie served them drinks. Miss Sylvie and the daughter were busy with the baby. Did she know, or was it his mind playing the damn fool with him? He wanted to go over. It felt intrusive. Still, it felt good to have her in the house after so many years. It felt good to see her again. This daughter that was his own flesh and blood. This daughter that Cecil had forced into him. This daughter that he'd not wanted at first. This daughter that was the burden to him until Miss Sylvie came and took over her upbringing, and then he could finally love her. "Congrats!" Lowe pealed instead to the husband, and the husband beamed again, just like Cecil, and Lowe felt sick to his stomach.

"Come." The little boy tugged at his legs. "Come and see the baby." Lowe was grateful. The boy rushed up to the women, pushed against their fused hips, and Lowe's daughter looked up, finally acknowledging him.

"Pa," she said breathlessly.

"Congrats," Lowe said, and hugged her. She smelled of milk. Did she know?

She showed him the baby, and he thought it resembled the student, then he was ashamed of himself and he flushed. He couldn't think of what to say to her. He couldn't think of what to say to this daughter that he loved so much.

The baby took one look at Lowe and began to cry. The women belled over it again and smothered it with kisses and completely ignored Lowe and he went and sat beside the husband. He remembered their last meeting.

"Come," Lowe said after a while, and he took him outside to

show him the compound and pointed him in the direction of the stables, the acres of cane, the orchards of oranges, and the husband took it all in.

"Cecil leave all that," he said with awe in his voice.

"He was a good man," Lowe said, surprising himself, and then he remembered again how Omar had burned down the shop and how Miss Sylvie wanted them to move and for him, Lowe, to turn now into a woman. After all these years.

"You know him well," the man said. "How you meet?"

"On the ship," Lowe said, and coughed. "He was a good man, a good captain." He ran his hand over his face, but there was no mustache to save him and he worried that the floral scarf at his throat was too feminine.

"I feel like I know him. Liz talk bout him all the time."

"Yes," Lowe said absently. "I wish we were closer."

"You and Cecil," the man asked.

"No," Lowe said, "me and . . ." He stopped, suddenly embarrassed. "Me and Liz. You know how . . ." He searched for the mustache again.

"Father and daughter," the husband said.

"Yes," Lowe said, "father and daughter."

"She don't talk much bout you," the husband said. "In fact she don't talk bout you at all."

Lowe's stomach throbbed. He massaged it. The anguish was like no other. Then Lowe grew bitter. "Am sure she only talk bout Cecil and Sylvie. Only bout them." He turned. The old murderers! The blackmailers!

The husband said nothing; he looked at Lowe, then searched cautiously for words. He found none. They walked on in silence and Lowe could find nothing to fill up the space between them. The storm in his stomach raged.

"How the thing you building?" The husband's voice was mild, and Lowe remembered again the fight, the daughter's complicity. He wondered if this man was laughing at him, had come to his house to shame him.

"Coming along," Lowe said. "Coming along." He tried to be

casual. These days now there were just the poles sticking out of the foundation and all of the material lying down there collecting dust, the colored glass for windows and doors, the stone monuments, the wooden benches, ready-made. Things were so tenuous now with Miss Sylvie and her obsession with moving, he had to be careful how he asked for things. He had been placating her, every few days going over the dilapidated maps with her, bringing pencil and white paper each time, outlining itineraries, drawing out potential routes. She had been pleased, and her happiness had prompted several journeys into town, the drawing up and signing of official documents. He was just waiting now for Miss Sylvie to sign more paper and hand over the funds; he had used up close to all of his savings.

"The building coming along well," Lowe said again. "I may not need the daughter to help me run it after all."

"She have her hands full now."

"Yes," Lowe howled. "I happy for you." He was certain the husband had impregnated her on purpose. He shook his head. Children of vipers, they should be called! Murderers and blackmailers!

As was to be expected, Miss Sylvie usurped his daughter. He did not see her. If they weren't fussing over the ugly baby, they walked slowly throughout the house, heads close together, holding hands. They whispered. When he tried to interrupt, to say two words to the daughter, they looked at him with annoyance carved out on their faces and were brisk in their responses, as if pressing matters were at hand. When they broke into laughter not long after, he was positive they laughed at him. Murderers, he muttered under his breath, and walked away. He hated the husband, who walked round sullen and distracted and who made Lowe think always of Cecil and those months on the ship.

He tried to make friends with the boy while the husband napped. He gave him an abundance of white paper and Miss

Sylvie's paints, and much to his chagrin, the boy wanted to draw only ships.

"Even you too," Lowe growled, suddenly put off.

"What about me?" the boy asked.

"Even you too obsessed with Cecil."

"Yes," the boy said, putting sails on a boat he'd just drawn.

"You don't want to know bout me or bout China?" His voice was beginning to crack.

"Well, yes, if you talk bout it." The boy's tone was flippant, and Lowe wondered if his parents had put him up to it. He studied the figure prostrate over his art and squatted down next to him and produced, in a most detailed and picturesque flourish, a fleet. "Junks," Lowe cried in a proud voice, jabbing his finger at their thin slender lines, at their high sterns, flat bottoms, and horizontal sails, at their windowlike rudders and the cleverly crafted trunkways. The boy said nothing, only swallowed, and Lowe felt impelled to outdo himself. He drew pig boats and duck boats. He drew boats for scavenging and thieving and boats for honest trading. He drew boats for barbering and marriages. He drew boats for feasting and for theatricals. He drew boats that housed only lepers. He drew the slender-lined coffin boats dotted with row upon row of black and red lacquered boxes. He drew boats that were floating houses and filled to the brim with cackling hens and barking dogs and mewling cats and generations of families who lived and died afloat.

When he saw he had finally gotten the boy's greedy attention, he pressed on even further. He deftly produced the huge sleepy duck that was the outline of China, its breast jutting into the Pacific sea. At the bulging curve of the breast, Lowe dotted in the names of the coastal provinces and of his own, Kwangtung. He penciled in the circuitous route of the Yellow River and explained how it got its color from silt and loess and was a river most notorious for rising above its bed and breaking through dikes and drowning millions of people and inundating their fields.

Then he drew in the sinuous Pearl River and its numerous

waterways, and then he channeled it into the South China Sea, bypassing the rumpled hilly terrain. Then he broke down the divisions in the Pearl River delta: the Penti, the Dan, the Hakka. "We are Hakka," he told the boy, who stared at him unblinkingly. Lowe proudly drew for him the yellow dragon of the Chinese flag. Then he was silent, aghast, for he had no authentic word for his grandson; nothing to prove he was indeed Hakka, he had so successfully erased his language. He had so successfully forgotten. Was that possible? For if language was the carrier of culture, then he'd erased his culture too, and so now what was a person without language and without culture? What was he there on that island, what had he become?

"Tell me a story," the boy said, interrupting his quiet plummet into despair.

"All right," Lowe said, thankful for the distraction, and made himself more comfortable beside him on the rug. His limbs trembled with some great fire and he did not know exhaustion.

A girl who used to be a wife . . .

"Who is this girl?" the boy wanted to know.

Lowe sighed. "It don't matter," he said. "Just listen."

"What is her name, at least?"

"Lau A-yin."

"The same name as you."

"The last name come first always," Lowe said.

"What is your first name?" the boy asked.

"Look," Lowe said, "you want to hear the story or not?"

"Okay," the boy cried. "But one minute." He turned his head sideways to look at one of the funeral junks he had copied. He turned it the other way and one eye squinted. He touched up the figure with several more strokes of charcoal. "What you think?" the boy said.

Lowe was impressed and with his foot he silently nudged away the productions of Cecil's ships.

"Okay," the boy said with a cocked head. "Story." He pulled out a new sheet of paper and chose different colors this time.

Lowe began.

"Wait," the boy cried again. "What about a title?"

" 'Last Good-bye,' " Lowe groaned.

"Hmm," the boy said thoughtfully.

A girl who used to be a wife but is now a father's daughter again wants to see her father one last time. The girl leaves the forest of boats moored at the docks and twists along the narrow stone-paved lanes choked with tiny shops and hordes of people. It is almost dusk and the dim light of the town bathes everything in a yellow haze. In the distance, tall and menacing, are the foreign ships waiting in the harbor for emigrants. She pushes past the crowd of men milling outside Old Chen's Tavern and spies her father at the far end of the counter, hunched over a stool, sipping from a bowl of wine. It's her last night. Soon she'll be on the ship. Soon she'll be away from here. She doesn't know for how long. She doesn't know when she'll return. Only that she must go. Must leave. There is no future. And she wants to live.

The girl doesn't know if she'll pull it off. The bar is crowded with drunken men who line the wooden counter that runs the length of the room. She hasn't seen him since the betrayal, since the old man they owed a debt to came and took her away. Frightened, she had started to scream, to pull away from the man's iron clasp, and her mother's stinging slap had silenced her. And her father, when she turned around, had been nowhere to be found. There had been no ceremonial baths, no decoration of costumes. No go-between, no rituals with sweetmeats, no ride in an ornamented sedan, no accompaniment of musicians, no firecrackers, no pretense of loud weeping. Nothing but an arrangement and the one suit of clothes on her back.

Still, the girl wants to say good-bye to a father she may
never see again. A father who had infused her with his
dreams so she could still live, despite everything else. A
father with whom she had been bench and bottom, hand
and glove, eyes and socket. A father who had betrayed her.
He is an old man now, with a line-striped face patchy with
liver spots. He is an old man now, with trembling hands
and an unkempt beard and a long gown, dirty and tattered.
The bartender journeys back and forth between customers,
he ladles wine from a keg into their bowls. The girl wears
the shaved forehead and the long imperial queue, as the
men do. The girl wears the wide-legged trousers and the
padded jacket. There is the bag slung across her back.

It is a room full of hard and boisterous men. The girl
swaggers like a man over to the broken-down picture of a
father. Over to the wreckage crouched there near the door
facing the water, which is restless this evening. Junks rock
crazily on the agitated brow. People pass by. There is the
steady slap of oars, the cries of the fishermen. Inside the
room there is the constant spill of laughter, clutches of
conversations. The girl pulls up a stool by the old man and
he turns. There is a tremendous gasp, then there is nothing
at all. They stare. The old man starts to recite a jumble of
phrases, and then he stops. They stare. The girl puts a
warm hand on the trembling barks to keep them still. The
girl tells him she is leaving. She is going to see the world.
Inside her head are the humming pictures he had given
her. His gifts.

The old man calls the bartender for another round. For
two, he cries. There is froth foaming at the corners of his
mouth, with the remaining twelve teeth. He is an old man
now, decrepit, with the sharp thin blades of his shoulders
sticking out. The voice is still the same. Faltering voice
outlining magnanimous expeditions by sea. She smells the
glue on him, the wood shavings in his shirt, the varnish on

his skin. There is the smell of ink. The girl refuses to meet the eyes of the bartender.

Outside, the sky is slowly darkening, except for the red ball in the west. Beyond, there are the steep jagged hills marked with tiny houses, the endless rice fields, the mud-flats. Back there is the cripple. By now he has sounded the alarm, alerted the villagers. But she is far away. There are the eyes of the bartender in her neck. Can he tell? The girl remembers again the room with the parchment maps, their fragile and moldy skins. The bartender rinses bowls and glasses, lines them up sweating on the counter. Then he picks up the big copper kettle with tea and moves through the throng of men guzzling at their drink and talking of opium and of war.

The father lifts a creaking hand and presses it against the bartender's rag. My son, he says in a creaking voice and nods toward the girl. The bartender looks at the sharp thin face and sighs; his face reveals nothing. Bah, the old man growls thickly, and lapses into silence. He does not touch the bowl. He does not look at the girl. His head is bowed. His red-rimmed eyes do not move. Finally the old man speaks again.

Try not to forget about Old China, my son.

The old man's voice is wistful. The old man speaks as if he has forsaken China, he has turned his back on her children, on his daughter. The narrow eyes glazed by time are filled. The old man searches the pocket of his gown. He comes up with just the coppers for his wine. He has nothing to give her. Still, he presses the empty fist into her palm, then pulls his fingers away quickly as if scorched by the soft wet warm fleshiness of the palm.

Thank you, Father. The girl speaks in her own voice. It is the voice of his daughter. And of the wife he had sent her to become. The old man has turned away. Has returned to his bowl. She hops off the stool. She steps out into the evening. There is the rippling water ahead. A river surging with overloaded barges, Mandarin boats with dragons painted on the bow, which skim the water. Whampoa, with its smoking factories, with its fleet of emigrant ships that will take her, lies twenty miles beyond. The girl who used to be a father's daughter. The girl who used to be wife. The girl with her dreams. The girl steps into the evening.

Lowe and the grandson grew close. He brought him down to the construction and explained to him the necessity of the Pagoda. He told the boy it would one day be his to run, though it was a shame that the boy didn't look more like him or his clan but resembled more the father's people except for his red hair and his slightly bronze complexion, which got deeper every time Lowe saw him. He brought the boy to the Heysongs' and bought him a soft drink.

"Grandson," he told Mr. Heysong, who queried them both with one brow raised.

"Yes," Lowe said, wishing the boy at least had a hint of his eyes, for he didn't like this man's face. "My daughter visiting," Lowe said, tugging at the waist of his trousers and pulling it way above his navel. "She have new baby, a girl."

Mr. Heysong wagged his head up and down slowly and smiled with the face of a wolf, the one brow still raised, as if not certain he believed. He did not call the wife from the back to meet the grandson, he did not bring out the baby.

Still, Lowe pressed on. "Artist," he cried, shamelessly pulling from his pocket the smudged and meaningless colorings of the boy. He spread them out on the counter and made a mental note never to set foot in this man's shop again. Could he tell, Lowe wondered, did he know? And was that why he was so insufferable?

Lowe made the grandson a pair of catapults and they set off for the woods to shoot birds, which Lowe then plucked and roasted, and they ate the skinny legs with salt and chewed up the fine bones. Then Lowe brought out paper from his pocket and paints. And on the sheets he colored in colossal centipedes and benign-looking dragons, then folded them into kites, attached a fluttering tail and a ball of string to each, handed one to the boy, and together they went shrieking in the woods with the kites darting through the tall grass until they ended up in trees and were torn to shreds. The boy was exhausted. As was Lowe, and his heart rattled uncontrollably in his chest. He decided that he liked the grandson after all, he liked the boy's spirit, his inquisitive mind. He had never played with his daughter like this, he had never made her toys or told her stories. He had never showered her with affection. He had been so aloof and silent and desperate. He had been so anguished.

The grandson wanted to hear more adventures of the girl named Lau A-yin, but a happy story this time, he said.

"I don't know any," Lowe growled, his heart clanging like a bell.

"You never been happy?" asked the boy.

"Never," Lowe said, and then he was quiet.

They sat in the tall grass popping with grasshoppers and screaming with crickets. They sat in the tall grass shaded by trees. Surrounding them was the enormous countryside.

"Well, maybe when I was your age," Lowe said, vaguely remembering a breeze at his back and skippers unmooring a ship, bringing her slowly like a dead body to anchorage. "But then I didn't even know who I was and am not so sure of all that I remember."

"What's this one called, then?"

"A father's betrayal."

"Same girl?"

"Same one."

The bacchanal lasted one full week. They stayed up way past midnight every night and disturbed Lowe with their violent laughter, with their hushed mutterings that thundered throughout the house. He tried on two occasions to get the daughter alone. She seemed tense around him, she laughed too loud and at nothing in particular. She seemed uncomfortable in her body, she walked stiffly, and there was always the fussing baby between them that absorbed her attention completely. He brought her to his study intending to sit her down and show her the letters, talk her through them, but once they sat down he found he knew not where to begin. He could not meet her eye-to-eye, and the fear in his chest just kept hammering at him. He called her attention instead to the fading picture of the Manchu emperor Ch'ien-lung on the wall.

"A great man," he cried, his eyes creeping over to the bundle of letters. "He ruled for bout sixty years, and when he inherited the country it was reeking with wars and corruption and starvation. But he turn round everything. The country got prosperous. There was relative peace. He start up all kinds of literary projects. But after he died, the country just went to hell. God, so many wars, so many invasions, so many . . ." He grew quiet, his father's voice still clanging in his head. His eyes swept over the letters again, and with a sigh tinged with defeat, he eased her and the fussing baby out of the study.

After a week, the daughter left, and a great silence stole upon the house again. Miss Sylvie took to weeping, to wringing her hands as if washing out clothes; the incessant cough flourished all over the house again and he saw the depression hunting her. One day he went to their room and found the mirror on the dresser cracked to pieces, the priceless vases on the mantel in shards on the floor, the glass lamps crushed and piled up into a heap, and all her bottles of medicine swept off the dresser and leaking brown juice over the white rug and the bed. Chairs were overturned, the books on her night table thrust against the wall. He stood, nailed there, in silent observance until he remembered Miss Sylvie and found her crouched in a corner, her eyes wild, her pink face puffy and full up with blood.

"Sylvie!" He finally found voice and bounded over.

She lunged at his eyes with her curled fingers, and he fell back into a heap of foul-smelling bedclothes, still sticky from the brown medicine.

"I want to leave," she said, in a voice he did not recognize. "I want something else. Another kind of life. I want to move on."

His heart sank. "But, Sylvie . . ." He tried to disengage his feet from the sheets hovering at his ankles. "But, Sylvie . . ." He was so exhausted by her, and he thought again of the Pagoda that would one day be run by the grandson. He thought of the new generation of Chinese that would never have to suffer as he had done, never have to live the kind of lies he had lived. And then he pictured himself smothering inside one of Miss Sylvie's tall frocks with the billowing hips. He pictured his feet bunched up into one of her round-mouthed shoes, not to mention the frightful corset that Omar and Dulcie would have to fight to get him into; he pictured the pile of hair on his head.

"But, Sylvie," he cried again, so disappointed. "We could travel, we could . . ."

As if in response, she pulled one of the picture frames off the wall and hurled it against the door. He held his arms up against his bowed head until it had splintered. He rushed after her and tried to pin her arms, but she was strong and she sent him reeling against the wall. He knocked his head and the blood spilled into his hands. He bawled out, certain he was dead.

Dulcie and Omar appeared. They held Miss Sylvie down. She heaved against them, she bucked and bit, she kicked at them and cursed. They pulled her out of the room and into the drawing room. She growled. Lowe followed behind, holding a pillowcase to his head to stop the flow of blood.

On the couch, Miss Sylvie's pink face was sullen. Her eyes seemed stunned. He went and sat next to her, holding the pillowcase. He pulled her into his arm with the free hand. She fell in as if without life. She started to weep. He stroked the thin, patchy hair. The whole house was bathed in the sour smell of her grief. Omar and Dulcie left him there. "I want something else," she said softly, slowly, with barely any strength in her voice. "I want to move." She said it over and over until she fell asleep in his arms. He stayed there with her. What she wanted he did not know but he could well imagine: a place where she'd be free from her memories, from the past, a place that would absolve her somewhat, wash her hands clean. But there wasn't such a place, that he knew; look at how far he had come, so many thousands of miles, running and running, and look how he'd brought everything intact. Plus just a few weeks ago she had spilled so much of the past, had allowed herself to move through such a painful history again, had opened herself up so utterly and completely to him, of course now she'd want to move. Now she'd want to run again.

His arms, heavy with Miss Sylvie, soon grew cramped. He raised her up and settled her into one corner of the couch. She slept. He covered her. She slept. He listened to the liquid rattle in her throat, watched the slack jaw, the dark pools of her eyes shutting out the world. He leaned over and rested his cheek on her neck. He had never felt a greater love. And the rush of it through his veins made him shiver. He tiptoed out of the room and up the stone steps and into the kitchen. What did Dulcie think of all this? he wondered. Dulcie too was weeping. As was the parrot she kept in a cage. He fell into their melancholia. She blew her nostrils into the tail of her dress and drew Lowe tea leaves. She handed him a mug and took one herself. He sat next to her on a turned-down mortar and watched her slowly bring the mug to her lips. She half closed her eyes and blew on it. The steam sweated her shiny face. She slurped. The parrot did the same.

"Is the baby," she said.

"What?" Lowe said. It was the first time they'd ever spoken so intimately. His head throbbed and the dazzling stripes the sun laid out on the stone steps hurt his eyes.

"It bringing back all kinds of memories. She can't stand to sit down in one place. She tormented."

"Yes," he said, nodding in agreement and thinking again of all she'd told him and how deeply she must've suffered and how much he loved her, for all of a sudden she seemed soft and human and vulnerable to him. "You know where they are," he cried out into the hazy afternoon as an idea assaulted him.

"Who?" she asked.

"Who?" cried the parrot.

"Her children."

The mug trembled in her hand. "No, Mr. Lowe. Please don't open up that, sir."

"We could invite them," he said, thinking of the house choking with the laughter of Miss Sylvie's children, thinking of the tables, like old workhorses, sagging under the impossible weight of so much food, thinking how his daughter could come again and how there would be no end to the bacchanal.

"Without her permission, Mr. Lowe. Those old bones, sir. A grave long covered up."

"But maybe it would heal up some old thing. Take me and my daughter now, for instance." He said the word "daughter" as if it were pure gold in his mouth. "We still have far to go, but it feel so damn good to have her round, just hear her laugh, just know that her eyes touch on the same things I like." His eyes gushed with tears and he slurped noisily from his mug. "Sylvie could have that too." He tried to call up pictures of her children in his mind, but to no avail.

"Indeed, Mr. Lowe, but all that was a long time. Elizabeth at least grow up with you. Hard as it was, Mr. Lowe, sir, she was here with you before whatever differences cause her to leave. Miss Sylvie, now, she don't know any of them. Mr. Lowe, it was so long ago, sir. She was like a grip for them, a carrying vessel, sir, is not the same. You had Elizabeth here, growing up with you, playing with you. But Miss Sylvie, now . . ."

"What you remember?" Lowe pressed, staring at the one eye that was a bursting shell and dismissing the whine in her voice. "Which one of them could come?"

"Mr. Lowe, I don't want to, sir. Is not my place, or yours, either, to bring them here. What if she not ready? What if—"

"Come now, Dulcie, you see her there. You see her there suffering. My God!" Now it was his turn to whine.

"No, Mr. Lowe."

He pressed harder.

Still she said no. And the silence between them flowed without heed until finally, with a great shuddering sigh that frightened even Lowe and the parrot, she relented. But her voice, when she spoke, rumbled out as if from a deep and faraway place. As if she were remembering again her arms weighty with the neat warm bundles before she dropped them off like a thief in the night at the church door. She spoke as if for years and years she'd wanted to arrive at this very moment where she too could cleanse herself of some of the past and move on. Not run like Miss Sylvie, but cleansed, finally. And when she looked at Lowe again, he saw a resignation lurking there that told him she had packed up and already left. For good.

8

A correspondence began. As Dulcie could neither read nor write, she dictated, and Lowe wrote to the adoptive parents of the boy, an Anglican minister and his wife who lived in Falmouth, saying he was Miss Sylvie's second husband, the first having died suddenly from a tragic fall, and Miss Sylvie was ailing now, and wouldn't the man please get in touch with the son. The response was prompt, and Lowe collected it secretly from the post. The minister said nothing doing, he had raised the boy as his own son, he'd never told the boy otherwise, this was all they needed now, this confusion and botheration in their lives. Lowe was undaunted. He wrote back, he said Miss Sylvie was on her last legs. And desperate. And on her deathbed each day, she thrashed about and rolled in delirium, begging forgiveness from God and asking only to see the boy. Just one look. Before she closed her eyes and moved on home. The intent wasn't to cause contention, but as he must know, being a man of God, people often had regrets later in life.

The letter was effective. The man said he would send word to the son but that the rest depended only on the son. He was a big man now, he couldn't twist his arm.

They waited.

The luminous red wood for the cylindrical columns of the center were delivered and installed. The tiered and sloping roofs with their gray-green tiles came after. And all day long the square throbbed with the sawing of wood and the hammering of nails. All day long the square shrieked with the cry of vendors who had set up rickety tables of fried food that attracted flies by the construction site and gave Miss Cora stiff competition. Children ran their tires through the bustle and stray dogs and cats roamed listlessly, carefully eyeing choice pieces of meat. Sometimes murderous brawls broke out and people had to peel the bloody fighters off the cobbled concrete. By dusk, though, the crowd had all but disappeared and only a few of the men stayed behind.

One evening Omar appeared on the scene with a shovel and another wheelbarrow, and the men disappeared. At first he and Lowe did not speak, or meet up eye-to-eye, but each evening he came, he mixed the mortar for the bricks, he wheeled away with stones and carried some of the cords of timber. Something had shifted between them, though there were no words, and Lowe even went as far as to invite him to Miss Cora's shop one evening for a drink.

Omar stiffened, then he told Lowe with a low growl that he did not drink.

"What about a soft drink, then?" Lowe said. He had forgiven him. He had forgiven him for burning down the shop, for he saw clearly how they were all thrown in and piled up on top of one another and vying for power and trying to carve out niches.

Omar wiped his forehead with the tail of his shirt and the two walked slowly and abreast in the approaching dark toward Miss Cora's shop.

What was he thinking, Lowe?

People thronging the road stepped off the asphalt and waited in the wild wet weeds until they passed. It was Friday. Omar had slighted the salaries of his workers. They were foul with anger.

Shouldn't he have brought Omar over to the Heysongs', taken the drink together on the veranda up at the house?

Outside on the shop steps in the vapid dark were the rose-tipped cigars, the heaving blue smoke, the huddled band of men collected around a board game, the sole flaming torch. It was Friday. Payday. All week long from sunup to nightfall, they had worked themselves out on the various estates, these thin and wiry men with backs almost broken down, with curved brittle chests rattling from the fine cane dust. But here and at this moment, they could forget, or at least push back, the starvation and poverty that dogged them, the humiliation they suffered daily at the hands of foremen and overseers. Here and at this moment, they could forget. They shook the dice in a tin, then with a flick of the wrist sprang them onto the board. There was the hushed silence as they waited for the numbers to settle. Then the thunderous roar, their shrieking cries. They quarreled with one another and with themselves. They battered back and forth in confusion and hurled insults at dead mothers and strayed wives. They laid out astonishing bundles of cash, and the rose-tipped cigars glowed and dulled, the undulating smoke seeming to steam from their ears.

Shouldn't he and Omar have gone elsewhere?

It seemed an eternity for Lowe and Omar to reach the piazza, and once they set foot on the steps, the stooping brown mass rose up. "But what the hell is this, though?" one of them gave out, as the terrible silence tumbled on the night.

Lowe said, "Howdy do," and Omar mumbled from way down deep in his gut some incomprehensible thing, and the men abandoned their game and stared out into the cruel night with unblinking eyes. It was Friday, payday. He had slighted their salaries. And which one of them had he insulted today, which one of them had he lashed, as if they were children or dogs? As if they were women? Lowe and Omar tunneled their way through the crowd of men. It was the longest walk ever up to the counter, where Miss Cora stood solemn with a white turban tied round her head, her lips turned down at the corners, and her sagging jaws that were once full and round now swinging into her neck. The men inside the shop had cleared away into the corners, where they pressed up against the walls, and the ones outside had crowded in, packing the doorway with their threadlike limbs. Lowe's lips felt cracked and dry, and he had never known a more furious thirst.

"Two aerated water, Miss Cora." He laid out the coppers on the counter, and hidden somewhere behind him in the deep shadows he sensed Omar's unnatural breathing.

It took Miss Cora a long time to return with the bottles, and she inspected them first with her bulbous brown eyes and then she polished them slowly and carefully with her dusty white apron before popping the tops. They hissed.

Lowe brought the flavored sugar water to his lips.

In the deepening shadows the men did not speak, though the corners of their eyes darted toward Lowe and then toward Omar and then over to Miss Cora's face sheathed in wood and then back again. Miss Cora grunted often and paused to clap her enormous chest and to bawl out "Gas" and "Please excuse me."

Someone belched and cried out "Excuse," and the fetid fragrance flowered in the room, and another man punctuated the silence with "Ah, sir" and nothing else. There was the curling smoke from pipes.

Then they heard laughing and joking—for after all it was payday—as a gang of laborers slowly descended on the shop. The sounds broke the tension for a while or maybe they heightened it. Lowe did not have a weapon on him. But their cutlasses were there, their hoes and shovels and trowels and hammers and pickaxes were there, leaned up against the wall in crocus bags and in easy reach. Sometimes the sharp silver tines of a pitchfork shimmered in the brown of the shop. The men hemmed in closer and the heat and smoke thickened in the shop and all eyes turned to Omar's forefinger that reached up to flick the sweat from his brow, but the water spouted back just as quickly and his irritation crinkled his black brow and he tried masterfully to suppress it.

The gang of joyous laborers staggered into the shop, took a look around, and lapsed into immediate silence. They did not order. They stepped out again, and Miss Cora's face grew even more wooden. Lowe drank swiftly and wished that the swallowing didn't create such a ruckus. He tried to think of a joke. Nothing came to mind. Were they expecting him to choose sides? Choose between them and Omar? Jake and a few of the workers were there. He tried to smile at them and he knew his face must've looked horrid. They rested the empty bottles on the counter, and Lowe glanced at Miss Cora's brown face, now permanently set in concrete, touched Omar, said good night, and tried to walk out with dignity.

A violent outburst exploded inside the shop and followed them outside, and they turned the corner at the whitewashed wall that gleamed in the night and they heard the rattling of dice in a tin again and the tremendous roar again of voices. They lumbered two abreast, and ahead of them dodging and appearing from behind trees like a giant silver moon was the glimmering white house. Beside him Omar sighed often and spat.

They walked quickly, and alone in their minds they replayed again and again the raw hostility that had been unleashed inside the shop. They walked quickly, and alone in his mind Lowe realized that whatever caustic acid Omar had stirred up among the villagers would one day spill into his face. But that was Omar's business with the villagers, he decided. Still, were they expecting him to choose sides, those people? Hadn't Omar injured him as well, burned down his shop? And didn't they know it, those people?

They walked quickly and quietly, and Lowe smelled him again in the dark, smelled the carbolic soap on his skin, the blue in his white shirt, the polish on his shoes, for it was payday, he smelled the castor oil on his clean clear pate. They turned left again with just the thud of their chests between them, just the scrape of their shoes on the ground recently wetted by rain, and they turned left again and were swallowed up into the dark by a thicket of trees with towering trunks, and Omar's hands were at Lowe's waist and Lowe stopped suddenly and turned slightly: "What is it Omar, what!"

"Nothing, sir, nothing, I just . . ." He dropped his hands and fumbled for words, and they started walking again, and again Omar was at his back, his hands at Lowe's waist, and this time Lowe took the hands, which were surprisingly warm and soft.

"What is it, Omar?" His voice was softer, less frightened. "What, Omar?" They had stopped again, and he pressed himself against Lowe, and whatever fire Lowe had had before fled his skin.

"Sorry," he said, gasping. "Sorry."

Ahead of them was the dodging house like a silver moon and around them the chorus of all the barking dogs in the village, and the tears bubbled up in Lowe and he said nothing at all, not one word, just held on to the hands and allowed the body leaning into him to rest there. "Is okay," he said in a voice set on howling at any moment. "Is okay." And then he was quiet. He would have wanted to thank Omar, for in a funny sort of way, the destroyed shop had freed him. In a funny sort of way, Cecil's death had freed him, had freed all of them. But how do you tell Omar thanks? How do you tell him thanks for murdering someone without implicating himself? The police had never returned. To Miss Sylvie they had sent some sort of correspondence, but to Lowe nothing. They hadn't even asked him the value of what he had lost. How long he'd had the shop. They had jotted down some eyewitness accounts and had even gone as far as to rough up some of the villagers. Young men mostly, whose looks they didn't like. Two youths had been hauled off for questioning. But they didn't stay overnight in lockup. They had been let go. And no one had pointed a finger at Omar. Still, they must've known, those villagers. But then again, perhaps not.

Maybe it was Miss Sylvie they hated, who had moved them off their land so she could turn around and hire them for a pittance. Maybe it was Cecil they hated, and now Omar would pay.

The secrets inside that glimmering white house and in that village had been so tightly hemmed in that sometime soon they'd all be choking. Lowe wondered if he should bring up the business of the blackmail and of the land, the savage slaying of the dogs. The voice that had summoned him that night. But he decided against it; it was too much. Too soon. Lowe squeezed the hands again and Omar loosened his grip and they were two abreast again and the night charged with the smell of jasmine swallowed them.

They waited for word from the son. Nothing. And in the meantime, Miss Sylvie grew gaunt, the ring disappeared from her voice, her eyes grew glassy. She had no precise illness, yet every day her eyes ached, her head had to be bandaged with medicinal leaves, she complained of jangling nerves, she took heavy doses of Epsom salts and others of Dulcie's nostrums, she became preoccupied with her incessant dry coughs that produced no phlegm, she was often fatigued, her stomach was delicate and she had lost her appetite and so at dinner she ate only mousy portions, if anything at all. She cried often, always with the big hands churning in her lap.

Lowe sent for doctors and they came. With solemn faces, they shook their heads and pulled at the scraggly beards at their chins. They played thoughtfully with the rings on their fingers and removed their glasses to rub their watery eyes. They all had furrowed brows and sat in silence for long moments as they wrote up prescriptions after prescriptions. Bundles of notes were doled out. The cough only worsened. He made several trips into town and came back with various pamphlets of travel, ship itineraries. But the flicker in her eyes had been extinguished.

Then a telegram arrived that the son was to be expected, and for the first time Lowe felt the sheer weight of what he had instigated. For two full weeks he walked around with the note hidden deep in the crevices of his trousers pocket. When he finally told Dulcie, she said nothing at all, only sighed her trembling sigh, which made him worry even more. Still, he told her to ready the guest room. "Maybe the son will come with his family." He was trying to make light of the situation. "Maybe he'll stay awhile so they can catch up." All he really wanted was for the rust to return to Miss Sylvie's cheeks, all he wanted was for the throttle to return to her laughter.

Lowe decided he would ride into the square and waylay the man and surprise Miss Sylvie. Dulcie wanted to tell Miss Sylvie so she'd be prepared, Lowe didn't see the point.

"So she can jump on her horse and disappear? You know how Sylvie's head come and go. She might say she don't want to meet the boy at all."

Dulcie only wailed and emitted long staggering sighs, and Lowe decided that she was just completely incomprehensible, for what had to be done simply had to be done.

The appointed day, Lowe went to meet him. Lowe was nervous. He tried to put himself in Miss Sylvie's shoes, then abandoned the idea. He consoled himself with the memory of his visit to his daughter. Things weren't perfect, but he'd opened the door. Now there was room, perhaps, for friendship. Room for trust. Room for truths. He wore a flowing white linen suit, unstarched, and a white wide-brimmed hat to match. He had a drink at the Heysongs' shop to bide his time. "Guest coming," he told the man, who seemed impressed with Lowe's attire. It was the first time Lowe ever got a rise out of him, and he didn't at all like the man's suspicious smile, as if a certain knowledge brewing all along in his head had been finally confirmed. "Son from her first marriage," Lowe growled.

Not knowing what time to expect this man, Lowe had been waiting since ten. It was now after twelve. He was hungry and thirsty, his suit was no longer crisp and white, his feet swelled inside the leather shoes, and his bunions rebelled. His eyes were red from the heat, his head ached, his face was inflamed from the sun. He was all set to return to the house when suddenly he saw a thin black disfigured donkey slowly moving across the horizon and Lowe knew it was he. He paid Mr. Heysong, whose oily face was suddenly twitching with smiles, and stepped outside.

The donkey took forever to reach them. It paused often to nibble here and to nibble there, and the rider seemed none too perturbed. Outside on the Heysongs' piazza, Lowe fanned with his hat, and his toes tried to arrange a comfortable position in the shoes. The donkey ambled forward.

"So she dying, eh."

Those were the first words out of the son's mouth, and Lowe was taken aback by the open hostility in his voice.

"Well, not exactly." Lowe tried to remember what he'd said in the letters.

"Is a joke." He grinned with his horrid yellow teeth. "Am an undertaker."

He was thin like the donkey and tall and funereal and effeminate and shy. And inside his deep-brown face there was a pair of taciturn blue eyes. His hair had already dropped off completely, and he wore a hat that was too big for his head. They rode two abreast and in silence for some time, and Lowe wasn't sure he should point out the borders of her land just in case he too was hankering after her money. He smelled of ammonia and of balm.

"So you the husband."

"Yes," Lowe said; he didn't like this man's frankness. "But I not your father."

He made a disgusting sound with his teeth, and Lowe wondered if he had made the right decision. When they rode up to the house in silence, Omar took the decrepit animal at the veranda. Miss Sylvie was sitting there, and when she heard his footfalls on the steps her face lost its distracted look and came to attention. Lowe did not recognize her face. It looked neither younger nor older but as if it existed in a time before him.

"Matthew," she said softly, and got up out of the chair.

Was that the name she'd given him? Lowe wondered. And was she losing her head!

"No," the son said. "Is LeRoy." He took both her hands and kissed her on both sunken cheeks. Then he took off his hat and sat down on a chair across from her. Miss Sylvie said nothing, only stared openly at him, with that same face and with unmoving and unblinking eyes, as if trying to discern the meaning of all this.

Dulcie watched him as well and also Omar, and they all carried a face Lowe did not know. For the first time, Lowe began to regret.

"Water, eh."

"Of course," Dulcie said, having forgotten altogether her manners, and Omar appeared with a tumbler. The son leaned the glass to his head, and all eyes were on the throbbing Adam's apple and the drops that leaked out by the corners of his mouth.

"Food?" he asked.

"Of course," Dulcie said, and Omar appeared again, with a plate full of curried mutton and rice on a tray and utensils. He attacked the meat at once, cutting up each chunk into even smaller and careful strips before placing it in his mouth. He chewed slowly, endlessly, and like a horse, with his mouth open wide and his rusty teeth clicking.

Miss Sylvie was the first to recover. There was the growing grimace on her face.

"You have children?" she asked.

He took so long to respond, they thought perhaps he had not heard. He rested the utensils on his plate and wrestled with a bone and then brought it to the corner of his mouth and crunched with his powerful jaws and sucked out all the marrow and then leaned the shards white and clean in a neat pile among others in a corner of his plate. With a discreet hand he picked his teeth with a sharp shard and wiped his mouth with the napkin and drank from the tumbler, and Omar filled it again to the brim from the jug he held behind his back.

"Twelve," he said. "Six sets of twins."

Omar whistled.

"Yes," he said, "a hell of a thing. Plenty mouths to feed and people not dying quick enough."

"Undertaker," Lowe moaned, and everyone breathed again.

"For a while there was a breakout of TB, fifteen deaths every month. Oh God!" He looked incredibly unhappy. "We ate like kings. But must be they find cure." He drank again. The Adam's apple bobbed. He turned to Miss Sylvie. "People dying down here?"

Dulcie looked away and busied her hands.

He shook his head. "People not dying like they used to. People living longer now." He turned down his lips and looked as if about to cry. Omar took the tray from him. "Thanks," he said, softly and morosely, "thanks. Is a nice dinner." Then he grinned into his lap. His eyes were red. He turned to Miss Sylvie again. "I look like you son, Mother?"

Lowe winced.

"I look like me father?"

Miss Sylvie stared out at the row of Ortanique trees, her face set in granite. She did not answer. Over in the corner, Lowe suffered.

The son stood up and shook out his legs. "You've picture, Mother?"

But he did not wait for anyone to respond. "Mr. Chin here said he wasn't my father. What he die of, natural causes? Was a white man?" He paused to look at Miss Sylvie, and she stared back at him with pure hate. The look must have disconcerted him; he turned to Lowe. "See, I tell you, people today living longer." He sighed and sat back down in his chair.

Then there was the stilted silence that wheezed in the tin-colored afternoon, and during that time he inspected each one of them carefully and each one pretended not to notice his prying eyes. His gaze lingered longest on Miss Sylvie's face, and when he was done, he sighed again and, in a voice riddled with sadness, said, "Well, I must go now." His face betrayed no other emotion than the deep sadness it carried at all times.

Lowe turned to Dulcie. She would not meet his eyes. And he saw how very wrong he had been. How so damn wrong. And he saw now how she must have known all along. All along she must've known this wasn't the way, wasn't the right thing.

Omar brought his donkey, with a white star branded on its forehead, and the son told them he'd had it ever since he was a boy of ten. The donkey, as if understanding every word, brayed and farted at the same time. The son tugged at Miss Sylvie's hands and brushed her cheeks with lips that smelled of ammonia and camphor. His whole person smelled of formaldehyde. Then Omar held the reins while he mounted up, fixed his hat squarely on his head, and took the bridle and muttered to the beast. Unable to face each other and themselves, they watched him until he was but a black thin speck.

9

Early one morning Lowe looked out his window and saw an apparition moving slowly down the hill and away from the house. He thought maybe it was Dulcie, the rock and sway of her walk, the drag of the limp foot, the solid back and the wide shoulders set far apart. But it had rained overnight and the mist still lingered. Still, he pulled on his shoes and went after her, calling. But she did not stop or turn around. She dragged the broken-down limb, and it crawled along behind. Finally he reached her, his face flushed and his lips trembling from exhaustion. He tugged at her hand that was missing the three fingers dropped off from gangrene.

"Dulcie," he cried.

She turned slowly so as not to unsettle the box on her head. Inside was the parrot and the craven lazy cat, Hazel. They eyed him suspiciously.

"Dulcie." He tugged at her hand again, holding on to the big wrist.

"Is all right, Mr. Lowe."

He didn't recognize her deadpan voice. He didn't recognize the hardness in her dark hollow face, the left eye without a window. The eyebrows crouching in the middle of her face.

"Where the hell . . . what is this!"

"Is for the best, Mr. Lowe."

"But, Dulcie. I mean, you friends all these years. You family for each other all these years. Maybe I interfere in things that don't concern me, but is my fault, it was—"

"Is better this way, Mr. Lowe." And she turned to go again, and he realized he was still holding her hand and the bird and the cat still watched him. But there was such a finality in her voice. He squeezed her hand and he remembered again how in the kitchen she'd never wanted to send for the son, how she'd sighed that long everlasting sigh, and now she was leaving as if she knew it would come to this. As if she'd waited all along for it to come to this so she could finally leave. And with good reasons, after all these years.

Miss Sylvie was watching from the steps of the veranda when he dragged himself back to the house. Lowe did not speak. He brushed past her. He stepped inside the house. He wasn't used to the stillness. He dashed back outside. "Is my fault." He yelled it at her.

"Dulcie know best." Her voice was steely. "She been in this family for years. She know when she overstep her bounds."

"But it was me who tell her to send for him." He tapped his chest. "Me."

She said nothing.

He hated her. All this power she had. All this power in her alabaster skin. "You damn selfish." He slapped her with it. All these people he kept losing. Now Dulcie.

"Selfish!" His voice whipped out at her, but on the brim of it was the worry that he was the one who'd overstepped bounds.

"And what make you think I wanted to see that idiot? That fool? That monster that come here posing as son? Calling me mother with his nasty mouth."

He didn't recognize the spitting voice.

"Every mother wants to see her son," he said softly. He had never been so foolish, so wrong. So blasted blind.

"Maybe you," she cried, "maybe you. And how long it take you," she said. "You think what good for you good for me as well. You don't know me," she said. "You don't know me. Did you ever ask me one word about me since you live here?" she said. "One word? Maybe you the selfish one with your cement circle round you, with your wall of pain. Your cardboard box of disguises. You only see me when you want, Lowe, when you want clubhouse. And even so, what the clubhouse have to do with me? Even so. Ain't the clubhouse bout you and your people? Ain't the clubhouse meant to absorb you again like the shop?"

"Sylvie . . ." His voice failed him. He hated the horrible accusations. "Sylvie, I was only thinking of you. We old people now." Were they all true? The horrible accusations.

"Yes, we old people now and our hands empty now and still we can't turn to each other. Still we can't turn. You pick up now with the married woman Joyce. All of a sudden now Dulcie your best friend. You and Dulcie conspiring to help me. To do for my own good. You know if I have a mole on my backside. Thirty years now. You know that my left nipple is a hidey. You know . . ." She stopped to catch her breath. She stopped to sigh and to hiss disgustedly through her teeth. Then she went inside.

That evening he and Omar cooked. They did not speak but acted out silently and intimately in the close quarters of the smoky kitchen, as if in their gestures, thoughts came alive. He did not eat at the table with Miss Sylvie, he took his plate to Dulcie's room instead. He sat on the edge of her hard iron bed, sinking into the coconut-brush mattress, which immediately swooped to the floor. There was just the one tiny square window in this low-ceilinged room made of wattle and plaster, which reminded him of the abandoned slave quarters on the deserted estates he rode past on his way to Kywing's. She had taken nothing, Dulcie. Her Bible with passages underlined over and over in red was still on the table, as was the handsome white Jesus on the wall that stared down morosely at Lowe. Was he selfish? My God, what had possessed him to send for her son? Was it anger? But hadn't he done it for her? She'd been so ailing, so desperate.

The little lamp on the table by Dulcie's bed smoked. He saw that the wick needed trimming. He laid the plate by his feet and stretched out on her bed. He thumbed through the boxes of trinkets on the table and wondered why Miss Sylvie had subjected her to live in this kind of squalor all these years. And why Dulcie had subjected herself to it. He wondered if Dulcie had had a lover. He had been so locked up in his self, in his survival, more and more he saw how he did not know them. Had not figured out how to read them. Was it true, all of what Sylvie said about him, was it true, was he selfish? And had he intended to push Miss Sylvie away with his actions? Did he hate her, Miss Sylvie? Did he? Was all this anger!

Night waited at the wide-open doorway close to his feet. He slipped off his shoes and watched for Omar. The brush that nestled his head clawed at his neck, and the rusty springs groaned every time he turned. Maybe they were all selfish. Maybe they were all murderers. And it was only a matter of who could slay whom first. He must have dozed, for when he awoke the night had stepped in and a slight wind whistled through the cracks in the wall and tugged at the edges of the newsprint pasted there. There was the ringing of insects.

Lowe waded out of bed and pawed his way down the treacherous stone steps and into the warm safe house. Miss Sylvie had moved back into the guest room she had shared with Whitley. He tried the door handle and it refused to turn. So much was unraveling. He called. He pounded on the door. He rattled the latch. He sat down on the floor with his back braced against the door and his head in his hands. He wept.

He went back to Dulcie's room.

The following night, he slept there again. And the night after that. And again he watched the black grow blacker as the night deepened and the forest smudged away. He waited for Omar, and the smell of coconut oil in the pillowcase nestled him to sleep. He grew used to the smoking lamp, the soot that blackened the walls, the cloth mat at his feet that covered the cool and uneven and shiny concrete floor, the lip of light that leapt through a crack in the zinc in the early morning, the fowl that sometimes strayed in with her clucking chick. He could recite the newsprint by heart.

The swooping bed rested on boxes, and he picked loose the knotted cords that secured them. There were letters tied with a red ribbon. He knew she could not read. He tried to follow the gnarled handwriting, to piece together the decayed sheets. It was impossible. Was this her history outlined here in the faded ink on the yellowing sheets, and that of the protesters? The jagged scrawls he could not make out and as a result was misreading and misinterpreting. Was this her history here tied up in the carton box with ribbons, was this how things got set down, by people misreading and misinterpreting? All that was left now were the villagers' speculations. Was that to be the history now, the stories they would tell their children and their children's children about Dulcie? Was that how they made history? He would have no history for his daughter; he had told her nothing, taught her nothing. What would linger then on villagers' lips but the story of the Chinese man and his burning shop? There'd be nothing there of his river town, and nothing there of the ship journey, and nothing there of the conditions on the plantations. Nothing! She had been silenced by her experiences, Dulcie, the protesters had been murdered in cold blood. She had been beaten to bits. And now she was gone. Nothing left but the scraps of papers somebody could easily put in the stove to fuel the fire. Night after night he pieced together the lingering marks and thought of

Dulcie and his daughter until he dropped down dead asleep from exhaustion.

In the days, Lowe made Miss Sylvie's meals. He washed and polished the floors. He brought her tea each morning on a tray as Dulcie had done. He tidied the kitchen. He sorted the bundle of soiled clothes she left in a hamper by the door, scrubbed them and left them out on the stone heaps to bleach. He polished her mahogany furniture and her silver. He starched and ironed her petticoats, and every night he was swallowed up in the falling blackness of Dulcie's room, his back almost touching the carton boxes of old letters, old clothes. He and Miss Sylvie spoke less and less, but to Omar she complained that the mutton was too tough, the gravy too salty, the rice too runny, the tea too bitter. To Omar she griped about the unpolished silver, the streaks in the glasses, the abundance of starch in the ruffles of her skirts. To Lowe she said nothing. For what was there to say? A gulf. A tea tray. A hamper of dirty clothes. All these had erupted between them. Shifts, erosions, had fallen into place.

He lost interest in the men at the shop. At night he read the letters and picked out from the faded sheets the business of walkouts and shutdowns, the business of burned-out factories, of riots and arsons, of censorship, the business of uprisings all over the countryside, unjust imprisonment, unjust hangings. And then he fell asleep to the breathing black, Dulcie's earrings clipped onto the lobes of his pinnae. When the rains came, in crawled droves of insects through the space underneath his door. Pilgrimage of worms. Cavalcade of ants. Through the thin walls, he heard water dripping and dribbling on the wood floor of the buttery next door. When the rains ended, the earth's steam rose and he lay parched and sweltering in her swooping bed.

Piece by piece, he went through the boxes. He tried on a blouse, and his throat chafed at the stiff white ruffles. He unwrapped the gauze of cloth that banded his chest and slipped on her undergarment. It puckered around his thin chest. Outside, the forest had disappeared into a smudge of black, and still he waited and still Omar did not come and still he carried a yearning in his gut, deep beyond words.

One evening, a little before dusk, from the window of the kitchen, he saw Jake shambling up the hill. He had forgotten completely about the Pagoda, his Chinese people. He heard the chugs of Jake's water boots climbing up the steps to the veranda. He heard Miss Sylvie weakly calling for him. And when there was no response, he heard their muffled tones on the veranda. Jake told her how the people had taken to stealing the pieces of posts to build up their houses, how they had chipped away at the slabs of marble to sell at the market, how the children were breaking up the panes of colored glass and carrying them away. What a shame it was that the foundation was turning to bush. And the building was so nice already; this design in curves. What a blinking shame! Miss Sylvie told him to build a fence round the compound, put up a sign, and let loose a dog. Several days later, Jake returned, with the squatting sun glistening on his gaudy face and on the black hole that was his mouth. He told Miss Sylvie that an example had been set, that the dog had bitten one of the children, who had to be carried right away to hospital, where they cut off the foot. Miss Sylvie paid him, told him well done, and Lowe grimaced over the boiling pot.

How many days now, how many nights? Two dark figures with the howling silence between them, with the anguish laboring against them, with the past like smoke hanging motionless about them, with the thirty years between them dogging and dogging their steps all day.

One morning early a cart appeared, drawn by horses with orange plumes waving on their foreheads. Was she leaving?

There were the boxes and suitcases that the attendant was piling up into the back of the wagon. Twelve in all. Was she leaving? There was no sign of Omar, there was the shifting soil in his stomach, and the horses stomped and pawed at the earth and the plumes on their heads waved. Was she leaving? She did not utter one word to him. She did not offer a blinking eye to him. Finally she swung her voluptuous hips into the cart, and the white dress and white-brimmed hat disappeared in a flurry of dust. He could not speak. He watched till the orange plumes disappeared across the flats. Then he hobbled inside.

The atlases were gone. The compass. The itineraries he had drawn. There was no note. Piled up like a load of filth outside the door of the guest room were the unopened letters he had written her, trying to explain. She did not say when she would return. He imagined she had gone back to Whitley. He imagined she had left for good. He imagined her now ridged in the arc of Whitley's arms. He imagined the bells of her laughter flourishing again. What was he now without the shop counter and without the porcelain skin, with just the bower full of memories and some fallow plans that kept collapsing? What was he now!

One by one he removed her pictures from the walls, the gilded tapestry, the watercolors and oils, the daguerreotypes. One by one he removed the nails that had held them, stopped up the gaps, and painted the walls till they glowed again, a shimmering off-white. He did not have pictures of his own to hang in their stead, and the blazing concrete beamed at him. He dragged the spread from their bed, tore doilies from bureaus, knocked knitted throws from chairs, shook cases from pillows, ripped curtains from windows, and the dazzling light immediately gushed in. He no longer wound the clock that ticked in the shadowy hallway. Her plants wilted and died of thirst, and he pitched out the brown stringy carcasses. When there was nothing left to unhinge, his hands took to buckling, the fingers corkscrewing. He sat on them. He kept them clasped, and still they vortexed. As if his beating heart were in the balls of his fingers. He watched them, throbbing entities separate from himself. And there was no Dulcie to ask for a bush, except that Omar must have noticed, for he steeped Lowe a brew and they grew calm again.

10

The days now, even longer and more indeterminate, minced along, and each morning, in the bright streak of dawn, he rose to pound coffee beans in the mortar, to grind them to dust in the mill, and then to let it steep so Omar could sip the virile brew before he trundled off into the forest.

"Just us men now," Omar said, grinning, one morning, scratching at his bald pate. They sat at the table in the big house, Miss Sylvie's house, where neither Omar nor Dulcie had been allowed to sit.

Lowe scowled at him, and then he railed. "Don't you all know? Don't you all know? Why play the damn fool?"

Omar said nothing, only stared, the grin beginning to set like concrete in his face.

Maybe he did not know. Maybe. Anything was possible. So many secrets. "What about you mother?" Lowe barked at him. "You don't miss her?" So many disappearing acts. "Where she gone to?"

Omar slurped, he looked out at the winking dawn, he waited for the crowing rooster to shh. "It was time."

Who were these people? Who were they? Finally he found voice. "Time?"

"Yes, sir. She been wanting to leave for years now. But she so scared, after what they do to her in jail, after all that. How to face the world again. How to go on. Her spirits so crushed. Nothing left but to take care of the people that save her. Nothing left but to live out her life with them. But with Miss Sylvie reunited with her son, she feel like her business here finish, like she must go on, try something else."

"So was it Miss Sylvie who put up the money?" He was stunned.

"Yes, sir, and Cecil, and her husband was the lawyer that defend her."

"The same husband that was still shipping Negro people from Africa and selling them?" He was aghast.

"Yes, sir."

"So where she now?"

"Gone back to live with my father."

"You father," Lowe said, his voice turning to cardboard.

"Yes, sir."

And so was that where she went those Sundays she left in her floral red frock speckled with green and the matching turban, with the bad leg snaking behind that other one, which tumbled on ahead? And was that where they went those Sundays Omar left with her, his pate shimmering in the heat and haze? He had never asked, and if he'd wondered, he'd quickly smudged his curiosity. For if he didn't ask questions, people wouldn't ask them of him. Wasn't that how he'd lived? Protected. An armored man.

"You and him close?" Lowe's voice was hollow. So much unraveling.

"Pretty close."

And Lowe just stared at the lips wrapped round the rim of the mug. He was so jealous, so envious, so enraged. Here he was close to fifty, his father dead, but here he was still trapped in some ridiculous fantasy. For what kind of father stopped loving a child because it turned into a girl, because it turned into what it had always been? How does a father turn off like that, just stop loving? All those stories, all those trips, those excursions by sea, all those expeditions to those foreign places across the sea. How does a father stop loving like that, enough to give away a child? How? Lowe bayed the conundrum of thoughts. He studied the lines in his hands he could no longer unravel. He stared at the broken nails of his dirty fingers, at the shabby khaki sleeves of his shirt, at his weathered trousers and cracked boots. He started to giggle.

Omar glanced at him through the steam of his brew. The sun had begun to beat them down with heat.

Lowe started to laugh; his hands drummed on the table and the mug trembled and splashed the brown juice on his fingers. He laughed some more and with great agility. He took turns letting out thunderous roars and thin curvaceous whines that leaked out from the edges of his belly. And then he stopped altogether. He turned to Omar. "You know I'm a woman."

"Sir?" Omar brought the mug to his lips.

Lowe grinned at him, his face pleated into a thousand lines and his eyes tiny. He began to unbutton his shirt.

"Oh God, Mr. Lowe." Omar flung back his chair, the big glowing eyes like coals.

"No, wait. Wait." Lowe's voice was kind. "You don't want to know anymore? Didn't you ask me once, not so long ago? Isn't that why you burn down the shop, kill Cecil? You suspect something. And it bother you so much. All these years. Me and Miss Sylvie and Cecil." He tugged off the shirt and hung the loathsome thing over the chair.

"Mr. Lowe." Omar rose again.

Lowe pressed him gently at the chest. "No, sit." His voice was still kind, though some wild thing shimmered beneath it. He unbuckled his belt. He slipped off the boots, he tugged off his moldy socks.

"Oh God, Mr. Lowe." Omar was starting to cry.

"All right. All right." Lowe soothed him. He removed the trousers and stood there in his white merino and shorts, his skinny arms and legs stuck out like pale trunks. "You know what love is, Omar?"

Omar croaked.

"Love is leaving you heart in a place. No matter how far you travel, it still there in that place, knocking, beating, waiting. Look at me," Lowe howled, tearing at the mesh merino, tearing at the swaddling band, plucking at the knobby nipples of his breasts, soothing the thin wisps of fur at his groin. "All these years. All these years. Stuck there. In that place. My father's child. My father's son. Can't bear to become the girl he hate. The girl that disappoint him. Can't bear." Lowe howled, his head in his hand, his hand at his chest. And then he stopped.

"And you know what hell is, Omar?"

Omar had disappeared.

"Hell is this. Hell is never letting go. It is leaving you heart in that place, knocking, beating, waiting, waiting. Is never facing that thing about you you father hate. For how could you, when it was you, the core of you, the essence of you? You." He sobbed.

By now the fingers of day had thrust themselves into the room, into the house. Lowe glared at the sun-striped bundle on the floor as if just seeing it for the first time. He pulled his shorts back on and for the first time felt the repulsive scratching cloth against his skin. His breasts rebelled underneath the cotton sheeting. And still he dressed, piece by piece, limping through the rooms of Miss Sylvie's house jabbering to himself, his hair damp from the heat and matted to his head. "And how you to love some other person when the body you inhabit not even yours? When the body you inhabit has more to do with somebody else's fantasy. The fantasy of somebody you love. But who it turn out don't even see the real you, really. And how you to truly believe, when later in life a lover say she love you, when the reason she was thrown into your life to begin with was because of someone else's fantasy and her own as well? Hadn't she seen me in the dreams, Miss Sylvie? Wasn't she looking for safety after the murder, and wasn't Cecil looking for a mother?"

"Mr. Lowe." Omar hung like a crusted effigy in the yellow doorway.

"Call me Lau A-yin," Lowe said. He was dressed again.

"Mr. Lowe."

"Call me A-yin, damn it. Call me by my blasted name."

"Mr. Lowe."

"You son of a bitch."

"Mr. Lowe."

"Yes, Omar?"

"You want some tea, sir?"

He began to love her. Miss Sylvie.

All through the house and all through the burning silence of the night he roamed, with a tense face, listening for footfalls that never dropped, listening for doors that never creaked open, the rumble of carriages that never appeared, the cackle of voices that never sounded, a heaving body in bed that never materialized, a smell that was always fading. He took to sitting at the great desk in her study, and on pads of paper he stroked her back to life, her laughter swelling again inside the house. He painted her red house perched on the cliff by the sea. He painted the large empty rooms. He painted their heads on the same embroidered pillow, Miss Sylvie's hair swiveling off her plump cheeks. He painted her white muslin skirts billowing up around her ankles as the silvery sea crisscrossed with sharp darts of light lapped at her toes.

He painted her gold throat, her wide-set eyes ablaze. He painted his black knob of head on her great bosom, resting. He painted the silver river cutting through the hilly land, the green unfenced pastures, the slimy marshes, the flowering flamboyant trees. He painted her sitting idly on the shore, staring at the dazzling sea. He painted frothy and frenzied and calm seas; seas gushing with blood. Hour after hour he painted, day after day, and at nights by candlelight or with the violet moon dodging and appearing. As if some great dam had burst open, he gushed into the sheets: a solemn gray river swelling through a rumpled hillside and gathering strength from a million tributaries; a river powerful and mighty, bending and dipping, crashing with a great roar; a river surging with overloaded barges, Mandarin boats with dragons painted on the bows that skim the water, houseboats, rope-drawn ferries, rafts. And farther south, near the trading post, forests of cumbersome junks, tall masts and latticed rigging of ships on a glittering sea.

He painted the low range of hills alongside the purple horizon, the tiled roofs and gilded eaves and columned edges of mosques, the majestic sweep of the river, the maze of interconnected waterways. He painted landscapes ravaged by typhoons, villages made sodden by monsoons, crowded squares packed with jugglers and fire eaters and food stalls and sideshows. He painted the lighted boats afloat on the brim of the water like moving cities, a dim shore rising and falling, and gray seabirds gawking above a gray swell. All these he nailed up on the naked walls until he was trapped by the shimmering colors, assaulted by the smells that swirled around him, the memories that set his blood humming.

He took to sleeping in their bed again. Sometimes he woke up with a start and screaming, bathed in icy sweat. And so he took to sleeping in her dresses and wrapping up in her sheets that he refused to wash, for the smells comforted him. When his anxieties were boundless, he nestled his nostrils in her pillows and inhaled her persistent odors till they quieted. He no longer cut his hair and it grew quickly, rushing past his neck and shimmering above his shoulders. Wasn't that what she'd wanted, for him to look like Whitley? Each day he sat out on the veranda in her favorite chair and sipped mint as she'd done. He labored through her cherished books. He hummed again all the songs she had loved, watered each day all the plants she had loved, which he picked in the forest and potted now and kept all over the house. He mimicked her serpentine movements throughout the house and recited in a loud voice all the awful poems she had written. Wasn't that all he had now, the lingering memories that wouldn't desert him?

He called Omar into the study one day and begged him to explain the accounts. He had not eaten for days, and the meals Omar had brought him lay covered up under trays. He felt slightly faint and his head throbbed. Black rings circled his eyes, which seemed to have traveled long distances. His shaggy hair trembled against his sunken cheeks. Omar stood next to him, with the ledger full of figures open wide on the desk. The room shimmered with the smell of paint.

"Look." His voice was hoarse and he felt clogged with too many feelings. "I want to finish the Pagoda. Since you the man of the place now, I want you to help me out with the money. I want you to go and get you mother. I want . . ." He was overcome.

Omar held him in his muscle-bound arms. "Mr. Lowe."

"I want . . ." Lowe began again, and the rest of his sentence dissolved into more jabbering.

Omar soothed the gray stringy hair. He patted the hot cheeks wet with tears.

"Mr. Lowe, you need. . . . Six months now Miss Sylvie gone, and you lock up youself with the paint." He squinted at the smudges nailed up on walls, which were indecipherable. "You need company, sir. I mean this is no way to live, sir, this is no way." Omar's voice trembled, and Lowe wept deeper. So great was his anguish. And old. And here he was now alone, just him and Omar in this house on top of the hill, here he was now after all that had been said and done, after Cecil and the burning shop and Miss Sylvie's departure and Dulcie's. It was just him now and Omar, cooking and cleaning and watching out for each other.

It was the middle of the day, and the curtains had been drawn to lock out the glare. But the furtive heat still crept in; it simmered about them. Omar handed him his handkerchief, and Lowe blew. His weeping subsided. His head throbbed, and against his chest, his heart hammered. He smelled Omar in the humid paint-washed room. He smelled the horse sweat on him, the dirt on him, the wet tobacco-leaf smoke on him, the rum on him. He took Omar's hand and folded the rough palm on his forehead where it throbbed, and against his temples where it throbbed, and against his cheeks, which were flushed, he took Omar's hand and boarded it across his throat, which was damp from the heat. The hand went limp, not a muscle moved, and Lowe nursed it back to life. He brought it back to his throbbing temples, his throbbing forehead, his burning cheeks, he brought it back to his fluttering chest, and with his fingers guiding Omar's, he unbuttoned slowly one by one the buttons on his shirt. Behind him, above his chair, Omar only swallowed, his breathing frenzied at some moments, completely silent at others as though his heart had stopped knocking.

"Mr. Lowe."

"Shh," said Lowe.

And he helped the trembling hands remove the horrid shirt that hung awkwardly between them and he helped the trembling hands remove the merino, the swaddling band, and they moved onto the cool wood floor, with Omar at his back, the roguish hands on his chest, on his nipples, the muscle-bound arms hard against Lowe's back.

"Mr. Lowe."

"Shh," said Lowe.

Their clothes lay in a heap on the floor. The galvanized roof tingled and pinged from the heat. They basked in the red glow of the heavy curtains and the smoky heat. The groping hands moved wildly, feverishly, on flesh no longer firm, on muscles no longer tight, on buttocks no longer round, on a waist no longer small, on a stomach no longer flat. Lowe felt the clumsy hands tumbling over his curving spine, tugging at the nipples, falling into the curve at his waist, dipping into the shrunken hips.

"Mr. Lowe."

"Shh," said Lowe. He did not want to face him, he did not want to read the astonished eyes, he did not want to kiss him, he did not want to talk to him. There was the organ between them, the throbbing hard thing between them. With stubby fingers Omar drew circles on Lowe's back. He soothed the stringy edges of Lowe's hair, he blew into Lowe's neck and rustled the fuzz that grew there at the nape, he hummed low jerky tunes of his youth, and his chest lay still against Lowe's curving back.

He must have slept, Lowe, for when he awoke dusk had come, the lamps were lit, and a tray of food awaited him on the floor. He smelled the humid leaves of burning tobacco and when he looked up he saw Omar watching him with unreadable eyes and Lowe remembered again a steady rock of a ship, the plop-plop of waves rubbing against the belly, the smell of salt. He pulled the white sheet closer to his throat and inspected his wrists to see if they had been bruised.

"You want pea soup, Mr. Lowe? It here getting cold."

He had washed, Omar, and his new white shirt sparkled in the darkening room.

He sat on the floor next to Lowe and spooned him soup. Then he removed his clothes and got underneath the sheets with Lowe and again there was the hot hard thing between them. He rested it on Lowe's hip and it lingered there on the sharp bones and in the silence and untapped desire between them, till it ebbed and Omar tucked it away.

"Did you know Cecil?" Lowe asked him. "I mean really know him?"

"Yes, sir. He was a man with his hands in everything. He was best friends with Miss Sylvie's husband. His family some of the richest on the island. But must be he fell out with them, they cut him off, so he run the coolie trade. He used to fund my mother's project, but they stop accepting money. Plenty Chinese and

Indian people and some Negro people he set up in business, if he take a fancy to them. But he was a man with his hands everywhere."

"And he never marry," Lowe said.

"No, sir, not as far as I know."

The night crept in on them, the two huddled there underneath a white sheet. The floorboards grew cooler.

"And children?"

There was the silence again, and outside, frogs and cicadas went wild in the night.

"Who is to tell, sir?"

"He save my life," Lowe said.

"Yes, sir."

" 'Yes.' One day you have to stop call me mister and sir."

"How, sir, after all these years?"

"You just have to try," Lowe said softly, "just try."

"Then what happened, sir?"

"Well, I was sick there on the ship, and he take care for me. And then he turn me into his whore."

"He turn everybody into whore, sir, man and woman. Young or old. He blackmail everybody, sir. So he operate."

"And then there was the pregnancy, and all through that he was so good. I didn't know bout the man markets, I didn't know bout the hellish plantations that kill people with work. You know how many Chinese die on the ship with me? I didn't know which life was better, the one underneath him whenever he want, the one tie up, shackle underneath the ship.

"And then he sew the clothes so people wouldn't know, in the heart of night he smuggle me out. Put me up at some friend or other. Pay some woman to help me deliver the baby, strengthen me again. Then he give me the shop. Give me the money, but every time coming back for more of me, wanting to humiliate me, remind me."

"Yes, sir, so he operate."

"I mean how you suppose to feel about a thing as that? How

you to lay a thing as that to rest? My daughter there, for instance. Oh God, Cecil can do no wrong. How you tell her otherwise, how you tell her how she was born? How you tell her a truth as that? How?"

"From the edges, sir."

"Yes," Lowe said, suddenly drowsy, the edges. He wondered what the hell Omar meant by that. Edges.

He must've dozed off again, for when he awoke day had come and he was alone with just the jug of coffee beside him and the suffocating heat.

He went back to see Joyce, and on the way the thin ragged children watched him from the side of the road with baleful eyes. Sometimes they ran after his mule with white dusty feet and threw pebbles at the beast and at Lowe. Small boys perched on whitewashed walls watched him and pointed and jabbered. Was it his clothes, the way he looked now? They took turns trying to piss at the mule and at Lowe. There was the dull clop of hooves in the cobbled streets, the rattle of a cart ahead of him, the clank of hammers from the smith's shop. Beneath him the mule wheezed. He passed the young girls with their faces painted, and they eyed him brazen looks. Wasn't that one his goddaughter? And was she laughing now at his clothes? A few outside cook fires smoked thinly in the sun. A cat appeared out of a blackened doorway and looked at Lowe and the mule without interest. He was thankful. She yawned.

Out in the fields that harbored mongoose, the stooped figures worked in the blazing heat. They picked the swollen red beans of coffee, they picked bananas, they picked oranges. Valencia and navel fruit. Crocus bags lay in heaps at their feet. He passed the hard-looking women with wiry men's bodies, overworked and with bundles on their heads. He kept his eyes on the ground. So profound was his shame. So much time on his hands now. What had he become among them? Sometimes when it was someone he recognized he cried hello, hoping to catch a glimpse of an eye, but they stared ahead with cagey eyes and made disgusting sounds with their teeth. He passed drunkards stretched out asleep. He passed dead dogs stinking in the heat.

Joyce waited on the veranda with tumblers of lemonade as if expecting him. Maybe she waited here for him every day. He eased down stiffly from the mule. He worried. He glanced around for Mr. Fine's bicycle.

"He at the station," she said as she hugged him. He heard singing in the back and the rinsing of clothes. "Just me and the housekeeper, Ilene," she said.

There was no mincing of words with Joyce. She brought him to her room, locked the door behind her, and pulled the blinds. She unbuttoned his clothes. She did not have to remove the merino or the offending swaddling band. His chest was bare and his breasts leapt out at her. There was no pause in her frenzied breathing, there was no flinch in her eyes. She said nothing at first, she only leaned into his neck and nuzzled for a long time. "You beautiful," she said finally.

He was thirsty.

She tugged at the belt of his billowing trousers and at the buttons of her own flared dress, nipped in at the waist. She fell on her knees before him, her green dress a garland at her feet, her head nestled on the mound. "You beautiful," she said again, closing her eyes and filling up her lungs.

He worried about his ashy knees, his sagging stomach, his sweat. What the hell was it that they saw?

She tugged at his hands, dangling at his sides. "Make love to me."

He said nothing at first, only swallowed. He was so thirsty.

She tugged at him again.

"I don't know how," he croaked.

"Okay," she said, and laid him out on the bed. "Tell me what you like."

She didn't ask last time, so why the hell she asking now? "I don't know," he said.

She peered down at him beneath her. "Shy."

"No," he said, suddenly exhausted. "I just don't know."

She nuzzled his cheeks and ingested his smell into her lungs with her widening nostrils. She nuzzled his ears and his nose and his temples and the shelves of his jaws. She nuzzled his forehead and the hollow at the base of his throat. "Open you eyes," she said. "Otherwise I could be anyone."

He stared at the lines on her nose, his chest a conundrum of sounds.

Years later, he would always remember that afternoon and how she had turned him into a garden of flowers and fruits. How she had made up a name for his slim and ashy ankles, for every inch of his strong broad feet, for each toe, which she sprinkled first with kisses before assigning them titles. His fists had become her flowering hibiscus, his elbows her marigolds, his breasts her star apples, his nipples her guineps, his knees her frangipani, his calves her turtleberry bush, his navel her iris, and down there, down there, how to call it, her tulip?

He would always remember how she kept his eyes open with her mouth full of orchids and how the iron drums rolled slowly and steadily off his chest. And how the great tongue throbbing in his mouth, that warm hot coiling thing, was no longer a wiggly fish choking him. He took darting stabs at it. He lolled it to one side, he lolled it to another side. She withdrew it. She nuzzled him. She talked to him of hyacinths and of nasturtiums. She unsheathed the organ inside his mouth. He nibbled on it. He pressed back against it as if they were wrestlers. He felt for a texture, he listened.

"Touch me," she cried, and she grabbed his hands. "Otherwise I could be anyone here with you." She laid them across her broad and stolid back. She laid them across her fleshy bosom, across the margins of her buttocks, she used them to strum the sides of her belly. "Plus you need to relax," she said. "Am not your enemy."

Was the texture different on the bottom of it than on the right side? He rubbed against the golden tongue. His stomach unclenched. Thin flames darted back and forth. He savored the underbelly of it, the hollow cave of it, the coiling steel of it.

"Touch me," she moaned.

He sent word to Jake and in the meantime went by himself to inspect the damages to his property. He paused at the fence that bordered his land. He eyed the ferocious dog, who had a penchant, it seemed, for children's legs. It frothed at the jaws and grumbled under its breath. It looked at Lowe with terribly unhappy eyes, with solitary and half-mad eyes. Ruination had come. Grass sprouted into the concrete joints, and birds had built pockets of nests everywhere. He saw the accumulation of tins and old pieces of furniture, as people had taken to throwing their garbage there again. He sighed, weary already from all the work that had to be done. All the pieces to be replaced.

He bypassed Miss Cora's and walked over to the Heysongs' shop. As much as he felt scrutinized by the husband, it was still hard not to go. He liked the wife. She was the only woman he knew from his country. He liked just to look at her, not even to say anything but just to be there quiet. He was relieved when she told him that the husband was out buying goods. She hacked off the stopper of the soft drink and told him it was on her.

Lowe smiled.

She looked away and immediately started busying her hands. "You been sick," she said.

Lowe nodded. There was so much tenderness in her voice. Around his shrunken hips, his trousers flowered, and his loose shirt ran almost to his thighs. Lowe pushed the hair out of his face and tucked it behind his ear. It was a new gesture. It curled at his cheeks.

"And the wife, you have news?"

Did the entire district know Sylvie had left him? He shrugged and sipped at his drink. He belched noisily. "How things back home?" he asked.

"Terrible," she moaned, and proceeded to tell him about the

festering rage that was breaking out against all outsiders, about the secret societies determined to rid China of foreign devils. "They murdering everybody," she said. "Missionaries, innocent people, tourists.

"And for what?" she cried. "More and more students leaving, more and more people rushing to gold-cap mountains in America, more and more Western books pouring in, translated, and then there's the Japanese, killing and torturing people, taking over. Terrible!" She moaned again and shook her head, wavering the lead pencil that held her glossy bun. They were just the two alone in the shop, and the China of which she spoke sounded distant and far away to him. Another country altogether. He liked her abrupt gestures, the short legs journeying back and forth as she dusted the counter and polished the glasses and swept the concrete and chopped codfish and weighed sugar and cornmeal and wrapped them in the coarse brown paper.

"It's not so easy even coming here anymore," she said, lowering her voice and slowing her movements to peer at Lowe with red-rimmed eyes that looked exhausted. "There's talk that the government setting up restrictions. Soon we have to pass English language test, we have to write and speak at least fifty or so words. Must pass physical exam too. Must pay fifty pounds."

"When I first come," he said, "there were no women. None at all on the island. That's why so many of us intermarry." Was he apologizing?

"Every man need a woman," she said, smiling at him with the horrendous gaps in her teeth.

And the plantations need steadier workers, he growled to himself, suddenly disappointed.

She cried excuse as people started gathering in the shop, and he finished his drink, belched, and left.

He saw Joyce once more after that and then he stepped back. Withdrew. Grew more remote. There was solace now only in the paints. He poured hours into searching for the precise scarlet that colored the tiles of the temples in his village, and then he grew obsessed with portraits. He surrounded himself with the glowing eyes and curling smiles of the men who crowded his father's coffin shop, searching among them for his father, his elbows soaked with sawdust, his ears ringing with the loud guffaws. Sometimes he stepped away from his paints, certain he had heard his father cough. He worked tirelessly, effortlessly, filling up sheets and sheets of paper, perfecting their gestures, every expression, and when he lifted his head and looked up, day had come twice and gone and come again, and now the night had been unsheathed.

One day he heard the creaking wheels of a carriage moving up the hill. She had been gone eight months. He dashed down the paints and rushed to the windows, pulling back the curtains. He could see nothing. The rose garden beneath the windowsill had turned back to bush. He stood at the veranda with his hand at his forehead, blocking out the glare. Omar had allowed the place to let go. The walls were cracked, they needed painting, the hedges trimming. The path leading up to the house was overgrown with weeds. The garden was full of twigs and dried leaves. Was that Sharmilla and Kywing slowly approaching the house in the carriage? His disappointment was boundless. As was his surprise. He felt for the mustache, but there was none. He pushed back the hair that tumbled past his cheeks, and the strands immediately bathed his face again. His hands were messy with paint. He tucked the shirt into his trousers and saw that he was wearing Miss Sylvie's blue fuzzy slippers on his feet. He looked up again and saw that they were upon him.

Sharmilla's cheeks were wet when she kissed him. "Man, Lowe, look how you meager down!"

Behind her, Kywing shook his head and fingered his mustache and rocked back and forth on his heels.

"Come in, come in," Lowe cried, suddenly finding voice. He gestured to chairs on the veranda. "Sit, sit." He went inside the house and realized he knew where nothing was anymore, since the cleaning woman who came once a week had transformed the place. He called out for Omar, but only hollow echoes responded. He started to curse, to knock glasses against walls, to throw the silver from the drawers.

Sharmilla held him. "Lowe." Her voice was firm and deep and reassuring. "Sit," she said. He sat at once, wanting so badly to obey someone, and he stared at the table in the dining room and the hands at his sides trembled. His shirt was besmeared with paint. He had not eaten in days, and his eyes were glassy. She found water and poured him a tumblerful and one for herself. She sat down across from him and began to drink. He felt her roving eyes on him, but it did not matter.

"Lowe," she said, after she'd polished off her third tumblerful and her heaving chest had subsided, "you look so . . ." She paused, bereft of words. She poured herself another glassful, this time slowly and without splashing the tablecloth, as if giving herself time to battle her thoughts before arriving at some kind of clarity. "You meager, though," she said in a tiny voice. "Your cheeks sink in, but you look so . . . with your hair and . . ." She was overcome again, and she swept her eyes along his legs and stopped. Kywing appeared in the doorway, and she poured him a glass and motioned him to sit.

"Miss Sylvie wrote us," she said to Lowe.

He rose his head and peered at her as if just seeing her for the first time.

"Yes, she told us how things had gotten from bad to worst between the two of you. How she had to leave."

"At this stage of the game you'd think two old people could fix up things." That was Kywing.

Sharmilla grunted.

"At this stage of the game now you just need companionship. Someone to help bury you. Not to pick up and leave and cause all this botheration." Kywing again.

"We come because it must be so hellish here, Lowe, by yourself and everything." That was Sharmilla. "She told us the housekeeper had left."

"You did knock her, Lowe?" That was Kywing, with an embarrassed face. "I mean . . ."

Sharmilla stormed at him. "You think all men make out of the same cloth!" Her many chins trembled. "You think that's the only reason why a woman would leave?" The brown pendules of flesh on her arms trembled, her many bangles clanked.

Kywing picked up his tumbler and slunk out.

"You never see it coming, Lowe?"

"What kind of nonsense question that you asking?" Kywing piped from outside.

"How can you tell a thing as that?" Lowe moaned.

"A woman can," Sharmilla said, and from outside Kywing hissed. Lowe turned away, suddenly uncomfortable.

"A woman can," Sharmilla said again, with a hard and obstinate voice. "They have to be able to. All they have is the man. Especially in this place cut off from everything, cut off from family, cut off from country. All you have is the man. And if he run off with another and left you destitute, you alone in this God's world if you don't have friends. So you have to read the signs. Is a skill every woman have to learn." She paused to look meaningfully at Lowe and to show her brown gums. He suffered. "And even then sometimes it does some women no good at all. Still you have to know if he hungry, even before he himself know, you have to know if he day ain't going well, you have to know. Is like another sense. For if he leave you and take another and he don't have the courage, don't have the gumption, to do right by you, you and you children could starve." She paused to drink, and her many chins trembled as she swallowed.

Lowe breathed easy again. It was good to hear her voice filling up the house. It was good to talk, to have company. For then it didn't feel as if all the walls and the ceiling were closeboarding him. He wanted to ask her what the letter said. What Miss Sylvie said. Where was she and was she coming back? And then again he didn't want to know. For what if she had no intention at all to come back? What if life was good now, and if she was happy now with Whitley, could give Whitley now all Whitley wanted?

The house shimmered with the smell of his paints, and Sharmilla's eyes watered.

"You take up coloring, Lowe?" That was Kywing, pouring himself another tumbler of water and squinting up at the sheets. Lowe winced.

"Them nice, Lowe." Sharmilla eased out of her chair to peer at the covered walls. "Them really nice." She blotted the tears with her handkerchief.

"Is our village that, Lowe?"

He winced, and Sharmilla took his elbow and led him outside. He was grateful. She blotted her eyes and sneezed. He wanted to ask her about this letter Sylvie had written. He wanted badly to know what she had said. Was it possible that after thirty years together and then a break, two people could get back? That they could put aside all the old quarrels, all the old resentments, all the old mistrusts, and start over? And all the secrets and all the lies, could they rise above them somehow and forget, blot them out and start over?

They took the path through the woods down to the shop. He had not taken the path since the night of the fire. It was overgrown with weeds, and damp and gnarled roots snaked around their feet. Darts of light tried to pry into the thick canopy of branches, but it was close to impossible. It throbbed with the smell of eucalyptus and with the chortling of birds. He stumbled over a trunk in the road, and Sharmilla steadied him with the heavy hand at his elbow. He wanted to ask Sharmilla if she thought there was a chance between him and Miss Sylvie. Maybe now when Miss Sylvie came to his bed he wouldn't have to run, searching for shoes and slipping through rooms. He had found voice. Now he would put her hand gently to his cheek, kiss the tips of her burning fingers, and try to calm the jumbled images in his mind so his chest returned to its normal conundrum of sounds, his limbs unlocked, his shoulders softened.

"Wait little," he would tell her, for he needed to make sure his wrists weren't tied, that that wasn't the heaving hull underneath him but the swaying bed, and the whirring sound he heard outside wasn't the gray water whisking by, and the harried moans he heard were indeed Miss Sylvie's and not those of some old cripple who had taken him in repayment for a debt.

Maybe with time between them, she would no longer have to carry round her hangman arms, wanting so desperately to fill them up with something, her abandoned children, her memories, anything, even Lowe himself. Now she would've had her own memories restored. Now she would've seen her son, now her hands would be filled up, and the words "wait little" wouldn't send her bounding out of so much control, as if he were slamming doors and sealing crevices in her face. His wish was that he would say those words and she would set little butterfly kisses at his throat, and at his forehead, which would indeed be damp, and she would say softly in his neck, "Is me, is me, Sylvie, just me and you. See." And she'd take his fingers splayed on her cheeks and one by one she'd press them on her big sharp nose. "See, is Sylvie's big nose," and she'd press them against her cherubic cheeks and say, "See, is Sylvie's octoroon cheeks," and she'd stick one of his fingers right into her ear. "Is whose ear?" she'd ask. And he would chuckle and not say a word, and she'd pry the finger even deeper. "Whose?" she would cry, sharp into the night.

"Sylvie's," he would moan, and she would ease off him a little and jab with the finger the tip of her breast that was the hidey, the one she claimed he had never seen, and cry out, "Knock knock, qui est là?" And he would break down there, just laughing and the tears trickling, and she'd smother him again with the butterfly touches, and this time when she entered his mouth, it wasn't a cold wiggly fish choking him and locking off his breath, it was Sylvie, his Sylvie, loving him and drinking him and tasting him and swallowing him, his Sylvie with the darting tongue, his copper bird.

"Is the center, that, Lowe?" They had approached the clearing where the shop once stood. There were tears in her voice. And he trembled just from hearing in there so much pride.

And she turned to him and he tried to smile and he felt like a sheep and he tried not to meet her beaming face and her eyes full of admiration and her eyes full of affection for him and her eyes full of so much understanding. His eyes darted away, and they wandered over his feet, and he saw that he wore Miss Sylvie's ridiculous fuzzy slippers still, and he brightened at once. She pressed him to her chest, and he was at once suffocated there against her heaving chest, suffocated there underneath her big arms with the pendules of warm flesh, suffocated there among her perfumes and body lotions. He did not move. He did not grunt. He smalled himself up and allowed her to smother him, to blot the last breath from his body, to absorb him completely.

She loosened her embrace when they heard crashing steps behind them, cracking the brush underfoot. It was Kywing, cutting through the forest with an intense face and haggard breathing.

"My God, Lowe, is the place that you was building?" He flew by them, sauntering through the trashing weeds and over to the foundation by himself. "My God, Lowe," he cried again, gaping at the tiled roof, the towering columns, the windows gleaming with stained glass, the wrought-iron gate at the entrance, the decorative fauna that the stonemason had carved out. Kywing shook his head and grunted at intervals. Sometimes he scowled, and every one of his scowls injured Lowe deeply. But beside him, Sharmilla, with his soft humid hand tucked in hers, only muttered, "Good work, Lowe, good work." And he tried to keep Sharmilla's repetitive recordings coiling in his head, he tried not to swing glances at Kywing from the corners of his eyes, he tried to see what it was Sharmilla was gaping at.

"Don't worry bout him, Lowe, he there just trying not to weep. I know him."

11

One night he returned to his desk with the flaming light at his elbow and began scratching again at sheets, the memories, like a cork undone, spilling into his fingers and fumbling them across the page. He asked after her health and that of her husband, he asked after his grandson and his granddaughter.

Did you get the box of food?

He had chosen for her the purplest of Negro yams, the most aromatic and juiciest of Julie mangoes, the darkest blue avocados, ripe and bursting, and he had boxed them himself and brought the box to the post office.

Loneliness is a hell of a thing,

he wrote,

and I miss Miss Sylvie so bad. Maybe she has sent word to you, but to me, nothing. Maybe I deserve it. Now that she left, I understand her more than ever. I love her more than ever. Maybe that means I never saw her when she was here. And all the things I was afraid of. Miss Sylvie. How she handled me with her tumbling hands, loved me with her wide mouth, with her oval eyes. How she desired me and what a ravenous appetite! And me, a little frail thing like a broken bird underneath her. And she with her hangman arms, wide and empty without her sons, wide and empty with all her losses, her memories.

Am an old person now looking to die, and still I never knew love. That's all I've lived, that's all I know. I mark off the days on the almanac. Two years now. No word. It's just me and Omar. Some days he cooks, other days me. Same with the cleaning. I lock off part of the house and he still sleeps up there in the buttery. He knocked down the wall between his room and Dulcie's and turned the space larger. I stay here with the colors and bring back the past, the memorable parts of it. I stay here with my hair grown way down to my waist, but thin and without any life, with Miss Sylvie's dresses on my back, with her colors on my nails, with her rouge on my cheeks, her jewelry on my fingers and throat. I don't go out much, health is too shaky, plus how to go out like this. The people would put me in asylum. Though am only just being me for the first time in my whole entire life. People don't like surprises. They don't like truth.

The center is there, maybe next year we can open it with a big ceremony. I have to send word to Kywing, who you never met, to Sharmilla. Maybe you'll send the grandson and the girl, it's for them. Their history. Their past. And yours too if you want it. I build it so you all wouldn't forget. So you all wouldn't end up like me, with not even one word of Hakka to speak of. I don't know which is worst, those years wanting so badly to forget the past so I could fit in, or now, forgetting so completely and still not fitting in.

Jake looks after things. He comes every week to give me the news. And he comes for money to pay himself and the worker, just one man now, Mr. McClean. He is a damn fool, Jake. He doesn't know what to do with his eyes, he keeps them on his shoes and still he calls me "Mr. Lowe." But then he jumps up every time, to pour water, to get me a chair, to open the door. I say to him: "Jake, is me, Lowe. Cut the damn fool." And he says: "Yes, ma'am, Mr. Lowe." I see him pretending not to peer into my chest, not to look at my behind.

I wait for Miss Sylvie to come back. Every evening I change the tumbler of water by her night table. The lamp is there, full of oil and with a new wick and shade, her pajamas are there, ironed and folded underneath the pillow. Her pad of paper is there and ink, for she loves to scratch notes to herself, to sketch. Her slippers are there by the foot of her bed. I know she hasn't passed yet, I would have gotten word. I wait. Sometimes I fall asleep and the creaking wheels of a carriage wake me up. Sometimes I fall asleep and she is there, pressing next to me and snoring lightly. Sometimes I fall asleep and there she is coming up the steep stone steps, laughing and laughing and laughing. Sometimes I don't want to fall asleep at all, for the dawn without her is hellish.

Maybe some of us not meant to have things in our lives forever. Maybe we meant to just taste and go on, taste and go on. Maybe Whitley can match her, desire for desire. Maybe now that she has seen her son, her hands won't be as empty. She won't need to clutch so much. Clutch and suffocate. And me, well, I have you. We can come together, and I can tell you what it's like to live as a man, what it's like to want to live so badly, and with some semblance of dignity, you'd do just about anything.

Maybe one day you'll take a ship and you'll show the little boy and the little girl where I was born. You'll disembark at Whampoa and a junk will ferry you across a great river and a cart will pick you up and run with you through the narrow roads of the town and you'll hear the crying vendors and see the marketplace thick and sweltering with people and another junk will ferry you upstream to my village, and along the narrow footpaths rustling with bamboo stalks on both sides you will see the meandering rice fields, our little fortresses on the hillside, the tiered red roofs of our temples dotting the landscape, the leaning gray monuments moss-covered and surrounded by cut flowers and blurred by the smoke of burning incense sticks. And you'll see the brim of the slate water and maybe my father's shop will still be standing, and you'll see the little lopsided red plaque above the entrance with just his name, Lau Shiu-t'ong.

At the back of the compound there'll be a little path, and across that a board bridge and against that a thicket of trees and then the riverside where we sat and listened to the murmuring springs and where he taught me to read and write, taught me his poems, recited his soliloquies, filled me up with his fantasies, his dreams, and where I absorbed them so completely I started to live them for him. Maybe you'll see his tomb and that of my mother and that of my brother. Maybe the coffin shop will be standing still and you'll hear the guffaws of my father's friends, the hopeless thread of their conversation, you'll see him there still elbow deep in shavings, you'll smell his wet wood smell, his oil smell, his paint smell, his sweat of glue.

And if you take the ferry across again you might come to another village, and there you'll see the shoemaker shop if you're lucky, and maybe in that town cemetery you'll see his tomb, the old man they gave me to, the cripple, to pay off a debt. That's what it amounted to. My father's fantasy, me, a debt. That was my value, my worth: an old man with no teeth at all in his head. With hardly a strand of hair, hardly any vision at all, but what a penchant for a young girl, what a penchant for her tough meat, her soft skin, her childish baby face, what a penchant for her innocence, her pure laughter, her zest for life. What a penchant! For the milk on her breath, for the tiny buds barely sprouting on her chest, for the wisps of hair underneath her arms. There had been a string of them before me. Maybe he killed them, maybe he sold them, maybe they hung themselves, maybe they sat watching at the window, counting the days like me, waiting. Watching the legs of men that pass. Waiting. Watching the swagger of men, the leaping and stolid walk of men. Waiting for a father, a broken-down shell of a father who never came. So I ran away. Like all the young girls before me, I was too infused with dreams to stay. And what did I run into? Cecil, your father, his ship, this island, you.

Did I ever tell you you never wanted to live? You took one look at the world and it mashed you. For one whole year, you hung on by just a thread. And who could blame you? You could sense my own worries. My own fright. The deep disappointment. This small hot place, those strange people who seemed at first so hostile and warmongering, the language that sounded like crushed corks, that was so inflexible it just turned body into stone. My breasts refused to milk. They grew hard and brittle and dry. The arms stiff at my sides, too wooden to move. Too wooden to touch you. Who could blame you? I didn't even know what songs to sing, what to say, which words to use, I had no dreams left to infuse you with, no fantasies. Who could blame you? There I was wanting so badly to forget the past, to leave it behind—my father that betrayed me, my father without the spine, my father that buckled under tradition.

It was the customers that brought you back. The little girls that peered at you through the netted window and stuck out their tongues and said "boo" and called you "red mongrel" and "chink." The little girls that envied the fire-red curls on your head. The women who brought you clothes they made by hand, brought you some of their own poor food. The men who talked stories to you, though they were black-up with rum. Still they put you on their knees and sang rum songs to you.

> *Clap hand Clap hand*
> *Till Mama come*
> *Mama bring sweetie for baby and me*
> *Baby eat the sweetie and don't leave none for me.*

You remember that? How they wrapped your little soft hands in their rough chapped-up ones and clapped?

They were the ones brought you back to life those early years when you weren't certain you should stay. Especially if it was just going to be me and you, me and you solely. But it must have been with those songs that you decided that maybe you could laugh. And Cecil when he came, stinking drunk and twice a year, his hands bloody with foreign bodies, he had not forgotten you. He brought pairs of red tiger shoes that were so big you had to grow into them, he brought you that one time a red embroidered jacket, and ribbons for your hair. Jade bracelets for your skinny wrists. What a celebration that was when he came. How he staggered round the shop piazza with you straddled on his neck, how he twirled with you and sang his bawdy ship music and how you laughed and laughed with just the one big tooth in your gaping mouth, how busy your hands were in his beard like a red forest, how you laughed yourself back into life.

Maybe you lived for just those two visits each year. Maybe you're a yearner like me. How you cried when he left, for days and days, this man about whom you knew nothing whatsoever, nothing except for his vigorous laugh, his sinister antics that made you chuckle, the red forest on his face. I don't know if there others of you he fathered. I don't know if he fathered them in the same manner he came to father you: a runaway girl with her hands bound on a heaving hull full up of stolen Chinese. I know almost as much about him as you. They say his family's big on the island, that they deserted him. So maybe he's like us, deserted, thrown away, rubbish.

I didn't know my mother at all. From so early my father had snatched me away from her, kept me for himself. I only remember the cheep-cheep of her shoes rocking on the ground. I only remember her hand on my face when I didn't want to go with the old man, I don't remember her eyes. Maybe she walked round with them closed all the time, refusing to look at the world, or maybe there just wasn't light inside them. But she was young, way younger than my father, though her skin was already darkened and wrinkled by the sun. And who is to tell the kind of man he was to her. Who is to tell. All day long she was out dipping and bending in the fields, with the pole between her stooped shoulders carrying water, carrying rice stalks, digging up bamboo shoots from the earth, collecting herb, gathering wire grass to make brooms, all day long. So who is to tell?

What can I tell you about life, my daughter? I feel as if I never lived it fully. I feel as if I lived it only halfway, only some of the time, and always sheltered, always through some kind of veil. I never embraced it fully, never ran with arms stretched out to meet it. And even then, it was still so cruel. Even then. With traps set up at every turn just to trip you so you'd fall and mash up your face.

Ask anybody, I been writing you this letter for years. But maybe the shop had to burn down first, maybe Cecil had to die first, maybe Dulcie had to leave and Miss Sylvie, maybe I had to lose every damn thing first and fall down so low and so deep that I almost hit bottom before I could finish writing it finally. Maybe it was just time to reach out to you in just this sort of way. Not last week, not next year, but now. And exactly with the words put just so.

Lau A-yin

A Note on the Type

This book was set in Janson, a typeface long thought to have been made by the Dutchman Anton Janson, who was a practicing typefounder in Leipzig during the years 1668–1687. However, it has been conclusively demonstrated that these types are actually the work of Nicholas Kis (1650–1702), a Hungarian, who most probably learned his trade from the master Dutch typefounder Dirk Voskens. The type is an excellent example of the influential and sturdy Dutch types that prevailed in England up to the time William Caslon (1692–1766) developed his own incomparable designs from them.

Composed by Stratford Publishing Services,
Brattleboro, Vermont
Printed and bound by Haddon Craftsmen,
a division of R. R. Donnelley & Sons,
Bloomsburg, Pennsylvania
Designed by Anthea Lingeman